———————— ★ ————————

The DANGER KEEP OUT sign posted on a wooden fence caught her eye. She found herself in a sandy area crammed with boats. One large boat with a hole in its bottom hung suspended from cables attached to a crane.

A muffled sneeze alerted Kelly that she was not alone. She heard a metallic clicking noise. She turned. A door in the wooden fence cracked open. She hadn't even noticed the door until now. Who was there? A worker or a deliveryman? Her heart pounded. She caught a fleeting glance of a man, dark clothes, something in his hands. Behind the man in the alley was a black car. The door in the fence was pulled shut.

Creaking sounds drew Kelly's attention to the crane holding the boat. The boat above swayed. The cable was shredding. She watched, horrified, as the cable snapped. She opened her mouth to scream. The boat teetered, swinging past her head. Kelly jerked back and tripped over a can of varnish.

The next thing Kelly knew, her head was throbbing, and black dots danced before her eyes. Scrawled in the sand by her foot were two words: *Leave Belvista*.

———————— ★ ————————

Diane Sawyer

The
CINDERELLA
MURDERS

W★RLDWIDE®

TORONTO • NEW YORK • LONDON
AMSTERDAM • PARIS • SYDNEY • HAMBURG
STOCKHOLM • ATHENS • TOKYO • MILAN
MADRID • WARSAW • BUDAPEST • AUCKLAND

As always, for my husband, Robert.

Recycling programs
for this product may
not exist in your area.

THE CINDERELLA MURDERS

A Worldwide Mystery/August 2011

First published by Avalon Books

ISBN-13: 978-0-373-26765-1

Copyright © 2008 by Diane Sawyer

Printed in U.S.A.

Acknowledgments

To Kirk and Linda Sawyer and to
Barrie and Luis Buenaventura for their encouragement,
love, and enthusiasm.

To Colin Sawyer, Cael Sawyer, and Sonia Buenaventura for
their unconditional love, wisdom beyond their years,
and joyful attitude about life.

To Grace Murdock and Peggy Nolan, gracious and talented
St. Petersburg writers and exceptional friends, for their
advice and continued interest in my work every step of the
way from the first draft to the last.

To Marjorie Jackson, writer and dear friend,
for her helpful comments and counsel.

To the many family members and friends
who encouraged me.

To the librarians and staff at the St. Petersburg Public
Library, South Branch, for their helpfulness and friendship.

To Faith Black, editor at Avalon Books, for her help with
the manuscript, especially character development, and for
her unflagging enthusiasm about my work.

And last, but not least, to Erin Cartwright Niumata,
editorial director at Avalon Books, for her patience and
insightful suggestions and her faith in me.

ONE

Arrival in Belvista

KELLY MADISON SNAPPED UP the handle of her luggage. The wheels *clickety-clacked* as she strode away from the bus station. She'd have answers soon. Real soon. Her floral skirt swirled across the tops of her Italian calfskin boots, a luxury from her recent business trip through Europe. Now she wished she'd stayed home and kept tabs on her sister, Meg. Tugging down her beret, Kelly hurried into the police station.

A ruddy-faced officer looked up from his desk as Kelly walked toward him, her luggage bouncing along at her heels. "I'm Officer Browning. How can I help?"

"My name is Kelly Madison. I'm here to find out about Meg Madison's disappearance. She's my sister. I couldn't get straight answers about whether a missing persons report was filed or if you have a case file on her. I'm so worried about her. Last night—"

"Let's start at the beginning." He gestured toward a chair.

Kelly parked her luggage by her feet and smoothed her denim jacket. "Last night I returned from a trip. A twenty-four-day trip, to be exact. Meg wasn't in our apartment. It appears she hasn't been there since I left."

"Where is your apartment?"

"In New York City."

His eyebrows arched. "And you came here to Belvista, New Jersey, hoping to find her?"

"Right. This is the last place Meg was seen."

"Go on."

"The day I flew to Europe, Meg came here to Belvista by bus. That was Wednesday, August 11. We knew each other's plans. She intended to spend a few days and return home on Monday, August 16. There were lots of messages on our answering machine. One from her dentist's office about rescheduling the appointment she'd missed on August 20. I had a message from a Justine Pruitt who owns Pruitt's Inn here in Belvista. She said, 'I have your sister's suitcase. Do you want me to send it at your expense?' She left a phone number and a gruff 'Don't call collect.' I called and was told Meg had been staying there and that she'd left with a man three weeks ago. She wouldn't just leave with a stranger. Something is wrong."

"Calm down, miss. What did you do next?"

"I checked with Meg's friends. No one had seen her."

"Did her friends seem alarmed?"

"No. It was more like, 'You know Meg. She doesn't stick to schedules. She'll turn up.'" Uh-oh. That line of talk wouldn't spur interest in Meg's disappearance. "Meg always left me a message if her plans changed."

"Then what did you do?"

"I called here last night and spoke to the officer on duty. He said that several weeks ago they had looked into the circumstances surrounding Meg's departure because of a call from Meg's innkeeper, Miss Pruitt, and that there was no sign of foul play." She leaned forward in her seat. "Time is passing. My sister—"

"Isn't it possible your sister extended her vacation somewhere else?"

"It's possible," Kelly said. "But Belvista is where she was last seen. This is the best place to begin my search."

"Pruitt's Inn, you said?" Officer Browning stretched his arms overhead. "That Pruitt woman likes to make calls. She phoned a few weeks ago, complaining about a young woman who'd run off without paying her bill, leaving her suitcase behind, and who'd been gone for two days. Like we'd bother with something so petty." The officer's eyes focused on Kelly. "Was that your sister Meg?"

"Yes." Kelly's breath caught in her throat. "Was Miss Pruitt worried about Meg?"

Officer Browning shook his head. "Nah. She figured your sister paid up front for the first two days and then skipped out without paying for the other days she'd reserved. You know, leave things in the room as a decoy. Miss Pruitt offered to store Meg's things."

Kelly shot him a questioning look.

"Miss Pruitt hinted she expected a reward for storing the suitcase if Meg returned. If you want my opinion…"

"Yes, please."

"She wanted the officers to document the disappearance so she could rent out the room. She didn't want a bad mark from the Better Business Bureau for double-booking. Our officers checked your sister's room and all of Pruitt's Inn and the grounds. That's routine. The officers found nothing suspicious, no sign of a struggle…but there was a nasty confrontation with Miss Pruitt."

"What happened?"

Officer Browning pushed aside his paperwork. "Miss Pruitt got huffy when our squad car drew a crowd of gawkers. When our officers messed with her rose trellises to see if a ladder had been put outside your sister's window, she went wild. She whined about the officers ruining her business and her rose bushes. She chased them away with a broom. Can you imagine?"

"That's where you left it? Without finding Meg? Did they think a ladder had been put outside Meg's room?"

"No. There were no broken branches or disturbed areas. No drag marks from a ladder. Think about it. A person up to no good isn't going to stop and cover his tracks." He cracked his knuckles. "Most likely your sister met a real charmer and took off with him."

"That's the kind of romantic hogwash I read in the Belvista *Bugle*," Kelly sputtered.

"Hold on."

"No, you hold on. Late last night I searched the internet for any mention of my sister. Nothing. Then I searched for Belvista, and up comes this." She dropped a photocopy of a newspaper article onto his desk.

"Simmer down," Officer Browning said.

Kelly leaned over and read aloud the section she had highlighted: "Transient beauty fished for a high style of life off our famous boardwalk. Apparently her 'lures' worked, and she traveled off into the sunset with her trophy. Her innkeeper, Justine Pruitt, confided that the young woman didn't even bother to retrieve her few personal belongings. It seems our own Belvista is the end of the rainbow after all."

Kelly slammed her fist onto his desk. "A big joke at my sister's expense. They left her unnamed, as if they feared a slander suit. An opinion piece stuck into an article about poor women chasing rich husbands. Sensationalism, not journalism. And that was the end of any search for my sister!"

Kelly slammed her fist again. "And let's not forget the South Orange *News-Record*." She dropped another highlighted article onto Officer Browning's desk. "They picked up on the young-woman-rides-into-the-sunset garbage. They claim there were several witnesses, local artists, who said that my sister, again unnamed, had been seen repeatedly with the same man in Belvista. A tall, dark, handsome stranger." She rolled her eyes. "Gee, where have I heard that before?"

Officer Browning tapped a finger on the article. "She was seen with that man her very first night in Belvista."

Kelly ignored his comment, which implied that Meg was chasing men the minute she arrived in town. "Something terrible might have happened. My sister's missing. I want her found."

"But it could be she fell for that handsome guy and left town with him."

"You don't get it," Kelly said. "Meg would never run off with someone she'd just met."

"Happens all the time in Belvista," Officer Browning said, crossing his arms over his chest. "It's like they said right there in the *News-Record*." He tilted his chin toward the article. "It's the Cinderella story all over again. You know, poor young woman, hoping to find a better life, comes here looking for Prince Charming."

Kelly clenched her teeth. "My sister doesn't chase men, and she's not poor."

"That sure goes against what Miss Pruitt said."

Kelly was stunned. "What do you mean?"

"Miss Pruitt said Meg was supposed to go for a job interview at the Erdlinger's home on Monday morning."

"Job interview?" Kelly's eyes opened wide. "What are you talking about?"

"A nanny job. According to Miss Pruitt, it was only temporary to tide Meg over while she worked out some business angle with travel agencies back in New York. You must know about that."

"Of course." Kelly swallowed hard. "Meg's trying her luck as a photographer. She came to Belvista to gather material to create brochures filled with facts and photos of quaint towns."

"Would that be only New Jersey towns?"

"I'm not sure."

"For which travel agencies did you say?"

"I don't know."

"Sounds like you didn't know what your sister was up to." Officer Browning's grin turned into a smirk. "In any case, we tracked down that nanny lead. Your sister never showed up that Monday, and the Erdlingers hired someone else." He shrugged. "Look at it from our side. No family member inquired about Meg Madison until now."

"I am her *only* family. As I mentioned, I just returned home last night." Kelly glared at Officer Browning. "You've had almost three weeks since Miss Pruitt reported Meg missing. You must have found out something more than what you've told me."

Officer Browning pushed off with his feet, rolling his chair to a bank of file cabinets. He opened the bottom drawer of the last cabinet, labeled August, and rifled through the folders. "Everything's in this file." He rolled back to his desk. "Give me a few minutes to refresh my memory."

Kelly settled back and thought about Meg. She regretted their quarreling over money their last evening together. She wished she could take back her harsh words. Tears welled in her eyes. She missed Meg. She missed their happy-go-lucky parents. She missed the life they had shared in their cozy apartment in New York City.

Ten years ago, when she was twenty and Meg was thirteen, a freak accident had shattered that life forever. As their parents were crossing the street coming home from work at a nearby catering company, a car sideswiped a bus and careened into several pedestrians. Their parents died at the scene. The funeral took place three days later on a gray November day. Numb with grief, Kelly and Meg had tried to stick to their familiar routines of work and school. Expenses overwhelmed them. There were no relatives able to help. They moved to a smaller apartment and struggled to make ends meet. Kelly worked hard to advance herself at work and provide for Meg. Their relationship was often rocky, but—

Officer Browning coughed and jarred Kelly back into the present. "Her file is officially marked *CC*," he said.

"What does *CC* stand for?"

"Case Closed."

Kelly leaned forward, tossing her wayward curls away from her face. "May I see that file?"

"You'll have to speak to a detective."

"Could you arrange that now?"

"No chance. They're all involved in a training session with Detective Luke Campbell. He's our consultant in crime solving."

"I'd like Detective Campbell to 'consult' with me."

"I'll pass the word when they break."

"This can't wait," Kelly said.

He sighed. "Wait here."

Ignoring Officer Browning's words, Kelly followed him down the corridor toward a room marked Conference. Through the glass panel in the door, she saw a well-dressed man who looked competent and organized—brown tweed jacket, brown slacks, polished loafers, snappy tie. Detective Campbell, she assumed. He was talking and waving his arms. The men and women seated around the table, some in uniform and some in plainclothes, looked up from their notebooks and laughed at something Detective Campbell had said.

Kelly was furious. The Belvista Police Department sat around laughing while her sister remained missing. She stepped past Officer Browning and banged on the door. Detective Campbell, a startled expression on his handsome face, opened the door.

"You can't go in there," Officer Browning said, blocking her way.

Detective Campbell cut in. "It's okay, Officer Browning. You can go back to your desk. Part of my job is to serve the people. Our new Open Door policy, instituted by this charming woman, should facilitate matters." He flashed a winning smile.

"Very funny, but your fake flattery won't work with me," Kelly snapped. She pressed her business card into his hand. "Call me when you and Belvista's finest are done joking around. I want answers!"

"Yes, ma'am," he said, his gaze challenging her. "I look forward to your questions."

Annoyed by Detective Campbell's flippant manner, Kelly turned and walked away, her boots pounding the oak floor.

Officer Browning looked up from his paperwork. "That was uncalled for."

Kelly faced him. "You wouldn't think so if your sister was missing and no one cared. Please remind Detective Campbell to call me asap so we can discuss the *CC*. That's within your job description, isn't it?"

"I'll have to check the fine print." He smiled, obviously

proud of his humor. "Did you receive any calls or emails or letters from your sister while you were away?"

"No. If I had, don't you think I would have told you before now?"

"Didn't that worry you?"

"I... Meg..." Kelly was ashamed to admit to their angry parting. "I couldn't be reached. I was traveling in Europe."

He raised an eyebrow. "Nice life."

"It was a business trip, choosing designs for a client," she said defensively. "I have to help support Meg. She's young, still trying to find the right career for herself."

"Let's put this into perspective," Officer Browning said calmly. "Now that you're here and can shed some light on your sister's habits and plans..." he cleared his throat "...at least those you're aware of, we'll get to the bottom of this. You can start with filling out these missing person forms." He slid the forms across his desk.

"Thank you," Kelly said through tight lips. "I assume Miss Pruitt didn't fill out any forms?"

"No, she didn't." His grin again turned to a smirk. "She was satisfied with our investigation."

KELLY TURNED IN THE completed forms and gave Officer Browning a photo of Meg. She started to leave when voices and laughter coming from the direction of the conference room caught her attention. She looked down the corridor. Detective Campbell was strolling toward her, surrounded by his officers. He was charming them, working them for laughs. He looked her way, held up her business card, and nodded. Kelly whisked her luggage across the floor and hurried away. Slim chance he'd make time to search for Meg. He'd have to tear himself away from his adoring audience.

Kelly descended the steps into the breezy sunshine, convinced she couldn't trust her sister's welfare solely to the Belvista Police Department. They had the necessary skills and technology, but she had the will and determination. Proceeding toward the center of town, she told herself to move quickly with her plan to distribute flyers that contained Meg's photo and a plea for help in finding her.

Looking left and right, Kelly crossed the street into the traffic of modern-day cars and old-fashioned, horse-drawn buggies. She remembered the town's motto from the internet: *The charming crossroads of Victorian and modern times.* Interspersed with fast-food places and gas stations were quaint shops with gabled roofs and spindlework porches. Their windows advertised goods with Victorian touches. The shopkeepers, who were bustling about with customers, wore Victorian clothes.

Meg would have lingered here, gathering material for her photography venture. Now that Kelly saw Belvista's charm, she regretted calling Meg's plan "one more foolish scheme in your string of financial disasters." A mechanical noise came from somewhere behind her, like a roll of film winding to the end. She turned to see if it could be Meg photographing the town.

There were cameras everywhere. Her eyes searched the crowds, singling out the women. Some wore contemporary jeans and tops.

Others were dressed in Victorian long skirts and frilly blouses peeking from prim jackets with puffy sleeves. Meg was not among them. A car door slammed, but all the cars parked in the busy street appeared empty. Her nerves were thoroughly frayed. After all, Belvista was a tourist town. Tourists frequently took pictures and even slammed car doors.

Kelly continued toward the taxi stand. Angry shouts came from across the street. Shielding her eyes from the sun, she looked over and saw that a black Lexus with dark tinted windows had gone over the curb. The people on the sidewalk had jumped out of the way, knocking over a table of sale merchandise. Somewhere behind her, a car backfired. Kelly gasped, thinking it sounded like a gunshot. Goose bumps of apprehension prickled the backs of her thighs as she hurried on her way.

TWO

Pruitt's Inn

KELLY HAILED THE FIRST empty cab cruising by. "Pruitt's Inn," she said, hopping in.

The cabby worked his wad of gum to one side of his mouth. "The scenic route?"

"The fastest, please."

"One and the same." He stepped on the gas. The taxi pulled away, dodging potholes, tossing Kelly about until Depot Road turned onto the smoothly paved Ocean Boulevard. Hedges clipped short along the route exposed the gorgeous ocean view. Kelly savored the salty sea air and hoped that Meg had photographed this beautiful section of Belvista.

Horns honked incessantly.

Kelly peered out the back window and saw a snarl of cars, cabs, and horse-drawn carriages filled with tourists.

"Move along!" cried one cabby.

"Out of my way!" shouted a carriage driver.

Kelly's cabby hollered out the window, "Put a lid on it!" He turned to her. "Tourists! They want to visit the slow pace of Victorian times, but they want a seventy-miles-an-hour speed limit to get them there!" He drove on, muttering. Soon the traffic moved at a slow, steady pace.

"One of Belvista's exclusive neighborhoods," the cabby said, nodding ahead.

Kelly marveled at the miles of boardwalk to her right that overlooked the Atlantic Ocean. Waves broke over jagged rocks, spewing their foamy waters skyward. On her left, magnificent restored Victorian mansions took her breath away.

"Have you heard of the Erdlinger family?" Kelly asked.

"Sure. Everybody has. Lots of money. Well-connected."

"Do they live around here? I want to see them today."

"Too late. Last week I took Mr. Erdlinger to the airport. A business trip, as usual. Mrs. Erdlinger and the children are back at their apartment in New York City."

"Do you know their local address?" she asked.

"Sorry. I don't reveal personal stuff about my regular customers." He chewed his gum noisily. "This here's my favorite." He slowed in front of a Wedgwood-blue Queen Anne.

"Very nice," Kelly admitted, "but I'm pressed for time. Could you speed up?" She wanted to speak to Justine Pruitt and search Meg's belongings. "I'll give you an extra tip."

"No problem." The cabby pushed his foot to the floorboards and passed several cars.

Kelly heard the sound of screeching brakes and looked over her shoulder. A black Lexus with tinted windows swerved past a maroon PT Cruiser. Was that the same Lexus that had caused a commotion earlier? She had the funny feeling someone was following her. She rummaged through her purse for paper and pen to copy down the license-plate number, just in case.

Kelly looked again. The Lexus was back in line. It stopped at the intersection, even though it had the right of way. The driver no longer seemed in a hurry. He wasn't following her after all. Relieved, she settled back in her seat. Signs sprouted like weeds on the way west toward Pruitt's Inn. Rooms by the Week. Good View. Off-Season Rates.

"Here we are," the cabby said, veering toward the curb.

Kelly peered at the dilapidated yellow Victorian. Her heart sank. "It's not quite what I expected." She opened her purse and pulled out the copy of the Pruitt's Inn brochure she'd downloaded from the internet. Looking at the drawing, Kelly observed the artist's clever camouflage. Vibrant roses obscured the sagging wraparound porch, and oversize weeping willows hid the encroaching inns on either side.

Kelly stepped out of the taxi and set her luggage on the curb. She read aloud the words scrolled beneath the brochure drawing: "Miss Pruitt, the friendly proprietor of this twelve-room inn in the West End's Victorian Sector, personally guarantees courtesy and service."

The cabby vigorously chewed his gum. "Don't believe everything you read. Or half of what you see." He squinted his watery eyes. "I'll be going," he said, and he pocketed Kelly's generous tip. "Good luck. You'll need it."

Kelly walked up the front path. She crossed the creaking porch into the foyer and wheeled her luggage to the reception counter. The place was deserted. She tapped the service bell bolted to the scarred mahogany counter.

"Miss Pruitt?" Kelly called into the darkened hallway. She glanced around the decrepit foyer. The floral-print wallpaper was yellowed with age, its edges curled. Could it be the original paper? Kelly wondered.

"Miss Pruitt?"

"Just a minute," came the muffled words from a back room.

Turning from the counter, Kelly followed the carpet's threadbare path into the parlor. *What a creepy time-warp experience,* she thought. But then the faded beauty struck her. Bloodred hues along the carpet's edges were all that remained of a once-vivid design. The soft September sunlight filtered across the mahogany furniture's graceful arms and legs.

Fascinated by the lily sconces that flanked the mirror above the mantel, Kelly walked toward the fireplace. She stopped, startled by a man's reflection in the mirror. Where had he come from? She hadn't heard the front door open or seen anyone descend the staircase near the reception counter.

"You frightened me," Kelly said, whirling around to face the man with wavy brown hair. *Calm down!* He had a friendly smile and didn't seem frightening after all. Her nerves were really shot.

"I believe you dropped your business card case," he said, his voice as warm and friendly as his smile. "It fell to the street when you got out of the taxi."

"And you followed me in." She felt riveted to the spot by his striking appearance. He reminded her of men in the fashion industry she often ran across in the interior design business. His clothes were expensive, in earth-friendly tones of brown that accentuated his deep-set brown eyes.

"Guilty as charged. I followed you." He held out her case. "I thought you might need the cards or that the case might have some special meaning." He took a well-ironed handkerchief from the pocket of his cocoa-brown Windbreaker and polished the case. He gave a final swipe across her monogram, *KM.*

Well, this man's direct and sincere approach sure was nice after the sneering comments of Officer Browning and the formidable bravura of Detective Campbell.

"I'm Alex Bradford," he said, pressing the case into her hand.

"I'm Kelly Madison."

"A nice Irish name," he said. "And a pretty Irish face to go with it."

She smiled. "I'd like to show my appreciation," she said, thankful to have her business cards. She planned to hand them out to anyone who knew Meg and might want to call with information. "Could we meet for a latte, say, late this afternoon?" She didn't hold back. He looked as if he would know popular places in Belvista for the twenty-to-thirty age group, the type of place Meg would have visited. "You must know a nice coffee bar."

"I have a better idea. I could show you around right now, if you'd like. I'm guessing you're new in town." He fished his keys from his pocket. "My car is just outside."

"I have plans for the rest of the day. Maybe tomorrow?" Kelly suggested. She handed him one of her cards. "First I need to find my sister."

"I'll try again at a better time," he said.

Kelly followed him to the front door, thanking him again. He turned to her and gave her "the look." She knew that look from singles bars and business conferences. It meant, *I'm interested. Are you?* She wasn't. She was intent on finding Meg. He wasn't her type anyway. He was too young, probably mid-twenties. And despite his friendliness, he seemed fastidious and uptight. She liked a more mature man with a good sense of humor. Curious, she glanced at both sides of the street. There were several parked cars but no black Lexus. She felt relieved.

"Kelly Madison?" a woman's raspy voice called out.

Kelly turned back to the reception counter. A gaunt woman with pursed lips and a pinched face peered at her.

"Strong family resemblance," Miss Pruitt said. "You're obviously the older sister."

"Yes. Meg's twenty-three, and I'm…older." Touchy about her age, Kelly hated to admit she was thirty.

"Sign here." Miss Pruitt pushed a guest ledger toward Kelly. "I won't mince words. I don't like your coming here and stirring up trouble. And I don't want any more police swarming around here. Do I make myself clear?"

"Perfectly," Kelly snapped, then immediately regretted her brusque tone. She couldn't risk being kicked out. This was the best place in Belvista to find out what had happened to Meg.

Miss Pruitt tapped a bony finger on the calendar tacked to the counter. "Several weeks remain before the tourist season dies down. My guests expect peace and quiet. Unsettling rumors about your sister's departure might give the wrong impression. Six couples, all related, will be arriving soon. If one leaves, they'll all pull out. This inn is my livelihood." She clamped the ledger shut. "The girl's gone. She's run off. Accept it, that's my advice."

"My sister has not run off," Kelly said calmly, steeling herself against the counter. "She's been missing for almost three weeks, and the police haven't taken her disappearance seriously. I intend to take matters into my own hands." She forced a smile. "Can you try to see this from my side? The *Bugle* insinuated Meg was a gold digger. Today a police officer called her Cinderella searching for Prince Charming. But my sister, Meg, is not like that."

"Let's set matters straight," Miss Pruitt said. "It's not my fault your sister disappeared during her stay here."

"Then may I count on your cooperation in finding the person who is at fault?" Kelly asked, honey practically dripping from her lips.

"Here's the key to 206," Miss Pruitt said, her eyes narrowed to slits. "Your sister's suitcase is in the room."

"Thank you." Kelly gripped the handle of her luggage and strode toward the stairway, pleased with her small triumph. She hadn't won over Miss Pruitt, but she hadn't made her an enemy, either.

"Benny!" Justine Pruitt shouted down the hallway. "Help Miss Madison with her belongings!"

"I can manage, thank you," Kelly said sweetly.

As Kelly walked down the second floor's narrow hallway, the rose-print floor runner muffled the sound of her footsteps. She peered with suspicious eyes at all six rooms. Could Meg have been dragged into one of them the night she disappeared? Officer Browning claimed they had checked for signs of a struggle and found nothing. But had they inspected every nook and cranny? Maybe they had overlooked a wisp of hair swept behind a bureau.

If only she could search each room. Perhaps she'd find some proof that Meg had been there. Overcome with a sudden curiosity about the layout of the house and the possibility of a secret room, she left her luggage, returned to the stairway, and tiptoed to the third floor. She stopped at the top step. Before her was a duplicate of the second floor—six rooms, doors closed, the hallway silent, the guests probably gone for the day.

Returning to the second floor, Kelly hurried down the hallway, retrieved her luggage, and unlocked the last door on the right: 206, Meg's room. The door swung open, and she stepped into the room that occupied the northeast corner of the three-story house. It was sparsely furnished. The few massive pieces of mahogany made the room appear small and cramped. A no-smoking sign, signed Management, was taped to the vanity mirror.

Kelly tossed her luggage onto the bed and rushed to Meg's suitcase, which was sitting on the vanity bench. Proof that Meg had been forcibly taken from her room would give her something to report to Detective Campbell when he called. If he called. Heart racing, Kelly hoisted Meg's suitcase onto the bed, unzipped it and dumped the contents.

The last object to land on the bedspread was their mother's watch. Kelly had saved that watch for years and given it to Meg as a college graduation gift. Meg would never have left it behind. Never. Meg had not willingly left Belvista.

She spread out the contents of Meg's suitcase and studied them. She had seen Meg pack. Was anything missing? Not at first glance. Even Meg's purse was there, and a quick check showed nothing unusual about the contents. Noticing a book of matches and a half-full pack of cigarettes, Kelly wondered if Meg, who was trying to kick the habit, was sticking to her limit of three cigarettes a day, one each morning, afternoon, and evening.

She went through every item of clothing. Meg's pajamas were gone. They were her favorite gray pajamas with draw-string pants and camisole top, the neckline embroidered with a chain of daisies. Kelly checked again. Meg's silk scarf with a daisy design was missing, too. Every evening Meg put on her pajamas and that scarf to keep her hair out of her eyes, then plunked onto her bed and read until she was sleepy.

Kelly rifled through everything, searching pockets, turning jeans, tops, and socks inside out, hoping to find a clue. A movie ticket. Restaurant check. Receipt. Nothing. She ran her finger-tips down the row of blue glass buttons on Meg's blue cotton blouse. The button on the left cuff was missing. Kelly caught her breath. That button could have rolled behind a bureau. She would find out where Justine Pruitt kept the master key, enter every room, and search for clues.

She started to zip up the suitcase, when she saw a shiny piece of paper poking from a side compartment. It was a smudged walking-tour map of Belvista's neighborhoods. Turning from one page to the next, she noticed the checkmarks next to several places of interest and Meg's comments in the margins, written in her distinctive flowery style. Great! Her plan to distribute flyers with Meg's photograph just became more precise. After first exploring the beach and boardwalk—the most likely places that Meg would have been seen—she would follow the very route Meg had taken, visit the very places Meg had gone to. Somebody would remember Meg, maybe recall a conversation about where she was headed, what she intended to do.

Kelly pressed the map to her heart. She didn't care if Meg wanted to try another risky business venture. She would continue to support Meg emotionally and financially as she'd done since their parents passed away ten years ago. All she wanted was one more chance to make things right with Meg.

She had to accept that she and Meg were very different. She had put herself through a two-year design program at a technical school, taking night classes while working full time and caring for Meg. She had gotten so used to watching every penny that even when she began to make a good salary, she continued to shop in thrift stores. She liked the retro-glam look. But Meg was cut from different cloth. Meg had expensive tastes. Kelly knew that in some ways she was responsible for that. She had sent Meg to private school, paid for dance and art classes, and dressed her to fit in with her wealthy classmates. She had taken out loans to pay Meg's college expenses.

Kelly opened her own luggage and pulled out her favorite photo of Meg and herself. With the edge of her skirt she polished the heart-shaped pewter frame and set it on the vanity. There was Meg hugging her, smiling, peeking through bouquets of daisies in their neighborhood florist shop. To Kelly, that seemed a hundred years ago. She had chosen another photo of Meg taken that same day in the florist's shop and had it printed on flyers.

Kelly checked her watch. Nearly an hour had gone by, and still no word from Detective Campbell. She traded her boots for sneakers, knowing she'd be walking in sand. She glanced at Meg's empty suitcase. Was anything else missing? She closed her eyes and thought hard. Meg's digital camera was missing! Kelly had surprised her with it on her birthday. Why would Meg leave, taking her camera but leaving her purse and wearing pajamas?

She called the front desk. "Miss Pruitt, this is—"

"I know who you are," Miss Pruitt rasped. "The room 206 signal is flashing."

"Did you happen to put Meg's camera somewhere for safe-keeping?"

"Are you suggesting I've got sticky fingers?"

"No. I was just asking if you'd seen her camera. I can now assume she has it with her."

"Let me tell you, missy, if ever my fingers are sticky, it's because I'm making cinnamon muffins for my guests."

"Thank you," Kelly said through tight lips, and she hung up. Being sweet to Justine Pruitt was a real challenge.

Before leaving, Kelly parted the sheer white curtains. She checked the view, noting the tool shed, the narrow side yard, and the alleyway running behind the house. The rickety trellises wouldn't support the slightest man. The wraparound porch, which would have allowed access to the second story, didn't extend to this side of the house. Officer Browning had said there were no visible traces of a ladder. If anyone had forced Meg to leave, he hadn't come through the window.

Kelly left her room and locked the door. Filled with a sense of expectation, she hurried down the stairway.

THREE

Sam Chambers

KELLY CROSSED THE BUSY street and approached the crowded boardwalk, which stretched as far as she could see in either direction. She climbed one of the sets of wooden stairs spaced at frequent intervals and stepped onto the boardwalk. She looked around. Shops selling beach supplies, souvenirs, and clothes fit snugly between cafés with porches that emptied directly onto the boardwalk. The cafés were doing a rowdy business. Designer names and logos emblazoned every shirt. Expensive cars, including Mercedes-Benz, Ferrari, and Jaguar, were parked nearby. Wealthy residents as well as tourists flocked here just as the *Bugle* had stated. As the *News-Record* had hinted, the social set loved mingling with the free-spirited artists, who, attracted by low rents, called the West End home.

Kelly set to work. She approached people seated on café porches and tried to strike up a conversation, but no one appreciated a stranger barging into their lives. Shrugging off the flyers with the photo of Meg peering through bouquets of daisies, they leaned across the brightly checkered tablecloths, gesturing and laughing. Drumming up help in finding Meg was going to be harder than she'd thought.

For one brief moment Kelly thought she saw Alex Bradford, the man who had followed her into Pruitt's Inn. Wasn't that him standing on the porch of a café farther down the boardwalk? She took a few hurried steps, straining to see, but whoever it was had disappeared.

Ducking into the nearest café, Kelly approached a pudgy-faced man who was busily seating people.

"Okay if I pass out these flyers?" she asked.

He barely looked at Meg's photo. "Sorry. The owner isn't here. I don't have the authority."

Kelly tried at the next café. "May I post a flyer in your window?"

The owner shook his head. "No garage sales, no lost pets, nothing. Too much clutter for my small place."

"Pets?" Kelly bristled. "She's my sister."

"Sorry." He waved forward a young couple.

Kelly tried several more cafés. No luck. Laughter everywhere. People having fun. She visited several shops. Merchants seemed afraid she'd drive away business. This was a waste of time.

She stepped off the boardwalk and picked her way across the sand toward the water's edge. The beach buzzed with activity. Banners draped across volleyball nets announced the annual kite competitions. They were scheduled to begin in forty minutes, at 2:30, on the beach. Lots of vendors milled around. More crowds must be expected. Good. She had plenty of flyers to pass out.

Kids and adults were already making trial runs with their creations. They flew everything from dazzling masterpieces to crinkled brown-paper bags finished off with scrap-fabric tails. People strolling along the beach watched the aerial ballet of single-, dual-and quad-line kites. This was such a pleasant place. If only she weren't so worried about Meg, she could enjoy herself.

Kelly spoke to dozens of people and distributed flyers. No one remembered seeing Meg. Kelly sensed that many people went out of their way to avoid her. She was discouraged but hoped the flyers would pique someone's memory. Or curiosity. Perhaps someone who knew Meg while she was here.

"Miss! You with the flyers! Hello!" a man's voice shouted.

Kelly turned. The man hurrying toward her waving a flyer

was of medium height, tanned, his brown hair gelled into blond-tipped spikes.

"You're the one distributing these flyers? Do you know Meg Madison?" he asked. Dressed in a plaid flannel shirt, khakis, and work boots, he looked like a construction worker.

When Kelly noticed his earring and the silver pendant dangling from a leather thong, she decided he liked the working-guy-chic look. "I'm Kelly Madison, Meg's sister." Her pulse raced.

"My name is Sam Chambers. I—"

"Do you know my sister?"

"I only know of her. Can we talk? It's important." He checked his watch. "Do you mind walking with me in that direction?" He nodded toward some cafés farther along the boardwalk in the opposite direction of Pruitt's Inn. "I'm on my way to a two o'clock meeting. It's urgent, but so is speaking to you about your sister."

"Then let's get started," Kelly said, thrilled to meet someone willing to discuss Meg. Without a moment's hesitation, she walked with him along the beach away from the kite crowds.

"Let me come straight to the point, Miss—"

"Call me Kelly."

"Okay, Kelly. I'm Sam." He steered Kelly past a group of kids collecting shells along the tide line. "Your sister's disappearance, which was alluded to in the *Bugle* and *News-Record,* brought me to Belvista. I'm an associate professor of journalism at Seton Hall University, on sabbatical. Crime reporting is my specialty. Criminal behavior intrigues me."

"Criminal behavior," Kelly repeated, skirting around a sand castle village. "Then you believe, as I do, that Meg didn't leave here voluntarily."

"Meg was definitely kidnapped," Sam said, and Kelly was so startled that she dropped her purse. "Three other young women have disappeared from Belvista during the past year."

A chill ran through Kelly as she retrieved her purse. He had put her worst fears into words.

"That's a high number for a town of nine thousand permanent residents. It's even high when the tourists double the population."

"Hold on!" Kelly cried. "Everyone says the women ran off with wealthy lovers. Nobody mentioned kidnapping."

"I'm saying there's a kidnapper, probably a serial killer, on the loose in Belvista."

"Serial killer?" Kelly choked on the words. She instinctively stepped away from Sam. "First kidnapper, now serial killer. That's a huge leap."

"No, it isn't. Disappearances of women and children in today's world often mean they've been kidnapped. Kidnapping used to be for ransom money, but with sophisticated techniques like DNA testing, kidnappers got caught, and juries showed no mercy." He checked his watch. "I've taken seminars in forensic psychology. The horrible truth is that today's kidnapper is often a sociopath who plays with his victims, then discards them."

Kelly shook her head in disbelief. "How come nobody but you is talking about a serial killer?"

"Let me lay the groundwork." Sam sidestepped several couples unpacking a picnic lunch. "Do you remember the Thompson serial-killer case from a few years ago?"

"Vaguely. Somewhere in North Dakota, wasn't it?"

"Right. Mrs. Thompson provided her son, the killer, with alibis. Everyone thought she didn't believe he was capable of murdering six schoolgirls, but it turned out she didn't want the women in her bridge club to consider her a bad mother."

Sam strode toward higher ground, away from runners kicking up sand. "Then there's the Delaware case—"

"I don't care about North Dakota and Delaware. Let's talk about Belvista." Kelly grabbed Sam's sleeve to slow him down.

"Okay. Try this on for size. Belvista's town fathers are afraid of losing tourist business, so they deny the possibility that the missing women were kidnapped and possibly murdered."

"Murdered?" The word finally sank in. "You think Meg's been murdered?"

"Like the North Dakota mother, the folks of Belvista are in denial. No one likes to hear my theory that some people not only deny the presence of serial killers, they even cover their tracks."

"That sounds a bit far-fetched," Kelly said, wondering about his sanity. She wished Detective Campbell would call, giving her an excuse to leave. "Why didn't reporters pick up on your theory?"

He looked over his shoulder.

"Do you think someone's following us?" Kelly asked, feeling jittery.

"I'm just being cautious. My meeting isn't open to the public. Now, about the reporters ignoring my theory, Ted Honeycutt, the owner of the Belvista *Bugle*, wants only upbeat stories. His so-called reporters are his nephews, well-paid to paint a pretty picture."

"Apparently no one challenges this Ted Honeycutt." Kelly couldn't decide if Sam was a whistle-blower or paranoid. She would listen so she could run all this by Detective Campbell.

"Honeycutt's a mere puppet," Sam said. "So far as I can tell, the Belvista Business Club and its president, Hal Dunbar—he owns Dunbar's Department Stores—run this town. All the merchants filling their pockets with tourist dollars are satisfied with the Club's schemes for economic progress. They squelched rumors about a possible connection among the disappearances."

"A cover-up? That's hard to believe," Kelly said, hurrying to catch up. "There must be decent people in Belvista who would speak up for the missing women."

"Don't bite my head off," Sam said. "But the women were poor. Family members, if there were any, didn't press for continued investigations. Maybe they didn't have money or didn't care. I don't know. I hate to say it, but the women were easy prey."

Kelly hated Sam's lumping Meg with women who'd been abandoned by their families, but she wanted him to continue talking. "If your cover-up theory is correct, then the police went along with the business community and showed little interest in the missing women."

Sam nodded. "Police Chief Clemmens promoted the theory that your sister ran off with a lover. And why not? Police salaries come from taxpayers. And many are business people who rely on tourism. I confronted Chief Clemmens with my theories. His response? 'No bodies, no case.'"

Kelly shuddered. "He should work on sugarcoating his words."

Sam checked his watch again.

"Didn't the initial news about the missing women spark fear in the community?"

"Not really. The disappearances got lost in the fun-stuff news. That often happens in resort towns. Plus, the women were outsiders and had only been in town a short time, so the people of Belvista never questioned much. They fell for that hokey Cinderella and Prince Charming scenario."

Kelly realized they had been walking for about twenty minutes. They had come to that part of the beach where the boardwalk ended. Farther ahead was a park with picnic groves and a playground. Beach Park the sign read. Dozens of bikes were parked near the entrance. The street that had run parallel to the boardwalk now veered away, back toward the town.

"I'm good at reading body language," Sam said with a mischievous glance, "and I sense that you don't trust me."

Kelly kicked clumps of sand from her sneakers. "I guess I don't understand your personal interest in this."

"You mean, what do I gain from finding the serial killer?" He checked his watch again. "Recognition in professional circles, for a start, followed by a promotion to full professor." He turned and looked her straight in the eye. "But you must believe me. The killer will strike again. Until now, I had no clue who might be his next victim. You're in danger, Kelly. If he sees you flashing Meg's photos, asking questions, he'll try to stop you."

"So the capture of the kidnapper will advance your career. And you'd benefit if I were kidnapped," she said calmly. "No one could deny the connection between Meg and me. They'd have to pay attention to your cover-up theory."

"I wish I'd had more time to present this in a better way," Sam said. "I came to Belvista about three weeks ago, right after Meg was reported missing. I've done lots of research on the missing women. I'd be glad to share everything with you. We have a common goal, to find Meg."

The public address system squawked, and then a man's deep voice thundered announcements about the first round of the kite competitions. Crowds of people rushed from cafés and picnic groves past Kelly and Sam toward the kite area. Two men in dark warm-up suits, their faces nearly covered by the jacket hoods and the armloads of huge kites they carried, charged at Kelly and Sam, kicking sand. Blinded, Kelly tried to dodge out of their way. Too late. They crashed into her and Sam, knocking them to the ground.

"Get out of this town now," one of the men hissed, tossing kites on top of Kelly and Sam.

Trapped beneath a web of paper, sticks, string, and kite tails, Kelly and Sam struggled to free themselves.

"Are you okay?" Sam asked, helping Kelly to her feet. Clearing their eyes and brushing sand from their clothes, they looked in all directions.

"I don't see them," Kelly said. "They must have disappeared into the crowds."

Several people stopped to help. Kelly asked if any of them could identify the men. It had all happened so quickly that no one had had a chance to see the men's faces.

"It's all part of kite mania," replied an elderly lady wearing a miniature kite-shaped paper hat.

As the people drifted away, Sam said, "I'm running late, Kelly. I have to leave."

"That was no accident," Kelly said, catching up. "I'm start-ing to believe your theory. The police bought that nonsense about Meg's so-called lover. They might have overlooked other suspects. I'd like to tell you what I know about Meg. It might help."

"Finally, someone on my side." Sam flashed his generous smile.

Kelly swallowed hard. "Do you think Meg is—" she hesitated, afraid to hear her own words and Sam's answer "—already dead?"

"We should never give up hope. We'll work on this together."

"I'm expecting a call from Detective Campbell. Maybe he'll help us."

"I wouldn't count on it," Sam said. "Campbell's a decent guy, but he's caught up in training his officers."

They were now a short distance from the playground and park. Kelly could make out designated walking trails through thick foliage.

"Don't come any farther," Sam said. "I'm meeting someone who promised me a good lead."

"I'd like to tag along. The person might know something about Meg."

"I promised I'd come alone," Sam said. "The business community has closed ranks. This person is taking a chance by coming forward and meeting with me in secret." He stopped and kicked sand from his boots. "Where are you staying? I'll call."

"Pruitt's Inn."

"Meg's room, 206?" Sam's expression turned serious.

Kelly nodded.

"You're playing with fire. You didn't know about the possibility of a serial killer when you came here, but you know it now. Move out of Pruitt's Inn. I'm a few blocks away at my Aunt Grace's inn on Ocean Way. I'll be in touch."

As Sam walked away, Kelly sat down on the sand and pulled off her sneakers. She removed her socks, shaking them, pretending they were filled with sand, and kept her eye on Sam. He spoke on his cell phone as he cut through the playground.

He was now heading toward the park. She considered following him. She wanted to know whom he was meeting and what that person might know about Meg. She stood up and jammed one foot into her sneaker.

Something moved in the underbrush between the playground and park. A flash of dark color. Was it a shadow? Leaves rustled. Could it be birds searching for seeds? Squirrels chasing each other? She turned her attention back to Sam, but he was already out of sight.

Kelly leaned down and retrieved her other sneaker.

Her phone rang.

"Kelly Madison?" a husky voice asked. "This is Detective Campbell."

"About time," she snapped.

"Have you had lunch?"

"No. I've been busy. My sister, Meg, is missing, or have you forgotten that?"

"I know a place with good food, the Barnacle Café. It's not far from Pruitt's Inn. Are you near there?"

"Yes." He rattled off the directions. "I'd like to welcome you officially to Belvista."

Kelly clenched her jaw. Grains of sand crunched between her teeth. "Somebody already beat you to it."

FOUR

Olivia Moon

KELLY HEADED BACK along the beach toward Pruitt's Inn and the Barnacle Café.

"Kelly, wait up!"

Kelly turned and saw Sam walking away from Beach Park toward her.

"That sure was fast," she said, and she noticed his smile.

"I got that lead I was telling you about, but it can wait." He linked elbows with her. "Let's go to a café. We can talk about Meg and the other missing women."

"I wish I could, but I'm meeting Detective Campbell."

Sam looked disappointed. "Here's my cell phone number." He passed her a card. "Call me later."

Screams coming from Beach Park pierced the air. "A woman's been hurt! Get help!"

Sam's face froze. "Please don't let it be Olivia," he said. He grabbed Kelly's hand, and they ran across the sand. A handful of people ran along with them into the park, toward the shouts.

"Who is Olivia?" Kelly asked, running fast to keep up with Sam.

"She owns the Moon Café. My first day in town, I stumbled upon the place. Great organic food. We've become friends."

"Olivia!" Sam called as they came upon a handful of people in the park, leaning over a ditch, shouting words of encouragement. A silver-haired woman in a green caftan was struggling up the side of the ditch, which was strewn with decaying branches. Several people were trying to help, but she waved them away. "I'm okay," she called up.

"It's Olivia Moon, that crazy fortune-teller," someone said as Sam, with Kelly trailing behind, rushed to the woman's side.

"Maybe someone didn't like the fortune she told," wise-cracked a man with a toddler.

Sam reached down and helped Olivia out of the ditch. He turned to Kelly and made hurried introductions.

"Let's get out of here before the police come," Olivia said. "Whoever did this is long gone." She was badly shaken, but there was no blood and no sign of injury. "I don't want a scene."

"What happened?" Sam asked, brushing leaves from Olivia's caftan.

"Go on. I'm fine." Olivia waved away the people. "People trip and fall. Count me among them."

"Talk to me," Sam said as the people wandered away, making snide comments about crystal balls and tea leaves. Sam and Kelly, one on either side of Olivia, walked with her back toward the park entrance.

"Some guy came out of nowhere, pushed me." Olivia's voice trembled. "I rolled into the ditch, landed facedown. I didn't see who it was. A man—that's all I know."

A shiver ran through Kelly. Only minutes before, she and Sam had had a similar experience. She looked around at the thick shrubs and dense underbrush. She had the creepy feeling that eyes were watching, that danger was close by.

"Could it have been anyone in the crowd?" Sam asked, looking over his shoulder toward the ditch.

"I doubt it," Olivia said, hurrying now. "He wouldn't be dumb enough to hang around."

"Could be he gets his kicks out of being nearby. You know, like an arsonist watching a fire he'd set."

Kelly remembered several men among the women and children who had probably been nearby at the swings and monkey bars. None of them stood out in her mind. She pushed aside a low-hanging branch as they left the park. "It could be one of those bozos who messed with Sam and me."

"Were they strong?" Olivia kicked a stone lying in her path.

"Yes," Sam said.

"So was this guy," Olivia said. "Strong and sneaky. I've got the planets, the stars, even the Milky Way on my side. I'll get this creep, and when I do, he'll regret the day he was born, no matter what sign he was born under."

"Let's get away from here," Sam said to Olivia as they walked from Beach Park onto the sand. "The fewer people who see us together, the better. And, Kelly, you probably shouldn't mention this to Detective Campbell. Olivia and I are considered nutcases by the police. They scoff at her psychic abilities, and they think I see murder plots everywhere. It won't help your search for Meg to admit you were with us."

"It will be our secret," Kelly said, willing to do anything to keep two allies on her side.

"You can get together with us later at Olivia's," Sam said, his eyes busily checking the area. "It's the Moon Café on Hamilton Street. If you've got Detective Campbell on your side, make the most of it. I'm going to take Olivia home."

"See you both later." Kelly checked her watch and took off running. Questions came with every step she took. Was it Olivia whom Sam had met in the park? She thought so, but she couldn't be certain. If so, did what Olivia revealed to Sam have anything to do with Meg? Would they share the information with her? The police might consider them nutcases, but she wanted to get to know them better and make up her own mind.

Kelly crossed the boardwalk and came to the street. From the corner of her eye, she thought she saw a black car. Brakes squealed. Was it that Lexus again? It turned a corner and was gone. This alluring vacation town was taking on a very sinister and secretive appearance.

FIVE

Luke Campbell

STOPPING TO CATCH HER breath outside the Barnacle Café, Kelly tossed her wind blown curls away from her face. She was nervous about meeting with Detective Campbell. At the police station, his flippant manner had irritated her. Everything was a joke to him. She'd seen how he entertained his officers, playing everything for laughs with amusing comments. She wanted him to take Meg's disappearance seriously and do something about it.

Kelly ducked inside the café, which was nearly deserted, and immediately spotted the detective at a booth near the rear door. He stood, flashed a brilliant smile that Kelly figured had melted the hearts of countless women, and waved her toward the table.

"Luke Campbell at your service," he said cheerfully as she sat down across from him.

She scowled.

He quickly donned a serious expression. "As I remember, you're a take-charge, no-nonsense, cut-to-the-chase woman. You said you have questions, and I promised answers. So, jump right in."

His rapid-fire speech and rugged good looks unnerved Kelly. "I have even more questions now." She gripped the edge of the table. "I spoke with Sam Chambers. He thinks Meg was abducted by a serial killer. If he's right—"

"You should eat something," Detective Campbell said. "You'll think better on a full stomach. I read Meg's file just before coming here. I was hoping we could discuss it rationally. What do you say?"

"Shall we get started?" Kelly flapped open the menu.

"Stick with the special," Luke said, plucking the menu from her hands. "Joe," he called toward the counterman, "two specials, extra slaw, iced tea."

"Detective Campbell—"

"Call me Luke, if you like, and I'll call you Kelly. Let's begin this discussion on a friendly basis. You certainly have a way of—"

"Let's talk about my sister, shall we?" Kelly tapped her fingernails on the table. She refused to be sidetracked by his charm.

He held up his broad, callused hands. "Okay. Let's review the facts and see if the officers missed anything."

This was going better than she'd expected. "Thank you," she said, and she stashed her menu behind the ketchup and mustard bottles.

"First things first. What brought your sister to Belvista?"

Kelly looked into his brown eyes and felt an irresistible pull. "She planned to spend several days photographing Belvista on spec for travel agencies and then return to our apartment in New York City on Monday, August sixteenth. Apparently she changed her mind and set up a job interview for that very morning with the Erdlinger family."

"That would be the land developer, Henry Erdlinger, and his wife, Alice."

Kelly shrugged. "I don't know anything about them. I heard they wanted a nanny." She opened a paper napkin and placed it on her lap.

"Meg needed money. Is that right?"

"Yes. Why do you ask?" She felt guilty because she had refused to finance Meg's photography venture.

"You're not going to like what I'm about to say." Luke dumped his silverware from its napkin packet. "Women who run out of money sometimes take foolish chances with strangers."

"So that's your theory?" Kelly pounded both fists on the table, and the silverware jumped. "That Meg propositioned strangers?"

"I didn't say *propositioned*—"

"You're falling for the Cinderella and Prince Charming baloney Officer Browning is spreading around the police station."

"I'll come straight to the point," Luke said. "You admitted to Officer Browning that you didn't know about Meg's job interview until he told you. And you said that you and Meg hadn't communicated for twenty-four days because you were traveling in Europe and couldn't be reached. Is that right?"

"Yes," Kelly murmured, fighting back tears.

"I don't mean to upset you."

"I'm upset with myself, not you," she admitted.

"Now we're getting somewhere."

Kelly smiled in spite of herself.

Luke pulled out his notepad and scribbled something on a page.

She leaned forward, trying to read upside down.

He turned the notebook to face her.

"Kelly Madison smiled for the first time on September fourth," she read aloud. "Guilty as accused," she said softly.

"Now, tell me why you're upset with yourself. I figure it's about Meg."

Kelly took a deep breath. "Meg and I had a fight the night before she left for Belvista and I left for Spain."

"Was this a door-slamming, I-hate-you disagreement?"

"Yes," Kelly murmured. "It was so stupid. It started about clothes and ended up about money."

"Give me some details to work with."

"I was wrong—"

"Details."

"Okay. Meg teased me about my thrift-shop wardrobe. 'You

look like a hippie,' she said. I laughed it off and told her, 'The look is considered artsy by wealthy clients, and I saved a fortune.' And then, the years of scrimping and saving to support Meg and myself got to me. I let her have it. 'Maybe an artier look would help you in your photography career,' I snapped. Meg shot back with, 'Why don't you say it? You're fed up with my asking for money.'"

Luke didn't say a word, so Kelly plowed on. "I didn't mean to hurt Meg's feelings. It's just that she had tried so many hare-brained ideas. Rollerblade messenger, penthouse gardener, whatever, and none of them panned out financially. She's crazy with money. I was worried she'd never be able to support herself as a photographer either. When we left the next morning and went our separate ways, we weren't speaking."

Kelly knew where this confession would lead. "There's something you need to understand. Meg was only thirteen when our parents died. I've raised her, struggling to be both sister and parent. Yes, we've fought, but basically we get along. Meg is good to me. I can't remember how many times she'd find me at the kitchen table, bent over my checkbook, worrying how to make ends meet. She'd coax me into watching a movie, and soon I'd be enjoying myself. Meg and I love each other. I need her back in my life."

"I know you're trying to put that big argument into perspective. But it's possible that Meg is punishing you, hiding out, making you regret what you said."

"Meg's not like that. You're treating this as a squabble between sisters and overlooking—"

"Lunch," Joe announced.

Kelly's eyes opened wide as Joe set down before her a platter overflowing with a grilled chicken sandwich on a Kaiser roll, coleslaw, and a mound of potato salad.

"Another pretty one," Joe said in a low voice, and Luke waved him away.

"This is too much food," Kelly said.

"You'll need your strength to pass out all your flyers." Luke dove into his potato salad.

Flyers? How did he know about that? She jabbed her fork toward Luke. "You've been talking to Sam Chambers."

Luke captured her with his gaze. "Sam called me minutes after he met you. He's concerned about you, that you might take foolish chances in your search for Meg."

"If the police aren't interested, then, for Meg's sake, I'll—"

"I've taken on Meg's case."

Kelly's jaw dropped. "You're going to help me find Meg?"

Luke scribbled his address and phone number on a napkin and pressed it into Kelly's hand. "Get word to me anytime, night or day."

"Thank you." She was at a loss for words. She had misjudged him. "Why Meg's case? Any particular reason?"

He nodded. "To encourage officers to keep an open mind and disregard public opinion. I'm guilty too," he said, gripping his sandwich roll with both hands. "Until an hour ago, I hadn't gotten involved in Meg's case or any other case. I came here six weeks ago, on loan from the Atlantic City Police Department. My job is to modernize the Belvista Police Department, helping them to coordinate with the forensic lab at Seagirt, utilize the latest computer databases, rework their antiquated filing system, and so on. The officers are great, but they've resisted innovations. I blame the Victorian ambience of Belvista's West End, where the police station is located. Would you believe that some of my men say they 'court' a woman? Not 'see' her or 'go out with' her. 'Court' her."

"Quaint, I admit," Kelly said, "but I don't see a connection with Meg."

"What I'm getting at is these officers like the romantic notion that Meg and other women simply stepped away from their poor, unhappy lives and ran off with wealthy men. They dismiss Sam Chambers' theory that a serial killer is rampaging through Belvista."

"What do you think of Sam's theory?"

"I've heard it from the officers and from Sam himself. They think it's a crackpot theory. But he's an outsider, and they don't cut outsiders much slack." He took another bite of his sandwich, and Kelly realized that he had already jumped that hurdle and won over Belvista's police force. "Since your sister may be the victim of a kidnapper, I'm going to work her case. But personally I don't buy Sam Chambers' theory. He's putting a spin on the news to make it fit his theory. Too much guesswork, not enough facts, but I'll keep an open mind."

"Thank you," she said. "I appreciate—"

"Before you get carried away, I have to admit I have a personal reason for getting involved."

She set down her fork. "I'd like to hear it."

"I may be partly to blame. I was so focused on meetings that I pulled the officers away from all but the most important crimes. Maybe—"

"They didn't give my sister the attention they should have." Kelly finished his sentence.

"I decided this morning—"

Luke's cell phone rang. "Sorry," he said, and he checked the caller ID. "I have to take this." He spoke into the receiver. "Hey, what's up?" He smiled. "No, there's no reason to send backup."

As Luke talked, Kelly studied him. There was no denying that he was ruggedly handsome. His zest for life was certainly appealing.

Luke snapped shut his cell phone. "Let me tell you what's already in the works." He counted off on the silverware he'd lined up. "I've asked my team to re-interview the artists who said they had seen Meg with a man her first night in town, to get specifics from the reporters who wrote the satirical articles about gold diggers, and to nail down everything about the other women who've gone missing. I'll add an interview with the Erdlingers to the list." He dropped his cell phone into his pocket. "Sam offered to share what he knows. It's a start, and

I can promise you a real team effort. Now, what do you say we finish our lunch?"

"I'm suddenly hungry," Kelly said. She picked up her sandwich and ate a few bites. She hated to be pushy, but… "Please find Meg fast. I have only one week in Belvista, then I have to return to work. Money is tight."

Luke took a swig of his iced tea. "Tell me about your work. You're an interior designer, right?"

Kelly nodded. "Freelance. Last month I gave up a secure job as associate designer at Interiors, Inc. to begin my own design business. A client I'd met on an apartment-complex renovation—I'd been doing on-site touch-ups at rehabs—" She caught his questioning look and laughed. "Very glamorous work, wearing a hard hat, lugging stacks of tiles and cans of paints, and carrying a toolbox."

"Quite an image, hard hats with jewelry," he said, reaching across the table and touching the colorful glass-bead bracelet on her wrist. "Now, what were you saying about this client?"

She shot him an amused look. "He hired me to design the kitchens at three upscale town-house complexes north of the city in Rockland County. One, the Grenada, will have Spanish-influenced kitchens. The Provencal, a French theme. The Tuscany, Italian style. He wanted bragging rights that all the designs were inspired on location in the country of origin, not copied from magazines. So he paid my expenses to travel around those countries to gather ideas. A real dream job. Right now I've got dozens of ideas in my head and some sketched out, but I need to get everything ready for a formal presentation. I've set all that aside to find Meg. I have no steady income, and I've got loans hanging over me, but I'm hoping for an advance." She laughed bitterly and sat back in her seat. "Funny, I accused Meg of poor financial management. Seems I'm guilty of the same thing."

"Maybe your client will offer more of an advance when he hears about your predicament."

"No," Kelly said firmly. "I don't want to begin a business relationship hitting him with my personal problems."

"Isn't there anyone who could lend you the money?"

She sighed. "Yes. His name's Kyle Weston. He's loaded. But I'd have to grovel."

"Not a pretty picture."

"I'd have to admit I needed the money because of Meg. We broke up because of Meg. He said I spent too much time and attention on Meg. Can you believe it? Jealous of my sister. But a girlfriend of mine tells a different story. She saw Kyle with another woman. Same old, same old."

"He must be a fool," Luke said.

"No, I was the fool." She took several bites of her sandwich. Luke was easy to talk to. It was his eyes. They held you, encouraged the words from your mouth. She thought about telling Luke about the black Lexus, which popped up wherever she went. She considered mentioning Alex Bradford, the man who had followed her to Pruitt's Inn and possibly shown up at the boardwalk. But she decided against it, for now. She wanted to keep the focus on Meg.

"As a designer, you'd get a kick out of the fixer-upper I just bought near here," Luke said. "It's a Carpenter Gothic. A real chance to use my woodworking skills. I plan to rent it out when I return to Atlantic City. Maybe in a spare moment, you could offer some suggestions."

"I'll make you a deal. If you find Meg this week, I'll design your kitchen as a thank-you."

"I don't take bribes," he said.

"It's not a bribe. It's a token of my appreciation. What do you say?"

"Deal." He reached across the table and shook her hand.

The warm excitement still tingled on her fingertips as she left the Barnacle Café.

SIX

Moon Café

AFTER LEAVING THE Barnacle Café, Kelly asked the man at the newspaper stand for directions to Hamilton Street. "I can do better than that," he said, and he sketched a map on a scrap of paper. "Don't get lost in that jigsaw puzzle of streets." He tipped his baseball cap as he handed her the paper.

Twenty minutes later Kelly turned the final corner indicated on her map and came to the fringe of the West End. Antique Alley read the street markers. Sidewalks made of octagon-shaped cement pieces defined the six-block area. Cafés, vintage clothing boutiques, and several upholstery stores were nestled among the many antique shops. Kelly picked her way past the chairs, curio cabinets, and tables overflowing with dishes, bric-a-brac, and jewelry that lined the sidewalks. She'd love to browse through the vintage clothing, but that would have to wait until she found Meg. Just beyond a bookstore, she saw a sloping green awning with the name Moon Café. As she came closer, the fancy calligraphy signs in the window caught her eye. Fortunes Told. Internet Access. Unique Gifts. Organic Cuisine.

Kelly opened the door and stepped inside. The pleasant aroma of flowers and scented candles greeted her. Harp music and the gentle sounds of wind chimes soothed the dozen or so people at the tables and counter enjoying soup and sandwiches. All six computer stations were busy.

Dazzled, Kelly took it all in. Open shelves from floor to ceiling overflowed with a conglomeration of candles, bath prod-

ucts, DVDs, and garden decorations. The ceiling was painted
a deep blue with glittery stars, a huge moon, and a white swirl
representing the Milky Way. A sign that said Yoga and Meditation Classes pointed to a curtained area at the rear of the shop.
BYOM. Bring Your Own Mat read the scribbled reminder
glued to the sign.

Kelly was intrigued. She and Meg both practiced yoga. They
used to take classes together before they started arguing so
much. It was hard to meditate when hostility crackled like
electricity between them.

Olivia, now wearing a purple caftan, came from a curtained
alcove labeled Consultation Room and bustled toward Kelly. A
few bandages on her arms covered the scrapes she'd suffered
in the park. After glancing out the window and scanning the
sidewalk and street, Olivia greeted Kelly warmly. "My customers expect me to dress like you," she said, nodding at Kelly's
outfit. "A renegade with romantic touches. Don't spread the
word, but I have a degree in informational technologies. The
occult started out as a hobby, but it turned into a successful
business. It's more fun than the corporate world."

Olivia led Kelly toward the alcove. "Sam and I were running ideas past each other. My daughter, Hazie, will be here
soon. You'll want to talk to her. She's the reason I met with
Sam in the park."

"Does this have anything to do with my sister, Meg?" Kelly
asked.

"Sam and I think so. Hazie does, too." Olivia smiled. "I met
your sister here. A real charmer, who wears her emotions on
her sleeve. I told her fortune."

"You talked to Meg? How was she? Did she say she was in
trouble?" The questions tumbled from Kelly's lips.

"She was fine except for some bad karma with a man. We'll
get back to that. First you need to talk to Hazie."

"Did someone mention my name?" A teenage girl carrying sacks of flour came from the storage area and nudged
the door shut behind her with the heel of one clunky sandal.

Kelly caught only a glimpse of a room chock-full of cans and boxes. Hazie, in black jeans and T-shirt, had her rapt attention. The teenager wore maroon lipstick, long straight bangs, and a stubby ponytail that spiked out like a raggedy Brillo pad. Spiderweb tattoos climbed one side of her neck. A gold ring dangled from her belly button, and a string of pierced earrings rimmed each ear.

"You must be Kelly," she said, flashing a mouthful of teeth with a slight overbite.

"And you must be Hazie."

"You're clairvoyant, like my mom," she said, and they both laughed.

Hazie set the sacks on the kitchenette counter. "My squash soufflé soup is holding its own." She nodded toward the Crock-Pots simmering away. "But my zucchini muffins are almost gone." She wiped her hands on her jeans. "I'll make another batch."

"Talk to Kelly first," Olivia said, smiling affectionately at her daughter. She slid aside the curtain that separated the alcove from the main room.

"Come on in, Kelly," Sam said, gathering scribbled pages of notes. Tarot cards, a crystal ball, and teacups sat in the center of the table. Shelves, which lined the walls, overflowed with books and magazines. "Welcome to my home away from home. It's a good place to think."

Olivia chimed in, "We think alike."

Sam smiled. "My favorite chef, Hazie, has an interesting tale to tell. It happened at Berne Community College, twenty minutes from here. She's a first-year student."

"It's better than high school. A lot less hoo-ha," Hazie said. She plunked down on a chair and crossed her legs, yoga-style.

"Start at the beginning," Sam encouraged.

Hazie nodded. "I was in the library computer room this morning, researching a history assignment. A big assignment!" She rolled her eyes. "Anyway, I printed out a page from the internet and went to the duplicating machine to pick up my copy.

Somebody else's copy was lying in the tray." She shrugged and crinkled her nose. "Hey, I'm curious. I picked it up along with my own and went back to my seat. Several minutes later, Jeff Traskell—"

"His father owns Traskell Insurance Company, and he's a big gun in the Belvista Business Club," Sam interjected.

"And he's an arrogant snot, just like his son," Hazie said. "Anyway, Jeff burst into the library and rushed to the copy machine. He checked the wastebasket. He stormed the aisles, passing by everyone at the computers, looking at their desks. He passed behind me. I could smell his angry sweat. He went to the librarian, pointing at the copier, and the librarian shook her head. I was safe. She hadn't seen me at the machine. Whew!"

Hazie wiped imaginary perspiration from her brow with the back of one hand. "Jeff spoke to the students sitting near the copier. They shook their heads and waved him away. No surprise there. Nobody likes Jeff Traskell. He gets his kicks from hacking and snooping into other people's business and spreading viruses."

Hazie uncrossed her legs and crossed them the other way. "I went into the restroom and read his hot document. It was a copy of an email he'd sent to his geeky hacker friends Adam and Ace. Jeff is such a nerd, keeping a hard copy. Anyway, I called my mom and told her to tell Sam." She tried to ruffle Sam's hair, but he ducked out of her way. "He's been working hard on his story."

Olivia said, "I called Sam and told him to meet me in the park at two o'clock. There are too many big ears at my café. But, as you know, the park turned out to be a bad idea."

Kelly blurted out, "What did the email say?"

Hazie plucked a folded piece of paper from her pocket and handed it to Kelly.

"Dear old Dad came through again," Kelly read aloud. "Five hundred buckaroos for hacking into emails between those geezer council members about construction bids. Ferguson thanked Dad big-time. See me for your cut."

"Ferguson runs a construction supply business," Sam added.

Kelly continued reading: "Dad gave me another two hundred for continuing to hack into the Cinderellas. Somebody was poking around the Cinderella sites late last night."

Kelly gasped. "The Cinderellas?"

"Traskell was obviously curious about their disappearances," Sam commented. "Knowing him, it was business related."

Hazie turned to Kelly. "Looks like when you went on the internet site about Pruitt's Inn, Jeff Traskell alerted his father that somebody new was interested."

Sam leaned forward. "They've probably been worried sick since you set foot in Belvista. You're the first family member of a missing woman to become involved."

Olivia came in. "Hazie honey, your regular customers are waiting for you." Olivia turned to Kelly. "My Hazie gives free internet help, and the customers love her. She's putting herself through college on their generous tips. She's one smart cookie."

"Mom, come on. You know I'm into muffins, not cookies," Hazie said, nudging her mother with one elbow.

"And she's cool under pressure," Kelly added, holding up the email.

"I see no reason to go to the police about that," Olivia said. "Sam has the information and can work with it. Jeff Traskell could hurt my Hazie. He's a bully. And Jeff's father is a big shot in the Business Club. He might retaliate for our putting Jeff into the police radar. He could find a way to shut down my café with zoning infractions. This is my livelihood and Hazie's ticket to college. Kelly, you understand my concern, don't you?"

"Yes, I'm the same way about Meg." Her voice cracked. "But I should have been more diligent."

"Meg will turn up. We'll see to that."

"Thank you, Olivia." Kelly patted the chair next to her. "Now, please tell me about Meg."

"Meg was upset about a man," Olivia said, settling herself

on the chair. "She didn't say who. But I think she was falling for an artist named Michael Duprey. Meg bragged about him—gorgeous, dark hair, really built, six-pack abs, the whole bit. She wanted to know if he would be in her future. I read the Tarot cards and looked into the crystal ball. No answers there. It happens sometimes. I told her to follow her heart. She liked that advice. She was only here about fifteen minutes. It was a Saturday. I know because our special of the day was raspberry tea. She was in a hurry. I figured she was planning to meet this Duprey guy. Later I saw his name in the *Bugle*. He was one of the artists who claimed they saw Meg walking the boardwalk with a man shortly after she arrived in Belvista."

Kelly was stunned. She couldn't believe Meg had gone to a fortuneteller for advice. Or that two men Meg had just met were so important to her.

"How about a cup of honey-orange tea for everyone?" Olivia asked, pushing herself up from her chair. "It's been a long day. It will perk us up. I'll get Hazie to throw in some sandwiches," she said as she headed toward the kitchen area.

Sam squared the corners of his pile of papers. "I was hoping you'd show up, Kelly. I went home and got my notes on the missing women. I'd like to run everything by you. Maybe we can see if Meg fits the pattern I've found."

"I'd like that," Kelly said. She felt hopeful. She would find answers here.

SEVEN

Profiles

SAM SET OUT THE ARTICLES from the Belvista *Bugle* and the South Orange *News-Record*. "Do you have any questions before I get started?"

Kelly stirred her tea. "How did you connect the dots and see random disappearances as the work of one serial kidnapper?"

"Luck, I guess. Certainly not from anything the police said or did. They investigated the disappearances—not very thoroughly, in my opinion. They found no indication of foul play, saw no likely motive, and heard little or nothing from the women's families demanding further investigations. To paraphrase Chief Clemmens, 'They found no bodies, so there was no case.'"

Sam sat back in his chair. "I was in my office at the college perusing the newspapers for stories that would reinforce my lectures. The Cinderella concept caught my eye. It seemed so naive and outdated. Poor women snare wealthy lovers and leave town." He shook his head in disbelief. "Most women today can support themselves, and the wealthy men I know want a woman from their own social circle. So I decided to come to Belvista to investigate. I quickly found out that Meg made number four. Maybe there were more."

"You found their names in missing persons' reports," Kelly reasoned.

"Yes. I spoke to the people who filed the reports. Granted, the first disappearance was back in April, and people's memories had faded, but you'll see patterns. I'd like you to read these mini-profiles that I've worked up." Sam slid the first sheet toward her.

Kelly read Sam's notes to herself. #1—Stacy Deems, disappeared on April 16. She came to Belvista from New York City by bus on April 14. According to Mario Salvo, the owner of the Dockside Restaurant, Stacy saw a Waitress Wanted sign on the bulletin board at the bus depot. Salvo hired her on the spot, and she took a room nearby. He said she went to a store and bought black pants and a white shirt—the required uniform—and was a good worker.

Two days later, when she didn't report to work, Salvo called her rooming house. She hadn't come home that night, according to Peter Zanovich, the owner. Zanovich didn't see any reason for alarm. However, he didn't know her or her habits. The Dockside Restaurant is an expensive eatery with wealthy clients. Stacy was pretty. Several men talked to her. Unfortunately, after this first disappearance, a police officer casually remarked that "Cinderella had run off with her Prince Charming." The *Bugle* picked that up, and it stuck. Her suitcase eventually went to Bargain Bins, a thrift shop. I went there, looking for possible clues among her belongings, but the suitcase was gone. It sold for three dollars, according to the manager, Luisa Prada. The contents, inexpensive clothes, were scattered throughout the store.

Kelly felt uneasy. Meg, like Stacy, had come by bus from New York City.

"Read the next profile, and you'll see a pattern forming," Sam said. He passed another sheet of paper toward Kelly.

Again, Kelly read to herself. #2—Kim Eberly disappeared on June 10. Kim came to Belvista from New York City by bus on June 7. She took a job at The Embassy Car Wash, advertised on the bus-depot bulletin board. Kim, like all the car-wash help, was a pretty young woman with a great smile. The Embassy Car Wash caters to a wealthy clientele who drive expensive cars. Lots of chitchat. Generous tips. When last seen,

Kim was wearing sneakers, jeans, and a blue T-shirt beneath a blue plaid shirt. She didn't show up for work on the third day. She hadn't returned to the inn the previous night. Her landlord tossed her suitcase into the garbage. The Prince Charming idea gained momentum.

"Several similarities," Kelly commented. Her stomach churned. Meg was pretty too.

"Here's a somewhat different scenario," Sam said, and he slid her the sheet of paper.

Kelly read again. #3—Mary Waverly, a jewelry maker, roared into Belvista on July second, can't say from where, in her old beat-up van for the annual Fourth of July weekend craft show. It's held in Pinecone Park just south of the bus depot. It's popular, crowded, draws people from surrounding counties. Mary paid a five-dollar overnight fee and slept in her van on the grassy area next to the parking lot. Many other crafters parked nearby.

On Monday, July 5, the morning after the show ended, a jogger found Mary's van, a dog whimpering inside, in the deserted lot. The police were called. Jewelry and money, but no Mary. People remembered her—pretty, talkative, customers liked her, she made many sales. A crafter named Jane Van Horn, specializing in silver and stone, had a table next to Mary's. I found Jane's address through vendors' permits at city hall and called her. She provided good information. I found the name and phone number of other crafters set up at nearby booths, but either their numbers were disconnected or they didn't want to get involved. Mary's address was unlisted, as was her phone number. Jane Van Horn said that Mary was a free spirit who lived in her van and traveled from one craft show to the next. Jane remembered several men asking Mary to go for a drink, lots of "What time do you get off work?" That fueled the Prince Charming rumors. Mary liked very colorful clothes. She told Jane that the colors worked like a magnet to draw in crowds. Nobody knows what she was wearing when she disappeared.

The van was old. Insurance had lapsed. It was towed away by Todd's Towing for scrap.

Kelly looked into Sam's inquisitive eyes. "Meg's story is different." She knew she sounded defensive. She couldn't help it. "Meg was well dressed. Her suitcase wasn't very worn." Kelly's words choked in her throat.

"And here's what I don't understand," she said. "All four women left their suitcases and belongings behind. If they were running away, surely they would have taken them along. Didn't the police find that suspicious?"

"You would think so. But here's what I dug up. A reporter for the *Bugle*—the nephew of *Bugle* owner Ted Honeycutt, who filters every story through rose-colored glasses—was hanging around a café that police officers frequent. He overheard an officer wisecrack that the women, the Cinderellas, left without their suitcases 'because their Prince Charmings probably promised to buy them fancy dresses and glass slippers.'" Sam shrugged. "Comments like that spread quickly and hindered the investigation. This town isn't used to major crimes like kidnapping. People keep making the facts fit the Cinderella fantasy. I don't know what it will take to wake them up."

Kelly swallowed hard.

Sam continued. "The reporters never linked the missing women—Stacy Deems, Kim Eberly, Mary Waverly, and your sister, Meg—by *name*. Just by insinuation. I blame Ted Honeycutt and his *Bugle* for that. The police too. I could go on and on."

Sam stacked the profiles. "Here's what I think happens," he said. "The kidnapper goes to the bus depot and spots his type. Young, pretty women who don't appear to have much money, traveling alone, come to Belvista for work. He follows them, finds out they don't have room reservations or steady employment. Apparently they don't have relatives or friends to stay with. They might easily give the impression, judging from their one worn-out suitcase, that they intend to stay for seasonal jobs and then move on. He stalks them for a day or so, learns their routines, and kidnaps them at night. The kidnappings occur about a month apart."

Sam fanned out his notes. "Four women, counting Meg, disappeared, mostly in the busy tourist season, and—"

The shop lights dimmed, blinked, and went out. Kelly gasped. She reached for Sam's hand. The café was cloaked in darkness. Customers shouted. Tables and chairs grated on the linoleum floor. Silverware clattered.

"Didn't you pay your bill, Olivia?" a woman's voice called out.

"Darn, I forgot to back up my disk," came a man's disappointed voice.

"The lights are on all around us," said Hazie, who had made her way to the front door. "We're the only place without power."

"I'll check the circuit breakers," Olivia said as she fumbled for a candle. "Stay calm, everyone. I'll have this fixed in a minute."

Kelly and Sam grabbed candles and followed Hazie and Olivia into the supply room. Olivia flipped the master switch. The lights came on. Cheers rose from the other room. Boxes of tea bags were scattered everywhere.

"What a mess!" Olivia cried.

"The Boston Tea Party all over again," Hazie said.

Sam stepped outside into the alley and looked both ways. "Whoever did this didn't hang around," he said. "But he wants us to know he was here."

"I'll call Detective Campbell," Kelly said, reaching for her cell phone.

"No." Olivia put a hand out to stop her. "Hazie and I have friends, Bill and Bob. They're brothers. We call them the Muffin Men. They stop in every morning for a muffin on their way to work. They own a gym just a few doors from here. They'd scare anybody away."

Hazie made a mean face. She cocked a skinny arm and pointed at her egg-sized biceps. "They'll look after us better than the police will."

"You got that right," Olivia chimed in. "We're like family here. We're not the Business Club in-crowd. We call those folks the in-laws. We're the outlaws." She chuckled. "Who knows what they call us?"

AFTER THE MUFFIN Men, Bill and Bob, arrived, Sam drove Kelly to Pruitt's Inn.

"I think we should tell Luke what happened at the Moon Café," Kelly said.

"Not unless Olivia agrees," Sam said, turning right at the corner. "I owe her that."

"Okay," Kelly agreed, but she felt uneasy. Sam was loyal to Olivia, and that was admirable. But Sam wanted to keep secrets from Luke. To her, that was a bad and possibly dangerous decision. She wanted all the help in finding Meg that she could get. She didn't know Sam or Luke very well, but if she had to choose which one to believe and depend on, it would be Luke. Sam had ulterior motives. Job promotion, fame, glory—all that good stuff. Sam was considered a crackpot by the police and didn't have their cooperation. Luke was respected and had every resource at his fingertips. Maybe Luke was right, that Sam was putting a spin on the news to make it fit his kidnapping theory. Could be Sam didn't have all the answers or a credible theory. But Luke might not come up with any better ideas. She would remain open to other people's ideas. She had nothing to lose and everything to gain.

Sam glanced at Kelly. "Luke might resent being disturbed on a Saturday night. He's having a fling with a perky little nurse named Jeannie Wilkins."

Like a bucket of cold water, disappointment struck Kelly in the face. Her jealous reaction surprised her. She had just met Luke. She was still getting over Kyle Weston. She was becoming man-crazy! It must be the air in Belvista, she thought. Or her hormones running wild.

EIGHT

A Busy Morning

CHURCH BELLS CHIMED as Kelly walked across the porch of Pruitt's Inn. "Darn!" She caught the cuff of her leather jacket on the railing and heard it rip. "Darn!" Her favorite jacket, a consignment-shop bargain. Sitting down on the step, she withdrew her sewing kit from her purse. She threaded a needle. As she repaired the damage, her mind drifted to a July evening eight years ago.

After her first day on her new job, promoted from seamstress to supervisor at a drapery factory, she had arrived home late, exhausted. Meg, who was usually talking on her cell phone to her friends, greeted her at the door of their cramped apartment with a smile. Then Meg, who disliked cooking, served a casserole and surprised her with the linen sewing kit to celebrate the promotion. The clumsy cross-stitching of the daisy-chain pattern made the gift very special. Meg had thoughtfully stocked the kit with needles, pins, thread, and two pairs of scissors.

Kelly suspected that this sudden change of behavior had occurred because Meg had dropped by the drapery factory for an advance on her allowance. Meg, who had struggled past the cutting tables, got sick to her stomach from the heat, the roar of sewing machines, and the odor of machine oil. Later, outside the factory, gulping fresh air, Meg had said, "I didn't know you worked so hard to support us. I'm sorry I've been such a brat."

Now on Pruitt's porch, Kelly, still thinking of Meg, trimmed the threads from her sleeve and returned the scissors to her kit.

Kelly looked up at the sound of whistling. A heavyset man, probably in his mid-thirties, was backing toward the porch. All elbows and knees, he was maneuvering a wheelbarrow overflowing with yard clippings. Before Kelly could jump aside, he'd plowed into her.

"Excuse me," he said, steadying the wheelbarrow.

"You must be Benny," Kelly said.

"Yes, I am. I work for Aunt Justine, even on Sundays." He scooped up the spilled leaves. "I know who you are. Aunt Justine said you was Meg's sister and just as pretty. She warned me not to stare."

"I can see you're a big help to your Aunt Justine," Kelly said, noticing his childlike honesty. "May I count on your help too?"

Benny shrugged. "I guess so."

"I have some questions about my sister, Meg."

Benny glanced at the house. Kelly followed his eyes and saw the curtains part. "When Meg stayed here, did you notice anyone talking to her or following her? Maybe a handsome man with dark hair walking her to the front door?"

"Like I told the detectives, I didn't see nothing. Didn't hear nothing neither."

Kelly handed Benny the trowel that had fallen into the flower bed. "You're doing a terrific job weeding, Benny."

"I'm the yardman for this entire block." He wiped his hands on his pants. "Aunt Justine won the community award for the most improved yard. After that, I got lots of work. Now we're trying for most improved street."

"You have quite the green thumb," Kelly said.

"It's not my thumb, Miss—"

"Call me Kelly."

"Okay, Kelly." He smiled. "It's the fertilizer. Most people settle for dried-out cow manure. I like mushy fish guts, fresh from the pier. They really perk up the shrubs."

"I don't want to be late for church," Kelly said, turning to leave. "If you remember anything about Meg, please tell me. It could be important."

Benny grinned. "Sometime we'll go to the pier. I'll show you those great fish guts."

Angling her brown beret, Kelly strode down the street. Her boots and comfortable, Moroccan-print skirt were a good choice for the hours of walking she planned. Checking Meg's map, Kelly turned toward areas surrounding the center of town that Meg had circled, possibly on her way to explore Belvista's landmarks. Meg had underlined the description at the bottom of the map: *A pleasant blending of diverse architectural styles, including Victorian Gothic, Gothic Revival, and Eastern Stick.*

Winding her way through the streets, she imagined Meg photographing the balustrades, fish-scale shingles, and octagonal cupolas. She grew suddenly anxious. Had someone tempted Meg to come inside, promising to let her photograph the interior? Kelly approached the center of town with her imagination running wild. She turned the corner onto Front Street, which bustled with traffic and pedestrians. Church bells clanged, scaring flocks of birds into the maple trees. The joyful bells continued, lifting the gloom from her shoulders. As Kelly walked toward St. Anne's, she passed young families, couples, teenagers, elderly people. Everything seemed as normal as could be.

Sam Chambers could be mistaken. This was such a peaceful town. An evil person would stand out here like a rough tile against a glazed one. Or would he? Nowhere was it written that an evil person would necessarily look evil.

Kelly entered the pretty church, fragrant with wood polish, and seated herself near the back. As the Mass progressed, Kelly relaxed. Familiar rituals comforted her. Father Shaunassey's lilting speech and birdlike movements reminded her of Father O'Rourke back home in St. Joseph's parish. Later, when he stepped to the front of the altar to make his final announcements, the light that streamed through the stained-glass windows cast colorful designs on the marble floor. Kelly felt he was looking straight at her as he scooped his hands through the colored flecks.

"The light is a reminder," he said, "that brighter days lie ahead...." His eyes searched the parishioners. "That God is the bright, shining light in our lives. He recognizes our weaknesses. He knows that we are sometimes driven to unpardonable decisions. He forgives...."

Father Shaunassey left the sentence hanging. Kelly wondered if he always gave emotional sermons in such an impromptu manner. Father Shaunassey then happily rattled off announcements about births, weddings, and the building fund. Then he sighed deeply. "Many among you have already heard the sad news about our young parishioner, Julia Newcomb."

His voice trembled. "After being a patient for several weeks at the Belvista Hospital because of injuries suffered in an automobile accident, our beloved Julia died yesterday morning from complications. She is now at peace in the Heavenly Kingdom." Coughing and sniffling, the parishioners shifted on the squeaking pews. "The family asked me to announce they will receive visitors tomorrow and Tuesday. The bulletin board in the vestibule contains further information."

When Mass ended, Kelly waited until the church emptied. She walked to a side altar and knelt before the statue of Mary. In the flickering candlelight she prayed for Meg's safe return. She wanted to linger, but time was slipping away.

As Kelly strode toward the vestibule, the hollow sound of her footsteps echoed across the marble floor. Stopping to retrieve Meg's map from her purse, she realized that the echoing footsteps continued. She whirled around.

"Oh, it's you," she said, relieved, recognizing Alex Bradford, the man who had come to Pruitt's Inn to return her card case. Sam's serial-killer theories were making her jumpy. "I had the crazy idea that someone was following me."

"Sorry. I didn't mean to frighten you," he said, apparently taken aback by her startled expression. "I'm attending Mass, as

I do every Sunday. I saw you and thought maybe today you'd have some time to explore our town." His voice was as friendly as she remembered from Pruitt's Inn.

"My nerves are frazzled," Kelly said. "Jet lag, lots of stuff going on in my life right now."

"Sounds intriguing. Why don't you tell me about it?" he said. "Maybe over a cup of coffee after a tour of the town? You were too busy last time we talked."

"I have time now."

"I know a nice bakery. On the way, there's something I'd like to show you."

Kelly wondered if she had misjudged him when they first met. He didn't seem so fastidious now.

"Sounds great," she said.

A tall, middle-aged man in a gray suit approached and nodded hello to Kelly. "Alex, I'd like a word with you."

"This should only take a few minutes," Alex said to Kelly, and he stepped away to talk to the man.

As Kelly studied her map, she noticed that the older man did all the talking while Alex listened. She was curious about what Alex wanted to show her. It could have something to do with Meg. Maybe he'd seen the flyers she'd distributed along the boardwalk. When he was done talking, she would encourage him to show her around Belvista right away.

She looked at Alex again. He seemed submissive, as if he were being scolded but couldn't answer back. The man, possibly his father or boss, seemed to be ticking off a list of things on a sheet of paper. Alex glanced at Kelly and looked quickly away as if embarrassed that he was being reprimanded.

Kelly folded her map. Alex and the man shook hands, and they both looked pleased. They must have decided to take their conversation elsewhere, because they started to leave. Alex looked at Kelly, threw up his hands, and shrugged, as of to say that leaving was not his choice. Disappointed, she went on her way, hoping she'd run into him again.

Passing by the bulletin board, Kelly noticed a photograph

of a beautiful young woman with thick, wavy hair wearing a beautiful, hand-embroidered dress. She read the announcement contained within the black border:

> *Julia Newcomb, who celebrated her nineteenth birthday last week, passed away on Saturday, September 4, surrounded by her loving family. The wake will be held at Kalinsky's Funeral Home, on Monday and Tuesday, September 6 and 7, from 4 to 6 in the afternoon and 7 to 9 in the evening. Julia will be buried at St. Anne's Cemetery on Wednesday, following a 9 o'clock Mass at St. Anne's Church.*

Father Shaunassey came up beside Kelly and rearranged several notices on the bulletin board. "Don't let me disturb you," he said. "I'm just tidying up."

"I was reading about Julia Newcomb," Kelly said.

"A terrible tragedy."

"There seem to be many tragedies occurring in the Belvista area."

Father Shaunassey frowned. "What do you mean?"

"The disappearances of four women, including my sister, Meg Madison."

"I'm sorry to hear that. I hope everything turns out well." He pushed a spare thumbtack into the bulletin board. "I don't know the individual circumstances, but things like this have happened for years. The media make the public more aware of it now. Missing persons, Amber alerts, children kidnapped, sometimes by family members. It's everywhere, Miss Madison." He drew her toward the bulletin board. "But there are good neighbors too. See here?" He tapped an index finger on one of the notices. "There's a covered-dish supper here at our hall this Wednesday night at seven, followed by entertainment. The winners of our talent contest are performing. Some are really good. Won't you join us?"

"I'll think about it."

"At three dollars, it's a bargain."

"Maybe some of your parishioners will remember seeing Meg or talking to her. Here's their chance to tell me about it." Kelly smiled. "The covered-dish supper sounds like a good idea. I'll see you there." Kelly turned to leave and then stopped. "Father, wouldn't a social event Wednesday night be disrespectful to the memory of Julia Newcomb? She's being buried that morning."

"Julia is now in Heaven. That is cause for happiness. The faithful recognize that and go on with their lives."

Kelly left St. Anne's. When she looked over her shoulder to wave good-bye, Father Shaunassey was scowling at the sky, as if he'd seen thunderclouds.

NINE

A Crazy Idea and a Clue

AT THE CORNER OF Main and Front Streets, Kelly turned right toward the library, the first stop on the walking-tour map. Uncertain how far away the library was, she sat down on a bench and checked the map pages featuring this neighborhood. Only six more blocks to the library. As she started to tuck the map into her purse, a faint but undeniable pencil marking on the last page caught her attention. She blinked and peered at the grid of Belvista's streets, dotted with tiny crosses for churches and other fitting symbols for schools, hospitals, parks, and so on. Beneath the grid, the symbols were explained. How had she missed it? Meg had underlined the word *Cemeteries.*

Kelly counted eight cemeteries. Beyond the hospital, there was even a potter's field for the poor and indigent. Belvista certainly had its share of cemeteries. She was surprised that a small town like Belvista would have a potter's field. A terrible thought crossed her mind. Was it possible that the missing women were buried in the potter's field? Maybe the directors of Belvista's funeral homes or the hospital personnel could answer her question.

She hurried to the phone booth on the corner. Flipping through the *Yellow Pages,* she stopped at the letter *F.* Her fingers trailed down to the listing for *Funeral Homes.* Two. Preston's and Kalinsky's. Her mind clicked into overdrive. Possibly the town fathers or charitable organizations paid funeral-home directors to bury the destitute.

As Kelly walked down the street toward the library, the

thought festered in her mind that death could be a moneymaking business for funeral directors even if there were no family members to pay the bill. Was it possible that an unscrupulous mortician would hire someone to kill poor women? What a crazy idea. But no crazier than Sam Chambers' kidnapping theory. She would ask Luke to investigate both the Kalinsky and Preston Funeral Homes.

Kelly walked past Henderson's Hardware, Tucci's Deli, the Traskell Insurance Company and the Belvista Bicycle Shop. All displayed the Belvista Business Club emblem in their windows. Sam's theory ran through her mind that the Business Club promoted the Cinderella idea to cover up any suggestion of kidnappings. She stopped to read the notice about renting bicycles. Darn! The store would be closed on Monday for inventory.

Kelly decided she would rent a bicycle on Tuesday and ride to the hospital, speak to someone of authority in the morgue about unidentified women, then continue to the potter's field at the edge of town. She didn't know what she might find there among the unmarked graves. But every place she visited, every lead she followed up, brought her one step closer to Meg.

Kelly continued three blocks west to the library. Standing on the bottom step, she looked up at the imposing stone building and the pillars that dominated the entrance. How could this cold, silent building reveal anything about Meg? She was wasting precious time. The library was closed, but she peeked through the windows and saw the computer area, DVD collection, and book stacks.

Perusing her map, Kelly saw that the Mariners' Museum, the next tour stop, had a popular outdoor display open seven days a week. Meg had noted that she'd shot an entire roll of film there. As Kelly turned to leave, something shining in the grass caught her eye. She bent down to investigate and found a quarter. When she moved the blades of grass to pick it up, several bits of pink chalk lay clustered nearby. She blinked hard and leaned closer. Was she seeing things?

Next to the chalk was the missing glass button from Meg's blue blouse. Meg had stood near this very window! She must have come to the library when it was closed, too. Possibly on a Sunday, the day she disappeared. But chalk? Meg never bought chalk. Maybe it belonged to someone who was at the library with Meg. A child, perhaps, or an artist. The newspaper article said that several artists had seen Meg with a man along the boardwalk. Was the man an artist too? Kelly blinked away her tears and placed the items in her sewing kit. She felt productive, closer to Meg.

This important clue, Meg's missing button, and the knowledge that someone might have been with her and might even know what had happened to her, brightened her day. She headed up the winding street toward the Mariners' Museum. She hoped more clues would soon come her way.

TEN

The Mariners' Museum

THE LOOSE-STONED pavement added old-time authenticity, but it made walking difficult. Several times Kelly heard the sound of pebbles rolling down the street. When she turned, no one was there. Stopping to catch her breath, she leaned against a building. A shadow crossed her path. At the sound of scattered pebbles really close by, the hair on her neck bristled. She looked up and down the street. It was deserted.

Suddenly a man stepped out of an alleyway. His chins drooped over his shirt collar.

"Kelly Madison?" He approached, the toes of his shoes jabbing the stones. "I see you're heading to the Mariners' Museum. I guess you've heard it's open on Sundays. I'll walk with you. Several accidents with cars sideswiping pedestrians have occurred on this narrow road."

Kelly stepped backward, ready to run.

"Who are you?" Kelly's voice shook. "How did you know my name?"

"Sorry, I forgot my manners. I'm Hal Dunbar, president of the Belvista Business Club. You came to my department store on the boardwalk. I saw you leave. One of my sales clerks showed me the flyer you wanted placed in my store window. You left before I could discuss the matter with you."

"I was upset. I still am."

"That's understandable. You're worried about your sister. I talked to her once, in my main store."

"Really? When was that? What did you talk about?"

"I passed by as she was buying a box of chalk from one of my salesclerks. It was about three weeks ago."

Kelly instinctively clutched her purse, which now held the pink chalk she'd found at the library.

"We talked about the weather, and I wished her a nice stay in Belvista," Hal Dunbar said. "Shall we go?"

Kelly hesitated. The street was deserted. This Hal Dunbar, if that was his real name, had appeared suddenly from an alley. She felt uneasy, but she couldn't give up any chance to find out about Meg. She decided to play along with him but stay alert.

"Did she say what she planned to do with the chalk?" Kelly asked, keeping his fast pace.

"No, but her cheeks had that glow of a woman in love."

Kelly noticed a stone marker along the roadside. Good. The museum was only one-half mile ahead. "What color was the chalk?" she asked.

"A box of Rainbow Mix, I believe." He tapped his chin with an index finger. "Come to think of it, your sister wanted pink, but the best we could offer was the mix." He chuckled. "I'm good at noticing details. I'd bet that pink was your sister's favorite color."

"You're very perceptive," Kelly fibbed, knowing that Meg loved blue best.

"She was wearing a pink shawl. Silk, with long fringe."

Kelly frowned. She knew every stitch of Meg's wardrobe. Meg didn't own a pink shawl, and there was no pink shawl in Meg's suitcase.

"Here we are, Miss Madison." Hal Dunbar pushed open the gate and leaned against the picket fence. "And now I'll leave you to James Ritter, the museum's watchman." He nodded to Ritter, who was directing visitors toward the wooden pathways that crisscrossed the crushed-shell yard. Taking a pen and notepad from his pocket, he scribbled a note and passed it to Ritter. "A recommendation about sweeping the path," he explained, but Kelly's glance had caught the last word, *trouble*.

"Enjoy!" Hal Dunbar turned and left abruptly.

Kelly wondered what the rest of the note said, but she quickly forgot about it as she took in the interesting surroundings. She couldn't believe the variety of nautical paraphernalia, apparently awaiting repair and restoration, jam-packed into one place. She meandered past the conglomeration of ships' flags, lanterns, steering wheels, and mastheads.

What would have captured Meg's interest? she wondered. Knowing that Meg disliked crowds, Kelly stepped off the pathway and picked her way through the tangle of ropes that looped around crab traps, anchors, and oars. She wandered toward a remote area at the rear of the yard. The Danger Keep Out sign posted on a wooden fence caught her eye. Meg could never resist a dare.

Kelly looked over her shoulder. Certain that James Ritter couldn't see her, she slipped through the gate. She found herself in a sandy area crammed with boats. Some lay on their sides, as if tossed there by a stormy sea. Others rested in wooden berths, surrounded by paint scrapings. Many, encrusted with barnacles, were stacked against a rocky wall. One large boat with a hole in its bottom hung suspended from cables attached to a crane.

A muffled sneeze alerted Kelly that she was not alone. She heard a metallic clicking noise. She turned. A door in the wooden fence cracked open. She hadn't even noticed the door until now. Who was there? A worker or deliveryman? Her heart pounded. She caught a fleeting glance of a man, dark clothes, something in his hands. Behind the man in the alley was a black car. The door in the fence was pulled shut.

Creaking sounds drew Kelly's attention to the crane holding the boat. The boat above swayed. The cable was shredding. She watched, horrified, as the cable snapped. She opened her mouth to scream. The boat teetered, swinging past her head. Kelly jerked back and tripped over a can of varnish.

The next thing Kelly knew, her head was throbbing, and black dots danced before her eyes. Gingerly she touched her right temple, where the pain was most intense. She felt something warm and sticky. She pulled away her hand. Blood. Dabbing at the wound with tissues, she tried to sit up. There was blood on a rock next to her. She staggered to her feet. She must have hit her head on the rock when she fell. Thank God, the boat that broke from the cable hadn't hit her. That could have done a lot more damage. She took a step and stopped. Scrawled in the sand by her foot were two words: *Leave Belvista.*

"Help!" Kelly called out. No one answered. She reached into her purse for her cell phone. It wasn't there. How could she be so stupid? She had left it at Pruitt's Inn. Frantic, she looked around. The sun was already dipping behind the trees, and shadows stretched across the sand. The visitors and James Ritter must have left. How long had she been lying on the ground? She pushed back her sleeve to check her watch. It was gone, and so was her glass-bead bracelet, a cherished gift from her graphics teacher at night school.

She searched frantically, scooping away the sand, sifting it through her trembling fingers. She gave up, frustrated, and fought back tears. In the shadowy light she spotted boot prints leading from the boat to the grassy area. A workman's boots, judging from the deep tread marks.

Kelly found her way to the front gate and staggered from the museum. Woozy from the blow to her head, she willed herself to keep moving. Every block or so she stopped to steady herself. If only she had her cell phone. Each time she heard a car on the loose stones or the sound of voices approaching, she ducked into the shadows. She was too weak to escape from a kidnapper and not sure whom she could trust. When she finally arrived at Pruitt's Inn, the night was pitch-black. She was on the verge of tears.

Justine Pruitt greeted her at the door. "That busybody with the crazy, serial-killer ideas telephoned. His message was that you should check your cell-phone messages. Didn't trust me with whatever was so darned urgent." She stared at Kelly's temple. "Take care of that cut. And be sure to tell people it happened elsewhere. You could sink my business once and for all."

"Thanks for your concern," Kelly said.

In her room, Kelly tended to her wound, then found her cell phone on the vanity, right where she had left it. Promising herself to keep the cell phone in her purse in case of future emergencies, she listened to Sam's message:

"Hi, Kelly, It's Sam. Must see you. Have found something that backs up my kidnapping theory. Have asked Detective Campbell to meet us at the Barnacle Café tomorrow morning at ten. This is very important. See you then."

ELEVEN

Sam's Discovery

KELLY STEPPED INTO the Barnacle Café, looking for Luke and Sam. They hadn't arrived yet. She waved to Joe and headed toward an empty table. She decided not to tell Luke about the missing button from Meg's blouse. He might think she was manufacturing clues. She would wait until he seemed willing to accept that Meg hadn't left voluntarily. She wouldn't mention a murder-for-profit mortician scheme either. That now seemed a crazy idea.

Luke arrived. "A full pot of coffee and three cups," he called out to Joe.

"Coming right up," Joe called back.

Luke took a chair across from Kelly. A startled expression crossed his face. "What happened to your head?"

Kelly touched the bandage, which she'd tried to conceal with her hair. "Someone tried to scare me at the Mariners' Museum, but I'm fine now."

"Tell me what happened." His voice was filled with concern.

Just then Sam came to the table. "Sorry I'm late." Kelly noticed that he was wearing work boots. For one brief second she wondered if he had been at the Mariners' Museum. This was terrible. Suddenly everyone was a suspect. Sam tapped his bulging briefcase and sat down next to Kelly. "It took awhile to make photocopies and… Jeeze, what's with the bandage?"

Kelly quickly ran through what had happened at the Mariners' Museum: the muffled sneeze, the man and black car beyond the gate, the teetering boat, her tripping and falling, hitting her head on a rock, the message in the sand. Once Sam got over the shock, he turned very protective. He and Luke asked lots of questions and urged her to be careful. Luke promised to investigate to determine if the boat's snapping loose was an accident.

"The black car has me worried," Kelly said. "I think it's been following me."

"Where else have you seen it?" Luke asked.

"I saw it near the police station shortly after I arrived in Belvista. Then it was behind my taxi on the way to Pruitt's Inn. And again on Saturday when I left the boardwalk area and came here to meet you for lunch."

"Did you catch any part of the license plate?" Luke asked.

"No."

"What about the make of the car?"

"A Lexus at the police station and behind my taxi. The other times, I know the car was black, but I'm not sure of the make."

"You should have told me this sooner," Luke said.

"I thought maybe I was seeing danger everywhere because I'm upset about Meg."

Luke opened his cell phone. "I'm going to have my officers run a check and see who in Belvista owns a black Lexus. We'll expand our search county-wide if necessary and see what turns up."

"Thanks for your help, Luke," Kelly said. "But let's set that aside for now. I want to focus on Meg, not me."

"It's not an either-or situation," Luke said. "You've both got my full attention." He flashed his winning smile. "You're hard to ignore in those dramatic clothes." He nodded at her honey-colored tiered skirt and matching top with cinnamon-brown embroidery on the neckline.

"Thanks again," Kelly murmured, and she knew she was blushing. "Now, Sam, tell us," Kelly said. "What did you find out?"

Sam's face lit up. "I've found a connection regarding the four missing women. But I'm not sure what it means."

Joe set the pot of coffee and cups on the table. "The same pretty face, twice in three days," he said in a low voice, and Luke waved him away.

Sam began pouring the coffee. "Yesterday I reviewed the newspapers I'd collected before, during, and after the disappearances. I've just about worn the ink off the pages." He set the cream in the center of the table. "As you know, the names of the missing women, including Meg, were never mentioned in the newspapers. They were just the Cinderellas who had run off with their Prince Charmings." He snapped open his briefcase. "Let me set the record straight. Their names are Stacy Deems, Kim Eberly, and Mary Waverly."

"And Meg Madison," Luke cut in.

"Okay," Sam said. "We're all on the same page." He reached into his briefcase and pulled out clippings from the Belvista *Bugle*. "I was looking for anything that would link the women. I went column by column. That's when I discovered a weird, off-the-wall coincidence."

"Get to the point," Luke chided, and he gulped his coffee.

"It was right there in black and white in the obituaries," Sam said. "Several days before each woman disappeared, a female patient at Belvista Hospital died. The kidnappings followed the deaths by just several days. Every time. Coincidence? No way. I see a pattern."

Kelly's breath caught in her throat. "I've read about deranged hospital employees who murder people for some sick challenge. Maybe—"

"I considered that," Sam said. "But the women died from whatever brought them to the hospital, without interference from anyone else." Sam gave them each a photocopied set of obituary notices. "Take a look."

Luke removed a pair of reading glasses from his jacket pocket and studied the material. Kelly thought the spectacles made him look distinguished. She read through the first three obituaries. Lisa McFarland died April 13 of a rare blood disorder. Sarah Lane, June 6, from congenital heart problems. Anna Morales, July 2, from cancer. When Kelly came to the fourth name, she saw that the woman who died when Meg was in Belvista was Elizabeth Brown. An inoperable brain tumor had caused her death.

Luke looked up. "Sam, were the deceased without families, like the missing women?"

"No, and that's where my theory breaks down," Sam said. "These women were very well off. They died from—"

Kelly's spoon tumbled from her hand.

"What's the matter?" Luke asked.

"Julia Newcomb died Saturday morning at Belvista Hospital. Father Shaunassey made the announcement yesterday."

"If I'm on to something," Sam whispered, "there will be another kidnapping very soon. I have no explanation, but somehow the deaths trigger the kidnapper to act, to kidnap another victim."

Kelly felt the blood rush from her face. Luke reached across the table and took her hands in his. "Nothing will happen to you, I promise. Stay in plain sight at all times. Remember, no criminal wants witnesses. And don't go out at night. I'll keep an eye on you, and so will Belvista's finest." He gripped her hands reassuringly.

"There's a problem. I'd planned on going to this Wednesday's covered-dish supper at St. Anne's to ask people about Meg. I don't want to miss it. It starts at seven and won't end until after dark."

"The problem's solved," Luke said. "I'll pick you up." He released Kelly's hands and removed his glasses. His concern showed in his soulful eyes. "Promise me you won't take chances. Until we sort out these hospital deaths and disappearances, you—"

"I can't just sit in my room and worry. I'm going to do my part. No one knows Meg better than I do."

"Okay, but promise me you'll be cautious," Luke said.

"I will, for my own sake and for Meg's. She's counting on me, and I won't let her down…not this time."

"You've done good work, Sam," Luke said. "I'll look into this possible hospital link." Kelly studied Luke as he underlined the deceased women's names, then folded the obituaries and tucked them into his pocket. His brown eyes darkened, the jet-black pupils dilating. He took out a notepad and pen and jotted down *5th deceased woman—Julia Newcomb, complications from an automobile accident.* Flecks of green and amber glittered in his eyes, and Kelly realized they were hazel. He continued writing, and she leaned closer. He had written a note to himself: *Was a black Lexus involved in Julia Newcomb's accident?*

"I'll be in touch," Luke said.

Sam crammed the newspapers into his briefcase. "I'm not trying to tell you how to run your business, Luke, but Chuck Lazenby, head of the records department at Belvista Hospital, might shed some light on the deaths of the four women. I've been trying to contact him all morning, but he won't take my calls."

"Leave the investigation to me," Luke said. "I'll call the hospital." He turned to Kelly. "I'll drop by Pruitt's after dinner to check on you." He cocked his head and peered at her bandage.

"Are you sure Justine Pruitt didn't sink her fangs into you?"

Kelly laughed. "Not a chance. She'd wait until she'd collected the week's rent."

Luke checked his watch. "I have to go," he said.

As Kelly watched Luke pay the check and leave, she realized how attracted she was to him. She couldn't wait to see him again. That kind of thinking had to stop…or at least be put on hold. She needed to concentrate all her energy on finding Meg. But she appreciated Luke's help. He had police officers at his disposal, files and records at his fingertips. New in town, he didn't owe any loyalty to the businesspeople who, as Sam pointed out, didn't want to hurt tourism with talk about women disappearing. He was more accepted by the locals than Sam, whose abrupt inquiries seemed to irritate them.

"See you later, Sam," Kelly said. "I'm headed to the artists' studios, another stop on Meg's walking tour."

"Remember Luke's warning. Stay in crowded areas."

"According to the information on the map," Kelly said, "the artists' studios are busy year-round." She touched her wrist. "Darn! I'm lost without my watch. I lost it yesterday at the Mariners' Museum. When I came to, it was gone. So was my bracelet."

"I doubt a thief just happened to be passing by and saw you lying on the ground." Sam shifted from one foot to the other. "It could be…"

"Sam, just say it."

The worry lines between Sam's eyes deepened. "Serial killers like keepsakes. I'm betting our serial killer paid you a visit yesterday. He probably followed you."

The words *serial killer* still made Kelly shudder. "But why didn't he just drag me away when I blacked out?"

Sam furrowed his brow in thought. "Someone must have come along and interrupted him. Let's put my theories to work. The second person, whoever he is, wanted to scare you away, so he wrote the words *Leave Belvista*. He didn't want you to investigate Meg's disappearance and bring attention to the missing women and hurt Belvista's tourist business. The kidnapper wouldn't have written *Leave Belvista*. He wants you here. He intends to kidnap you. I'd say two separate people are involved. They aren't working together. Their objectives are directly opposite."

A chill crept up Kelly's spine. "You could be right. You're good at figuring things out."

"The criminal mind is my specialty. I'll tell Luke about this."

"Sam, I'm having second thoughts about what we're keeping from Luke—the email that Hazie found, the attack on Olivia in the park, and someone messing with the lights at Olivia's café. I'm worried that all this is somehow related to Meg's disappearance and that by not telling Luke, we're hindering the investigation."

"I'll talk to Olivia." Sam brushed a hand across Kelly's cheek. "If you see anyone suspicious, back off and call for help." His fingertips trailed down her cheek.

Kelly found his touch surprisingly tentative for a man so sure of his opinions. A nervous feeling rippled through her stomach. Sam had shown up on the beach near Pruitt's Inn at the very moment that she was distributing flyers. He was calculating. A man on a mission, and it wasn't only about finding Meg. He wanted to prove his theory that the kidnapper's tracks were being covered by businesspeople intent on protecting Belvista's tourism income. Just now, he had made her stolen jewelry fit into his theory. Sam was hoping for a media-attention event, an exposé of small-town business practices. She didn't care about that. She just wanted Meg back. Were their aims compatible? Or, when the chips were down, would Sam do what was best for Sam, regardless of how that affected Meg?

TWELVE

The Artists' Studios

AFTER LEAVING THE Barnacle Café, Kelly crossed the street and walked two blocks north of the pier. She entered the area of narrow, twisting, brick-paved streets lined with artists' studios. Brochures at Pruitt's Inn told her that in the days when Belvista thrived as a whaling port, the studios had been saloons and inns bursting at the seams with itinerant seamen. Kelly mingled with the crowds, intrigued with this quaint area.

She peered into doorways and chatted with the artists. Most worked at their easels, others knelt on the floor with their metal sculptures, and several were at their tables, which overflowed with mixed-media pieces. She showed Meg's picture and asked if anyone had seen her. No luck. Several studios posted signs Will Return Soon. Inquire Next Door.

"Where has everyone gone?" Kelly asked a bearded artist in a paint-spattered T-shirt and jeans.

"You mean the landscape artists? They're off painting at the beach, wherever. These are working studios. Most of the artists can't afford to pay a gallery attendant. As you can see—" he pointed with his paintbrush at the portrait he was working on "—I'm a portrait artist. My subjects come to me. Anyway, we're all friends. We help sell their work while they're away."

Kelly held up the photo of Meg. "Have you seen her?"

He set down his paintbrush. "No, but with that face and those cheekbones, any artist here would want her."

AFTER AN HOUR, the studios began to swim before Kelly's eyes. She was very discouraged. None of the artists remembered seeing Meg. She turned a corner into a tiny cul-de-sac that sheltered three studios. Paintings of young women filled the middle studio's window. They were done in the Impressionist style, reminding Kelly of Monet. Light seemed to emanate from the women's faces. Their hairstyles and dresses were from the 1800s. There were women sitting at tables surrounded by blossoms. Women wandering along paths in front of shuttered cottages. Women standing in fields of wildflowers.

Kelly stepped onto the porch. The artist's name jumped from the sun-drenched colors. *Michael Duprey.* The man Olivia said Meg was interested in. Olivia said he was one of the artists who claimed to have seen Meg strolling along the boardwalk with a man her first night in Belvista.

Kelly raised a hand to shade her eyes and peered inside. A large painting rested on an easel. The portrait of the woman in pink, gazing out from under her parasol with half-closed eyes...

"Meg!" The word escaped Kelly's mouth.

Heart pounding, Kelly looked left and right. The two other studios were closed. The street was deserted. She plucked her cell phone from her purse, checked the napkin with Luke's number scrawled on it, and punched in the numbers. Dead. The battery needed charging.

Her reasonable nature told her, *Go get help. Stay where you can be seen.* But it would take time to find a phone and get through to Luke or one of his officers. She didn't dare waste a precious minute. What if Meg were imprisoned inside? Kelly made a bargain with herself. If the door was locked, she would immediately leave and get help. But if...

Kate tested the doorknob. It turned. The door opened. She looked over her shoulder. No one was in the street. No one was following her. Quickly and quietly she slipped inside Michael Duprey's studio.

THIRTEEN

Michael Duprey

EYES ALERT TO DANGER, Kelly surveyed the long, narrow studio. Paintings covered the walls. Tables overflowed with paints and brushes. An open staircase led to a loft. She began to lose her nerve. The faster she searched and got away, the better.

Dodging between easels and scattered stacks of canvases, Kelly found herself facing five huge paintings, draped with crumpled bedsheets, leaning against the staircase. In an attempt to uncover any secret, Kelly pulled away the first sheet. She blinked in disbelief at the painting. There was Meg, dressed in a shimmering pink dress and shawl, painted in the Impressionist style. Kelly yanked away the other sheets. Meg gazed at her from Belvista's beach and boardwalk. In partial stages of completion, the paintings glistened like pastel silks.

Kelly gasped. These paintings of Meg couldn't have been done in a few days. Meg must have been here for weeks. Meg must still be here.

"Meg! Where are you?"

Kelly charged through the room, searching for some secret passageway that would lead her to Meg. She pulled back the rug in the center of the room, hoping for a trapdoor.

"Meg, where are you?"

Silence.

Pushing past the table and chairs, Kelly searched for a clue to Meg's whereabouts. A bag of rags smeared with paint offered no trace of the gray pajamas that had disappeared with Meg. No sign either of Meg's silky gray scarf. She flung open the rear door and rushed into the alley, hoping to see a storm-cellar bulk-head door.

Nothing.

Kelly hurried back into the studio and raced to the loft. Nothing except Michael Duprey's paint-spattered clothing. Discouraged, she started down the stairs.

The rear door slammed open.

Kelly dropped to her knees. Crouching behind the paintings, she saw a man struggle into the room, easing a painting through the door frame. Kelly's heart raced. This man fit the description Meg had told Olivia. The handsome, brooding face. The dark hair. It had to be Michael Duprey. Kelly watched as Michael leaned the painting against a wall and adjusted the oilcloth covering. His back to her, he tossed his mud-caked jacket onto the back of a chair. His blue denim shirt and jeans hung loosely on his lanky body.

Holding her breath, Kelly tiptoed down the last steps.

Michael turned. His jaw dropped when he saw the paintings of Meg exposed and a woman he didn't know staring at him.

Kelly raced to the door. Michael followed, stumbling when his muddy boots became entangled in the sheets.

Kelly yanked at the doorknob.

Michael scrambled forward and fell against Kelly, pinning her to the door between his arms.

"I can explain...my sister," Kelly stammered into his chest.

"You have to be Meg's sister, Kelly." He stepped back, his eyes wide with amazement. "She said you looked like her. And you are just as surprising!"

Kelly tugged the door open. She rushed across the porch into the street, where she could call for help.

"Don't leave." He followed her to the porch.

Kelly faced him. "What have you done with Meg? I know she was here."

"I haven't seen Meg in weeks."

"I don't believe you."

"Come inside. Please. Meg would want us to be friends. We'll discuss this over a bottle of wine."

"We'll discuss this here in the street." Kelly backed away. "I won't risk being kidnapped."

"What are you talking about?"

"Don't play games. You've taken Meg. Now you want me."

"There's been some misunderstanding."

"Then straighten things out. Tell me where Meg is."

"I'll tell you what I told the police." He folded his arms across his chest. "I first met Meg on a Wednesday afternoon, about three weeks ago. She was photographing a sand-castle competition. I was painting scenes of the boardwalk." He leaned against the doorjamb, crossing one leg over the other. "Meg came over to admire my paintings. She called them tapestries." Enthusiasm crept into his weary voice. "She said you'd like them because you're interested in fabric design."

"Meg just struck up a conversation?"

"I can explain. My sister, Rita, and her fiancé, Greg Saunders, and her friend, Lila Putnam, were painting by my side. Meg felt free to stay and talk. One thing led to another, and Meg agreed to pose for me. I was glad. Even if I could afford a model, I never would have found someone with Meg's incredible features."

"But Meg was busy taking photographs."

"Meg said she could make some free time the next morning. I asked her to wear something pink." He studied her face. "I wanted to play up Meg's youth and innocence."

"Meg didn't take anything pink to Belvista."

"I found that out. My sister provided the pink shawl and parasol from costumes she uses in her work. I sketched her in pink."

"And just like that—" Kelly snapped her fingers "—you created five life-size paintings of Meg."

"After Meg disappeared, I couldn't get her out of my thoughts. I took the scenes I'd been working on and, with help from my sketches, painted Meg into them."

Pacing back and forth across the worn bricks, Kelly thought things through. Michael Duprey was convincing. He could be telling the truth. "Meg gave you pink chalk, didn't she?"

"Yes. She… How did you know?"

Kelly pulled the chalk from her sewing kit. "I found this outside the library, along with a button from Meg's blouse."

He shook his head in disbelief. "Meg worried about that vintage button. She told me you had found a set of them at a fair. We searched for it that Saturday night, and…" A shadow crossed his handsome face. "We had a fight. She said she never wanted to see me again."

"Did that fight have anything to do with the unidentified man your friends had seen her with?"

"Meg swore me to secrecy about him."

"You have to tell me. Meg may have been kidnapped." Her voice trembled. "And it could be the man with her on the board-walk."

"That's crazy. The police questioned me. They didn't mention kidnapping. Neither did the newspapers."

"Tell me about that man."

"Okay." He took a deep breath. "As I told the police, I didn't get a good look at him. It was Wednesday night, about six-thirty. He stayed on the boardwalk. Meg came down to the beach and talked to Rita, Greg, and me."

"Could you describe him?"

"Medium height. He had dark hair and wore black slacks and a gray shirt. But he was far away. I couldn't really see his face."

"Please. What did Meg forbid you to say?"

Michael stuffed his hands into his pockets. "His name is Tim Ramsey. Meg met him on the bus from New York to Belvista. She told him she was going to photograph the town. He said he was a professional photographer on vacation and could save her steps because he'd been to Belvista many times."

"Meg fell for that stupid pick-up line?" Kelly's hands balled into fists. "I'm sorry. Please. Go on."

"I saw Meg on Thursday, as I mentioned, when I sketched her in pink. On Friday she came to my studio around noon, wearing the pink shawl. I insisted she keep it to help her stay in the mood I'd created in the sketches. I was happy to see her and hoped to do more sketches. She was upset. She said Tim Ramsey was a lying creep."

Michael ran his fingers through his tousled hair. "He got her alone in a deserted area. He grabbed her. Meg pushed him away. He wouldn't take no for an answer. She whacked him with her camera case and got away. He didn't bother her again. She figured he left town."

"I don't understand." Kelly's voice rose. "Why didn't Meg call the police?" She was angry at Meg and at Michael too. He should have told the police about Tim Ramsey.

"She decided not to press charges," Michael said. "She wanted to spend her time photographing Belvista. I encouraged her to stay. I had fallen for her. Really fallen hard. I know how that sounds, love at first sight and all, but it's true."

"You saw her throughout the weekend."

"Yes. Meg and I took the walking tour, late in the day, after I'd finished painting. She and her camera were having a love affair with Belvista."

Kelly stepped toward the porch and gripped the railing. "Did you see Meg that Sunday?"

"No. We spent Friday afternoon and most of Saturday at the cattail marshes beyond the hospital, but she didn't show up on Sunday."

Kelly frowned. "Cattail marshes?"

"I was working on a series of contemporary paintings. They still consume me." He dabbed at the speckles of brown and black paint on his shirt. "Meg said the somber paintings, different from my usual sunny scenes, would make me famous. She wanted to pose for them. Just a minute." Kelly watched him disappear into the studio and return with the painting he'd left by the back door. "You're the first person to see this," he said, removing the oilcloth.

Kelly gazed at the painting of Meg standing in the misty morning, a melancholy expression on her face. Meg wore brown slacks and a brown and black checkered jacket. Kelly knew it well. She had given it to Meg as a Christmas gift.

"There are others paintings," Michael said. "They show Meg in different light, different shadows. The marshes change every hour." He smiled. "So does Meg."

"I'd like to see them," Kelly said.

"They're locked next door at Greg's studio. I didn't want that jerk Chambers to see them."

"Sam Chambers?" Kelly was startled. "What's he—"

"Chambers came here. He tried to get me to reveal some dirty little secret about Meg. Something he could sell to the newspapers."

Kelly was furious. "When I see him—"

"He didn't get a word from me," Michael cut in. The furrow deepened between his eyes. "If Meg is in danger, we... you need a professional detective."

"Detective Campbell is helping me," Kelly said. "Do you know him?"

"Not personally. I know he bought a home near here."

Kelly paced again, concentrating on the time sequence. Michael had seen Meg on Wednesday, Thursday, Friday, and Saturday. "You didn't see Meg on Sunday."

"We were supposed to meet at the marshes Sunday morning. Saturday, when she stormed away from the library, I said, 'I'll see you bright and early tomorrow.' She said, 'I never want to see you again,' and ran off. As I said, I was madly in love with Meg. I had been imagining marriage, happily ever after. When I came to my senses, I went after her."

"What did you do to her?" Kelly sputtered.

"I would never hurt her. I loved her."

"Then tell me what did happen."

"That night, Saturday night, the light was shining from her window at Pruitt's Inn. I tossed a handful of pebbles, and she came to the window. She looked so beautiful. I couldn't wait to see her." Disappointment crossed his face. "Her light went out. I waited, but she never came. I figured she went to bed and was punishing me, enjoying every minute of it. I left and went home."

"What was she wearing when you saw her at the window?"

"I don't know. From where I was standing, I could only see her face."

"Tell me what the quarrel was about."

"Meg saw me kiss Rita's friend, Lila Putnam. It was just a friendly kiss, maybe a bit too friendly. Lila is a passionate woman. Meg took things the wrong way." He shook his head. "It all sounds so stupid now."

"Stupid but believable," Kelly admitted.

"The next morning at six, I loaded up my van and went to the marshes. I set up my easel and paints and was making progress with the mists. By nine, when Meg didn't show up, I began to worry. I packed up everything and headed toward Pruitt's, thinking maybe she'd had an accident along the road. I had lent her my sister's bicycle. I sneaked around to Benny's toolshed. That's where Meg stored the bicycle. The shed was locked, and I couldn't see through the smudged windows."

"Did you ask Miss Pruitt or the neighbors if they had seen Meg?"

"No. I had some things to take care of. By nightfall I was frantic. Greg helped me comb the marshes. We turned the town and the beach upside down. I even checked St. Anne's Cemetery."

Kelly frowned. "Why the cemetery?" A shiver ran up her spine. Meg had underlined the word *cemeteries* on the walking-tour map.

"There's a cluster of tombstones at the back near a gnarled oak tree. The tombstones fascinated Meg. She thought they would provide a mysterious setting for my next painting. A wild idea struck me. She'd gone there, hoping I'd find her. You know how dramatic she can be. But Meg had disappeared off the face of the earth. When the police questioned me, I was beside myself with worry."

"What did you think happened?"

"Greg and Rita convinced me that Meg had returned to New York. They said I'd hear from her eventually."

Kelly clenched her teeth. "So you sat and waited."

"No. I tried to get Meg's address from Justine Pruitt, but she said it was privileged information. The Belvista police weren't helpful either. The New York City phone book was a dead end."

"We have an unlisted number," Kelly said.

Michael continued. "Crazy with worry, I went to New York, but I had little to go on except Meg's imaginative descriptions of neighborhood shops. My money quickly ran out. I tried to hire a private detective, but they wanted money up front. Frustrated, I returned to Belvista. I did the only thing I could. I worked night and day on the paintings, hoping to sell them so I could continue my search. The paintings kept me going. That and the thought that one day Meg would forgive me for our petty quarrel and return to me. Sometimes I convinced myself that my friends were right that Meg was punishing me and would pop back into my life." Pain emanated from his mesmerizing eyes. "What has happened to her?"

"I'm convinced, and so is Sam Chambers, that Meg was kidnapped. Detective Luke Campbell is investigating."

"I'm sorry, Kelly. I'm a lovesick fool, and I'm not thinking straight. I should have borrowed money and continued searching for Meg. Because of me—" He drew a deep breath. "I'll cooperate fully with Detective Campbell."

"Tell me," Kelly said. "Didn't you find it peculiar that Meg never contacted you after your quarrel?"

He rested his elbows on the railing and leaned close to Kelly. "You probably don't think I care, going on with my life, but I've been torn to pieces since Meg left. If you've been checking up on me," he said with hurt feelings, "you know that I've been seen with other women. But they mean nothing to me. I need a woman to keep the creative juices flowing. How else can I paint Meg's lovely face if I'm not surrounded by faces less lovely than hers? Comparison is essential to creativity. I'm sure you look at the kitchen and bath styles of other designers before you create your designs. Am I right?"

Kelly didn't know what to say. Michael's words jumbled in her mind. Was he being truthful? Sincere? Or did his flowery words conceal his sinister side? She felt confused. But one thing was clear. Michael had spent more time with Meg than anyone else in Belvista. Michael was her best hope of finding Meg.

Michael put a hand on the doorknob. "This news about Meg has me worried. I could use a stiff drink. Care to join me?"

Kelly nodded. "A scotch and water to steady my nerves. Will Greg Saunders be coming back soon? I'd like to meet him and the other artists who talked to Meg."

"They're visiting Lila's friends in Connecticut for a juried art exhibition. Greg doesn't miss any chance to show his work." Michael cocked his head to one side. "I'll let you in on a secret."

"I'm listening," Kelly said.

"Greg pays an assistant to blow paint through straws at his canvases. 'To build up layers of interest,' Greg says. Then he paints the top coat." Michael smirked. "Lazy, if you ask me. If he were as talented as he thinks he is, he'd create the entire work himself."

"Sounds like a professional rivalry between you and Greg Saunders," Kelly commented.

"Personal too," Michael admitted. "He kept asking me about Meg. He made it sound as if he wanted to paint her, but he doesn't paint people or anything that's recognizable. He just wanted to make another conquest. He goes after any woman I'm interested in."

"When will Greg be back in Belvista?" Kelly asked. "I'd like to talk to him about Meg."

"He'll be back when his fans in Connecticut run out of

money. Now, how about that scotch?" He extended a hand, and Kelly followed him into the studio. He took a bottle of scotch and two glasses from a shelf in the dining area and poured their drinks. Kelly gazed at the hauntingly lifelike paintings of Meg. Michael had captured Meg's rosy complexion, the dazzling green eyes, the dimpled chin, the graceful neck.

"Sometimes at night," Michael said, "I can't stand the loneliness. I light dozens of candles. I stand here, and I imagine that Meg is in my arms. She presses close to me. We dance."

When Michael slipped an arm around Kelly's waist, she didn't resist. She knew she should. But she was so tired of being the strong sister, the older sister that Meg depended on. For once she wanted someone to console her, to offer strength and understanding. She rested her head on Michael's shoulder and lingered in his embrace. His cheek brushed against hers. She felt the beating of his heart against her breast.

"I miss her," Kelly said, and tears rolled down her cheeks.

"So do I," Michael said.

They began to dance, and time seemed to stop. Kelly followed his lead, her body close to his. The paintings blurred, and bits of color, like confetti, swirled before her eyes. Burying her face in the folds of Michael's shirt, she felt his firm, hard muscles beneath the cotton fabric. She missed Meg. She missed having a man in her life. Loneliness overwhelmed her. Michael tilted her chin toward his face and kissed away her tears. His lips were warm and inviting. He drew her closer. Off in the distance, muffled voices came and went, like the ebb and flow of the tide.

Kelly pulled away. "I'd better leave," she said.

Michael stepped back, keeping her at arm's length. He held her with his vivid blue eyes and wouldn't let go. "I'm sorry. I got caught up in the moment. I wanted to believe that Meg was here with me."

Kelly felt as if she had awakened from a dream. Surrounded by the paintings of Meg, she had fallen for Michael's charm and believed his every word. "But Meg isn't here," she said.

"She's missing. And I hope you'll help find her." She was confused and embarrassed. She wondered if Michael's charm was intentional, if he had deliberately created a romantic mood to win her over. She picked up her purse and turned to leave. "Did Meg have her camera with her on Saturday?"

"I'm not sure."

"One more thing. Was your sister's bicycle that you lent to Meg ever found?"

"No. She stored it in Benny's shed at Pruitt's Inn. The police searched everywhere, including the shed. Like Meg, it disappeared without a trace."

FOURTEEN

St. Anne's Cemetery

KELLY STOPPED AT A pay phone. "Luke, it's me, Kelly," she said hurriedly after the beep. "The man the artists saw with Meg is Tim Ramsey. He pretended to be a photographer eager to help Meg. They met during the bus ride from New York City to Belvista. Find him. Do whatever it takes. Make him talk. Call me."

Ten minutes later, the iron gate at St. Anne's Cemetery creaked open, and Kelly slipped inside. She had promised Luke not to wander off alone, but she wanted to visit every place Meg had been. Something or somebody might pinpoint Meg's whereabouts on that Sunday in August. She stopped and reasoned with herself. She had taken a foolish risk entering Michael Duprey's studio, but he had revealed a great deal of information, and his paintings showed that he cared for Meg. With luck on her side, someone or something here could be helpful too.

Determined, she walked straight ahead. In the center of the cemetery loomed magnificent tombstones and above-ground burial vaults. Hurrying along the service road, she passed by a mound of freshly dug earth in a roped-off area. Julia Newcomb's grave, she figured.

A pickup truck was parked a few feet away. As Kelly approached, she noticed that shovels, grass clippers, and empty sod pallets filled most of the truck bed. In the corner was a plastic laundry basket containing candy wrappers and other unsightly items that would detract from the stately appear-

ance of the grounds. A second laundry basket, labeled Lost &
Found, held a child's teddy bear and an eyeglass case.

"You shouldn't be here," a man's harsh voice said.

Startled, Kelly turned. "Alex?" She blinked. Was this the
same well-groomed, designer-clothes-wearing man she'd met
at Pruitt's Inn and St. Anne's Church? His sinewy arms glistened with sweat. His mud-spattered jeans and shirt clung to
his muscular frame. But it was Alex, all right.

"I was hoping we'd meet again," she said. She was surprised
to see Alex working as a groundskeeper. When they'd first met,
she guessed he worked in the fashion industry. "You said you
wanted to show me something. But we never had that tour of
Belvista." She stepped aside as he flung down the shovel and
burlap sack he'd been hefting on his shoulder.

"Well, as you can see, I'm busy right now."

"Have I offended you somehow?" Kelly asked, startled by
his brusqueness.

"This isn't the best place to socialize." He picked up the
shovel and stabbed it into the soft earth. "When I said I wanted
to spend time with you, I didn't intend for us to meet here like
this." Frowning, he looked at his dirt-caked clothes.

There was that fastidious side to him she'd noticed when
they first met. "I'll only stay a minute." She smiled, hoping to
make light of the situation.

He scowled. "As I said, you shouldn't be here."

"I didn't know the cemetery was closed," Kelly explained.

"It's my responsibility to see that a grieving family's wishes
are respected. They wouldn't like visitors when a grave is being
dug for their loved one. You understand, don't you?" he said,
his voice soft, his manner timid.

"Of course," Kelly said. "I'll just go on my way."

"Look, I'm sorry I snapped at you," Alex said, stretching
his back. "But some people can be very insensitive." With the
back of the shovel, he packed the earth, then smoothed it, his
gloved hands moving rhythmically in small circles. "I like to
leave the earth looking cared for until the burial takes place."

He lifted squares of sod from a pallet in the truck bed and placed them in orderly piles near the mound. "Graves should be covered with a carpet of grass." He smiled, showing white, even teeth. "The carpet shouldn't be marred by bare spots," he said, and Kelly realized how proud he was of his work.

"Hello, Alex!" a voice called out.

The middle-aged man Kelly had seen talking to Alex in church walked over the crest of the hill.

"Keep up the good work," the man called out, and he gave Alex a two-thumbs-up salute. He turned back the way he had come, making notations on his clipboard.

"Who was that?" Kelly asked.

"Nobody important." Alex chuckled. "Just the director of St. Anne's Cemetery."

"He seemed pleased with your work."

"He's a tough taskmaster, but we want the same thing—a beautiful final resting place that meets the family's expectations." Alex packed down a few remaining loose bits of earth with the shovel.

The wind picked up and blew a strand of hair across Kelly's face. "You sure pay attention to details," she said, hoping a compliment would make him talkative. She wanted to know what he had hoped to show her. It had seemed so important to him yesterday in church.

Kelly heard a car engine start up. Could be the administrator leaving. She didn't like being the only visitor in the cemetery. It was creepy now as rain threatened.

"Looks like more showers." Alex scanned the darkening sky. "I'd better get a tarp to cover the soil."

"I won't keep you from your work."

Alex removed his gloves and wiped his forehead. "It's a labor of love," he said.

Kelly stared at his smooth white hands. He had the long, tapering fingers of a pianist.

"What's the matter?" he asked.

"You don't have a gravedigger's hands."

He laughed. "I'm not a gravedigger. I help Walt Preston at his funeral home, but I supervise here when I can. The groundskeepers don't always have the time to do things right."

Just then, a groundskeeper ducked beneath the branches of an oak tree and began clipping the grass that climbed up a tombstone. He waved to Alex and smiled. "Hey, Bradford, the boss is pleased," he called out. "A bonus is coming our way!"

Kelly breathed easier, knowing that another person was in the cemetery and that he'd seen her.

"It's about time," Alex said, and Kelly figured that the director had reprimanded Alex in church, but everything was now going smoothly.

"I've changed my mind. I'm going to walk back there." She pointed toward the lone oak near the back fence.

"Now, Kelly, why would you want to do that?"

"I've heard the tombstones are unusual."

"This is a sacred place," he said, "not a stop on a walking tour."

"I meant no disrespect."

"I'd best go with you. You might trip and hurt yourself."

The cemetery was shadowy and still. Keeping the groundskeeper in view, Kelly strode toward the oak tree. Alex followed. Beneath the oak's leafy branches, eight identical headstones, surrounded by flowers and potted plants, formed a circle. Eight matching footstones formed a second circle.

Kelly leaned over the headstone closest to her and peeked behind the red chrysanthemums. "Peter Bradford," she read. She looked up at Alex. "Peter is a Bradford too," she said, and Alex nodded. Kelly looked again at the tombstone. "He died November tenth, 1999," she said. She knelt at the second headstone. "Anne Bradford. She died November tenth, 1999." She looked up at Alex again. "Another Bradford," she said.

Kelly moved from one headstone to the next, astonished. At the last headstone, she looked up at Alex. "They're all named Bradford, and they all died on November tenth, 1999."

"You've met my entire family," Alex said. "They suffered

a terrible accident. My parents and both sets of grandparents, my aunt and uncle." He shook his head as if he couldn't believe his own words. "Father Shaunassey had his work laid out. The whole town did. Eight caskets, eight sets of funeral clothes, eight graves, and eight sets of headstones." He gathered the leaves scattered across the graves and stuffed them into the sack. "Preston's Funeral Home worked around the clock. Bill Kalinsky helped out, too. We rented hearses from nearby towns. There were flowers everywhere. Cards arrived for days."

Curiosity got the better of Kelly. "I'm so sorry about your family. How did the accident happen? Was anyone else involved?"

"There was a boating accident at Fisherman's Cove." Alex stood beneath the tree, his broad shoulders stooped, his faltering voice punctuated by the sound of the clippers in the distance. "When I arrived, two capsized rowboats floated near the dock. There was no one around, no one to call for help. I dove in, but it was too late."

"How horrible," Kelly said.

"It was my twenty-first birthday. It was a beautiful day, perfect for rowing and picnicking. I'd rather have gone out partying with my friends, but this was one of those family traditions. You know how that goes." He sighed, but Kelly sensed that he had enjoyed such traditions and the closeness of his family. "My family went ahead to Fisherman's Cove. I was to meet them there after I stopped at the bakery and picked up the cake my mother ordered."

Kelly felt such compassion for him. He knew the anguish of losing cherished ones. One day he had been surrounded by family, and the next, he was alone. Kelly stood in the gathering darkness, wondering how Alex had endured such tragedy. How had he mustered the strength to watch his entire family buried, to continue his life, coming home to an empty house? How had he gotten through all the lonely holidays during the past seven years?

"I'm sorry your family was taken from you," she said, embarrassed that she couldn't find more adequate words.

"Thanks. It's difficult alone." His face brightened. "You look like you could use a friend too."

"My sister's missing. I'm afraid something terrible has happened to her." Kelly tried to muster a smile. "Did you say you had met Meg here in the cemetery?"

His eyes fixed on hers. "I never had the pleasure."

Kelly was determined to find out what Alex Bradford had wanted to show her. "I'd like to see you again in a more social setting," she said boldly.

"I'd like that too."

"I'm going to the covered-dish supper at St. Anne's Church Wednesday night. Will you be there?"

"No. I have other plans, but I'll be in touch."

"Good." Kelly turned to leave, when she noticed something unusual about the footstones. Each bore the same design—two sets of *V*-shaped lines, the *V*'s turned sideways, like chevrons or arrowheads flying to the center toward one another. Kelly was about to ask Alex about the unusual design, but she was too late. He had disappeared.

Several minutes later Kelly called Luke from a pay phone. Still no answer. Where was he?

"Luke, it's me, Kelly, again. I've found another piece to the puzzle. The man who came to Pruitt's Inn to return my card case is Alex Bradford. He works for several funeral homes. He has a pickup truck, not a black Lexus, so I don't think he's the person following me. Call me."

She knew Luke would be furious that she had gone to the cemetery alone, so she didn't give any details about how she'd met Alex again. The less said, the better. She looked forward to returning to Pruitt's Inn. There had been enough excitement for one day.

FIFTEEN

Keepsakes

"ANY MESSAGES?" Kelly greeted Justine, who was standing at the reception counter of Pruitt's Inn.

Justine snapped shut her laptop computer. "I know what you're thinking. What's a computer doing in a Victorian inn? Well, missy, I know all about downloads, chat rooms, and blogs. In this business, you have to be modern." She cracked what might pass for a smile. "But you can't let the guests see you at it. They like quills and inkwells and all that frou frou."

Justine stored her laptop under the counter. "Yes, you have one message, from that smart-alecky Luke Campbell. Hand-delivered. I'm on to him. He could have telephoned or emailed. But oh, noooo. He wanted to snoop around, see if you were staying in some den of iniquity." Justine nodded toward the stairway. "I slid his note under your door. Don't worry. I didn't read it." She cracked another sly smile. "The envelope was glued shut."

Kelly hurried upstairs, looking forward to Luke's message and a relaxing bath. Entering her room, she noticed a bouquet of chrysanthemums—white petals around a yellow center—stuck in a rusty can sitting on the vanity. An envelope addressed to her in Luke's distinctive scrawl was wedged between two stems. That was odd. Justine said she'd slid the note under the door.

How did these get here? Kelly wondered, picking up the can and turning it in her hands. The chrysanthemums had a slightly sour smell. Bits of caked-on mud broke loose from the can and landed on the vanity. When Kelly brushed them away, she realized that the silver-framed photograph of her and Meg posing among bouquets of daisies was gone. She barreled down the stairs. "Miss Pruitt!" She rushed to the front desk. "Who has a key to my room?"

"Just you and me."

"What about Benny?"

"I said, just you and me."

"Someone put these on my vanity." Kelly waved the can under Justine's nose. "That same someone stole a photograph of Meg and me."

"It wasn't Benny. He's visiting his father in Atlantic City for the day. He'll be back soon. You can ask him yourself." Justine tapped an index finger against her chin. "There is one other possibility. Your sister had a key when she left."

"Meg!" Kelly exclaimed. "Meg has come back!"

"I didn't mean for you to get your hopes up. She might have dropped the key, and someone picked it up."

"But why would someone take my—" The answer came flying at Kelly like a kite in a windstorm. The kidnapper! He had taken Meg's key. He wanted more keepsakes.

"Hello."

Kelly turned at the sound of Luke Campbell's voice.

"You look like you've seen a ghost. Did my note have that effect on you?"

Kelly shook her head regretfully. "I didn't read it yet."

"You sure are difficult to impress, Kelly. I worked hard over that flowery dinner invitation. Although I don't remember adding the flowers."

Kelly stood there openmouthed, wanting to get a word in, but Luke plowed on. "Miss Pruitt," he said, "do I have you to thank for the floral arrangement?"

"I'm sick of all these accusations," Justine snarled as she retreated to her private quarters.

"Women," Luke muttered, "have a peculiar way of communicating." He smiled at Kelly and nodded toward the door. "Ready to go?"

"No, I'm not!" she blurted out. "Someone got into my room while I was out and left an old, rusty can filled with chrysanthemums. Whoever it was moved your note and stole a photo of Meg and me."

"I'll send someone from forensics to dust for prints." Luke made a quick call to the forensics lab in Seagirt.

Kelly massaged her temples. "I have so much to tell you about what happened this afternoon, I don't know where to begin."

"Over dinner," he said calmly.

She looked at her honey-colored outfit and saw wrinkles, paint dabs, and dirt smudges. "I'm a mess. I should change."

"Don't waste your time." He smiled. "Your paint-spotted clothes are perfect for where we're going." He touched Kelly's cheek. "Green polka dots. Let me guess. The latest fad from New York City?"

Kelly laughed despite herself. "It's a long story," she said.

"We have all evening."

SIXTEEN

An Evening with Luke

PULLING AWAY FROM Pruitt's Inn in his midnight-blue Honda Accord, Luke glanced at Kelly. "You promised to tell me how that paint got onto your face."

Kelly filled him in about talking to Michael Duprey and seeing his paintings of Meg.

"And Duprey told you about Tim Ramsey?" Luke asked.

She nodded. "Did you find out anything?"

"Lots of good stuff."

"That sure was fast."

Kelly noticed a two-story blue house on the corner as he turned right.

"Here's what we know." He took several quick turns, backtracking his route, and she wondered if he'd lost his way. "Tim Ramsey, the so-called photographer who assaulted Meg, is really Tim Rodgers, a married man. He's a skirt-chaser with a huge ego. Someone as beautiful as Meg was a real challenge for him." He turned right.

Kelly felt as if they were going in circles.

"I need to talk to Duprey," Luke said. "He saw Meg with Tim Rodgers but withheld that information. He hampered police work."

"Go easy on him. He gave us our best lead so far. He intends to cooperate." Kelly realized immediately how protective she sounded. "His friend Greg Saunders was interested in Meg, too. He might know something important. He's at his sister's in Connecticut."

"I'll ask him to drop by the police station."

"How did you track down this Tim Rodgers creep?" Kelly asked, quickly changing topics. She was embarrassed about drinking and dancing with Michael Duprey.

"First, let's get back to Duprey and you," Luke said.

Kelly thought he sounded peeved, maybe jealous.

"I'm surprised you're making Duprey out to be a nice guy." Luke swerved around the corner. "If he'd spoken up, a more thorough investigation of Meg's disappearance might have occurred." Luke took a sharp right, brakes squealing. "And I'm disappointed that you went exploring alone again. I asked you to stay where you could be seen. Was there a crowd of people at Duprey's? No, just the two of you. What were you thinking?"

"I'm sorry. It won't happen again," Kelly said, stunned by Luke's harsh words. But he was right. She had acted foolishly. "Please, tell me how you found Tim Rodgers."

"We tracked down the bus driver on Meg's New York to Belvista trip. He had a lot to say about Rodgers, who's a regular."

"The bus station!" Kelly snapped her fingers. "Sam believes the kidnapper chooses his victims at the bus station."

"I'm one step ahead of you. I've put a woman detective there, on the lookout for pretty women searching the bulletin board for jobs." Luke adjusted the rearview mirror. "Our database provided complaints about Rodgers in the past, but no charges were ever filed."

"I wonder what kind of complaints." Kelly glanced out the window. There was that same blue house again. Luke must be lost.

"The usual. Unwanted advances, harassment, stalking."

"Do you think Rodgers is involved in the disappearances?" Kelly asked.

"Rodgers has an alibi for when Meg went missing. We're checking on his whereabouts when the other women disappeared." He glanced at her. "You said you had lots to tell me. I assume the rest is about Alex Bradford, the guy you mentioned in your second phone call. Where did you run into him?"

"Promise you won't get mad."

Luke's jaw tightened. "It can't be worse than being alone with Duprey in his studio in a deserted alley."

Kelly took a deep breath. "I ran into Alex at St. Anne's Cemetery."

"Damn!" Luke slammed his fists on the steering wheel.

"I wasn't alone, and Alex seems nice…in a weird sort of way. He—"

"A cemetery! Will you please tell me—"

"This is the third time we've passed that house."

"I took the long way so we could get all this talk out of the way."

"Why?"

"So we can take a break. You know, get to know each other and enjoy ourselves. But I guess we have to get out of the car."

Kelly laughed.

"This isn't going the way I planned. Shall we call a truce?" Luke asked as he finally parked the car.

"Truce," she said, and she shook his hand.

After they exited the car, he took her hand and led her up the winding path to the blue house. Kelly glanced up and down the street. There were few streetlights. She felt uneasy, as if someone were watching from the shadows.

"The houses on either side are unoccupied. They're being rehabbed," Luke said, and Kelly noticed the overgrown shrubbery between the yards. "One day this neighborhood will be among Belvista's finest." He led the way up the steps to the porch, boasting about his two-story gabled home.

Luke unlocked the front door, a wonderful old oak door with burnished hardware. "Don't expect too much," he said. He stepped into the foyer and flicked several switches, illuminating the rooms. "What's your honest opinion?"

"It's …" Kelly searched for the right word as she walked into the living room. "It's promising." She tried to overlook the ladders, sawhorses, and lumber and visualized draperies, furniture, and rugs. Two huge boxes overflowed with hammers, screwdrivers, and tools for every conceivable task. "And loaded with charm," she added, taking in the spacious room with a fieldstone fireplace and oak baseboards.

Kelly followed Luke across the living room's hardwood floor. Their shoes left prints in the thin layer of plaster dust swirled with broom strokes. How thoughtful! He had tried to make his home presentable for her.

Luke led the way to the dining room. "Lucky for me, a family down the street sold off their furniture, and I bought their dining room set. I need a place to spread out papers when I work at home."

"It's lovely," Kelly said, as Luke stopped at the cozy table and chairs with carved arabesque backs set in front of the dining room fireplace. A laptop, fax machine, and papers filled the card table in a corner. Kelly figured he had moved everything there from the dining room table.

Luke knelt before the fire and poked the glowing logs, coaxing them to flare and hiss. "Warm enough for you?" he asked, prodding a stubborn log. "The furnace isn't up and running yet."

"It's perfect," she said, admiring the table set for two, the wrinkled cloth, the mismatched wineglasses, and everyday kitchen plates. She was touched by his attempt to create a warm and intimate setting despite the hodgepodge.

"There are other rooms on this floor that the neighbors tell me were once the study, the children's playroom, and the music room. But we can see them later. I think a drink is in order." Luke headed into the kitchen. "You've had quite a day. So pick your poison."

She leaned against the doorjamb. Four painted chairs surrounded a kitchen table covered with newspapers. The crossword puzzles were done in ink. A confident man, that Luke Campbell.

"Scotch and water," she said.

"Hmm." He arched an eyebrow.

"I work mainly with men. Contractors, plumbers, electricians. Sometimes on Fridays, we socialize. Beer and scotch—that's what the guys like."

"I don't think of you as one of the guys," he said. "You're more the…" He shrugged away his words, and Kelly wished he'd finished the thought. "The previous owners, the Jamisons, were married for fifty years. This was the only home they'd ever known."

After pouring scotch for Kelly and mixing a gin and tonic for himself, he opened the refrigerator and took out a lemon and a lime. "This came with the place," he said, removing a knife from the cutting block on the counter. "The cutting board too." He nudged it with the tip of the knife. "Matthew Jamison was apparently the romantic type. He carved a heart encircling their initials, *MJ* and *KJ,* in the handle." Luke sliced off a chunk of lime and dropped it into his glass.

He looked her way, his dark eyes glistening in the overhead light. "I assigned an officer to Pruitt's Inn to make sure you're safe." He handed her the glass of scotch. "But now that someone has a key to 206, you should consider moving to another inn or at least to a different room."

"He'll find me sooner or later," Kelly said. "The sooner, the better. He'll take me to Meg." Tears welled in her eyes. "I miss her so much." She dabbed at her eyes with a tissue. "I'm sorry. I don't mean to blubber."

"Let the tears flow," he said, removing fish fillets from the refrigerator. "The countertop needs a good washing."

Kelly laughed and sipped her scotch.

"Now, sit down and let me get to work." He removed his jacket and rolled up his sleeves. "I'll start with the flounder." He heated butter in a frying pan, scrambled an egg, and coated the fish with the egg and then bread crumbs. "Old family recipe," he said. "Equal parts crumbs and sawdust." He glanced around the kitchen. "My cat, Rusty, must be hiding. He usually comes out when he smells fish."

The scotch went down nice and easy. Relaxed, Kelly sat at the table, her back to the window overlooking the porch. She watched Luke move from the stove to the refrigerator to the counter, opening and shutting cabinets and drawers, apparently uncertain where things were stored. He was all thumbs as he measured out rice and dumped peas into a saucepan. Such a rugged, take-charge man, yet so vulnerable and inexperienced in the kitchen. She found that incredibly sexy.

"Coming up with ideas for my kitchen?" he asked.

"Yes. I'm compulsive. Everywhere I go, I mentally move walls, change wallpaper, and so on."

"Let me guess," he said. "You don't like the fake-brick linoleum or the wallpaper design." He nodded at the little bouquets of red flowers that dotted the walls.

She laughed. "You've got plenty of room here, and the pantry is a nice bonus." She tapped a finger against her cheek and studied the room. "Forget today's look—granite countertops, brushed-steel appliances, and glazed cherry cabinetry. Your kitchen needs authenticity—definitely an oak table and chairs."

"I like your advice. It's classy. You're a classy woman."

"Not one of the guys."

"No way."

"I'm being a terrible guest. May I help?" Kelly removed her jacket and draped it over her chair.

"Sure. My drink needs more lime."

Kelly moved the cutting board closer and passed her fingertips over the knife handle. The workmanship impressed her. So did the romantic sentiment. As Luke stepped aside to make room for her, his shoulder brushed against hers. There was a slight hesitation, an anticipation, their eyes fixed on each other's, a shared reaction to something—she didn't know what, but it was nice and warm and friendly. She reached for a paper towel to wipe up the lime juice, and he continued preparing the fish. Through the window she caught sight of a picnic table and benches on the back porch, visible in the light spilling out from the kitchen.

Startled, Kelly pointed at the porch. "Where did they come from?"

From the surprised look on Luke's face, Kelly knew he hadn't set the bouquet of chrysanthemums on his picnic table.

Luke unlocked the kitchen door, stepped onto the porch, and pulled a small card from the stems. "Greetings," he read, then shrugged. "That's the message. There's no signature."

"It's the kidnapper, taunting us. When I find him—"

Luke took the knife from her hand and set it aside.

"What's come over me?" Kelly exclaimed.

"You've had quite a scare." He placed his hands gently on her shoulders and coaxed her back toward the kitchen. "It's probably a neighbor, being friendly. Dinner will be ready in a few minutes. We'll share a bottle of wine and enjoy the fire."

"I can't shake the feeling that the flowers have something to do with Meg," Kelly said.

"Let's be logical," Luke said, following Kelly into the kitchen. "From what you've told me, Meg's favorite flower is the daisy. Her missing pajamas and scarf have a daisy print. The missing photograph of Meg and you was taken in a florist shop near bouquets of daisies."

"You're right about Meg and daisies," she said, turning her face inches from his. "She even cross-stitched a daisy design on my sewing kit. But I don't see what you're getting at."

"Think about it, Kelly. If there is a kidnapper, and if this kidnapper wanted to taunt you about Meg, he would have sent daisies, not chrysanthemums." He pulled out a chair. "Now just try to relax."

While Luke put the finishing touches on dinner, Kelly thought hard. She looked again at the chrysanthemums on the porch. "There's a message in these chrysanthemums—I'm sure of it—but we're missing it. What—"

Luke set down his spatula. "Okay, I'll admit the chrysanthemums could be an intentional choice. These chrysanthemums have white petals around a yellow center, just like oxeye daisies." He came and sat next to Kelly. "But why bother with chrysanthemums? Why not just put a can of daisies in your room?"

Kelly sighed. "I don't know. I think it's a clue."

Luke wrapped his hands around Kelly's hands. "Think about it. He couldn't be sure we'd figure out his clues."

"But I've heard people say you're smart."

Luke chuckled. "And you believed those rumors?"

"Yes, and you're a detective, and you do crossword puzzles. And supposedly I'm good with colors. So—"

"There are other explanations," Luke said calmly, taking a napkin from the table and dabbing at her tears. "Chrysanthemums are plentiful right now. This person could be a cheapskate."

Kelly sniffled. "He's trying to show us how clever he is."

"People in love often pull away daisy petals," Luke admitted, patting her cheeks with the napkin. "You know, 'she loves me, she loves me not.' This could be a romantic person. Maybe someone who wants us to fall in love."

"Who would that be?" She blinked away her tears.

Luke thought for a moment. "Justine Pruitt?"

Kelly laughed heartily. She was laughing and crying all at the same time.

"See?" He pulled a petal from a chrysanthemum. "At this point you're supposed to say, 'he loves me.'" He set the flower down. "I'll stop there while I'm ahead." He walked back to the stove and squirted lemon over the flounder.

"I can get carried away," Kelly said, standing up. She leaned against the doorjamb and felt the tension in her body melt away. "I'm sorry. I don't usually behave like this with someone I've known for such a short time."

"I'll take that as a compliment," he said, and he began heaping food onto two plates.

"You still don't believe there is a kidnapper."

"I have serious doubts." Luke uncorked the wine. "Don't keep the chef waiting." Hands full, he nodded for Kelly to follow him into the dining room.

They sat down opposite each other, and Luke filled their glasses to the rim. "Kidnapping women and imprisoning them happens in big cities, but this is a small town. Someone would notice. People talk." He unfolded his napkin. "I don't mean to get on a bandstand. Let's enjoy our dinner. We'll talk after."

Kelly tasted the flounder. "It's delicious," she said, wishing she were hungry. Luke had gone to so much work. The logs crackled, and their flames cast dancing shadows on the walls. Kelly glanced at Luke. He looked incredibly handsome as he worked his way through the meal with a purposeful expression on his face. She felt guilty, thinking romantic thoughts about Luke at a time like this. She felt guilty too remembering how she'd danced with Michael Duprey. Loneliness had engulfed her and worn down her self-control. She wouldn't let that happen again. She couldn't let her emotions distract her from finding Meg.

Luke wiped his chin with his napkin and pushed himself away from the table. "You want to know if there's a serial kidnapper here in Belvista. Let's look at the facts." He spoke calmly, as if he were reading a police report. "Meg's missing. A thief has a key to room 206 at Pruitt's Inn. Someone is delivering chrysanthemums to you or to us."

"What about at the Mariners' Museum—the sneeze and the message *Leave Belvista?*"

"It's allergy season. People sneeze. The message might not have been intended for you."

Kelly bristled. "Why are you—?"

"There is a slight possibility that you and Sam are on to something." He poured the rest of the wine.

"I can't wait to hear this."

"My officers ran down every black Lexus in town. So far, nothing promising, but you kept seeing the same car? That's a suspicious coincidence. Then when I followed up on Sam's obituary idea—"

"You discovered another coincidence." Kelly was enjoying this conversation.

He savored his wine. "Yes. The women who died at the hospital and the missing women were all attractive, all between seventeen and twenty-eight. Coincidences always jump-start my curiosity. So, I've asked Chuck Lazenby, a hospital administrator, to check his files."

"I appreciate all that you've done. You're experienced and helpful and…" The wine on top of the scotch was loosening her tongue. Compliments flowed from her lips. But how could she resist? Luke Campbell was not only handsome, charming, and intelligent, he was a man of action. "What do you think those files will turn up?"

"I'm not sure. But I want to know how many other young women died at the hospital during the past year. If there were more deaths than disappearances, then Sam Chambers' theory falls apart. Chuck Lazenby will have an answer for me tomorrow morning. I'm meeting him at eleven."

Kelly turned the stem of her wineglass in her slim fingers. "I was hoping you'd go with me to the cattail marshes tomorrow morning. The brochures recommend going by bike or horse. A bike sounds good to me."

Luke planted his elbows on the table and rested his chin on his fists. "So, you're inviting me to go bike riding. Are you one of those aggressive New York women I hear about?"

She laughed. "No, but I'm willing to make an exception just this once." She liked Luke. He always made her laugh.

"I'll come by at eight," Luke said, "and I'll bring a bike for you. What do you expect to find there?"

"I don't know. But Meg spent hours in those marshes with Michael Duprey. I won't be content until I've seen the area. I'd also like to visit the potter's field near the cattail marshes. I have a theory, but it can wait until tomorrow." She rose from her chair. "I've had a wonderful time, but I'm feeling woozy from the drinks."

"I'll take you home."

They stepped into the cool night air and were admiring the star-tossed sky when a pathetic whimper came from beneath the hedge.

"Rusty?" Luke called. He picked up the red fluffy cat and stroked his back. "How did you get outside?" Rusty cowered in Luke's arms. "Don't be frightened. This is Kelly Madison. Her bark is worse than her bite."

"Very funny," Kelly said.

Luke turned to Kelly. "I've never seen Rusty frightened like this. I don't get it."

"It's quite simple," Kelly said. "This evening, Rusty met the kidnapper."

SEVENTEEN

Justine's Offer

LUKE LINKED ARMS WITH Kelly and walked up the porch stairs to the front door of Pruitt's Inn. "I had a wonderful time tonight," he said.

"So did I."

Luke leaned against the wall, drew her close, and gave her a sweet good-night kiss. Kelly didn't resist. His embrace was so thrilling, his arms so reassuring, his lips so inviting. He kissed her again, this time with more urgency. One passionate kiss led to another. She didn't want the evening to end. She didn't want his kisses to stop, but they must. She didn't want Luke to feel that she was leading him on so that he would pursue Meg's case.

"It's getting late," Kelly said, pulling away.

"I'm disappointed," Luke teased. "I heard New York City women really knew how to kiss. Heart-thumping, knock-your-socks-off kisses. Based on a statistic of one, I'd say New York women are overrated."

She laughed. "Give me another chance."

"You've got one shot. Give it your all."

"All right, but just one." She wrapped her arms around his neck and kissed him long and hard. "There," she said. "That's how we kiss in the Big Apple. Are you happy now?"

"Very happy," he said, sweeping her into his arms and kissing her again.

Kelly's heart raced. "I'll see you at eight in the morning," she said, and she slipped through the doorway into the foyer. She backed up against the door and tried to catch her breath.

"It's about time!" Justine exclaimed, stepping from the shadows, dressed in black from collar to shoes.

Kelly gasped. "You scared the life out of me!"

"Thought you'd seen a ghost?" Justine cackled, and the dim light from the reception desk emphasized her yellow teeth and hawklike nose. She tapped her bony fingers on the registration book. "The Povloski clan I told you about, the six brothers and their wives, have settled in for the week. They've taken all five rooms on your floor and one on the third."

"You must be happy, Justine. Rooms full. Money coming in." Kelly wondered where this conversation was heading and why Justine was telling her this now.

"There's a problem. The Povloskis are very demanding. They want breakfast at five-forty-five sharp and insisted on sausage, pancakes, eggs, the works. They want sandwiches ready to go at noon. They'll return for supper at six on the dot, expecting a pork and cabbage dinner. The shopping nearly killed Benny and me, but everything's bought and stored."

"You must be exhausted," Kelly commented, still not sure what this conversation had to do with her.

Justine plowed on. "I can handle the kitchen or the upkeep of the guest rooms, but not both. My part-time girl, Elsie, ended up full time this week at the Sand Castle Inn. They're full up too."

"I thought the season was dying out. What's going on in Belvista this week?"

"Crazy rumors that Belvista might boom as a mall town—biggest mall and entertainment complex on the East Coast, a maxi-mall-megaplex or some dang thing. This Povloski clan is here to scoop up inns and rehab them. As many as a dozen, they tell me."

"Pruitt's Inn too?"

"No, this is too nice for them. They want fixer-uppers.

They're going to spend every day scouting for bargains. In a nutshell, I'm shorthanded. I was wondering—"

"If I'd help out."

"Could you?"

"I need time to look for Meg."

"What about helping me early in the morning before the town is awake?"

Kelly nodded. "That's okay."

"Good. You work on the rooms. I'll cook and serve and clean up."

"There's a small matter of—"

"Three-quarter rent for the days you work."

"Half."

"Deal." Justine shook Kelly's hand enthusiastically.

Kelly had never felt such a cold hand. "I appreciate this, Justine. I've had lots of expenses lately, and as a freelance designer, I only make money when I work."

"Sounds like you're at poverty's door," Justine said sympathetically. "I've been there. It's no fun."

Kelly felt guilty about exaggerating her financial problems. She wanted Justine to think this arrangement was all about money. But really it was a chance to search six rooms in Pruitt's Inn for traces of Meg. She would figure out a way to get into the other rooms.

"I promised the Povloskis clean towels every day," Justine was saying. "I'll expect you to clean both baths. Make the beds, plump the pillows, dust-mop the floors. And don't be shy about moving the furniture and cleaning behind it."

Kelly thought she caught the glimmer of a smile on Justine's lips. Was Justine giving her tacit permission to search for some trace of Meg that had been overlooked? "Are you saying—?"

"I'm saying, clean all six rooms." Justine's arms dropped limply to her sides, her hands still and lifeless. "I once had a sister. She died young, from pneumonia. There was nothing we could do to save her. I miss her and think about her every day."

"I'm sorry, Justine." Justine waved away Kelly's words.

"Start cleaning at five-forty-five, and don't quit until everything is spit-and-polish clean."

"Spit?"

"Don't get smart with me, missy. You know what I mean. Here's the master key." She dropped it into Kelly's hand. "Benny will show you the supply closet. He likes to help. You're patient with him. Many of my guests are not." She clapped her hands, and Benny lumbered from their private quarters behind the reception counter.

Kelly noticed that Benny's room was the first doorway on the right, opposite the staircase. With this vantage point, he probably served as night watchman.

"This way, Kelly," Benny said, and in the dim light he led her to a door tucked beneath the staircase directly across from his.

When Kelly turned to say good-night to Justine, she saw Justine entering the second doorway, next to Benny's. She had never noticed the door before because it blended so neatly into the wall. A chill went up her spine. It was like watching a specter walk through walls.

Benny opened the supply-closet door.

"This is very well organized," Kelly said. "Did you arrange it?"

"Yes," Benny said proudly. "Me and Aunt Justine can find everything we need, quick as bunnies."

He showed her all the items she would need. "Don't mess up, or Aunt Justine will get mad at you. And then she'll get mad at me, because I didn't teach you right." His eyes went as big as saucers.

"I'll keep things just as you have them," Kelly promised, and Benny breathed a sigh of relief.

The moment they were finished, Kelly decided to call Luke. She plucked her cell phone from her purse. "Darn! I forgot to recharge the battery," she said.

Benny whispered, "You can use Aunt Justine's." He took

Justine's cell phone from the reception desk and handed it to Kelly. "Who do you want to talk to?"

"My friend, Detective Campbell. This will be our little secret, Benny. Let's not worry Aunt Justine. She's got enough on her mind with so many guests. I'll put it back when I'm done. You go on to bed."

Benny nodded. He made his way past the reception counter, stepping this way and that as if to avoid squeaky boards, giving the impression he often crept around at night without awakening Justine. His door clicked shut.

Kelly sat in the parlor in the dark, waiting for Benny to fall asleep. She promised herself to recharge her phone that very night. She thought about Luke Campbell. She had practically thrown herself into his arms. She could blame the scotch and wine, or the strain of trying to find her sister as reasons for being so interested in Luke. But the truth was, he was easy to talk to. She had fallen hard for his good looks, bold personality, and quick sense of humor.

Kelly's eyelids drooped. She couldn't wait any longer. She called Luke. Afraid that Benny or Justine might overhear, she whispered hurriedly, "Luke, it's Kelly. Don't speak, just listen. I have a chance to search Pruitt's Inn for clues to Meg's disappearance. I need your help. Come for me tomorrow morning at exactly ten minutes to six, not eight o'clock. Please sneak past Justine. I don't want her to know what we're up to. I'll explain when I see you. I'll be waiting in room 206. We'll still be able to bicycle to the cattail marshes at eight. Thanks."

"May I speak now?" Luke asked.

"Yes," Kelly whispered.

"I'll see you at ten minutes to six. In keeping with the clandestine nature of our meeting, I'll park my car and our bikes away from Pruitt's Inn, on another street. Your obedient servant, Luke Campbell."

EIGHTEEN

Killing Two Birds

KELLY AWAKENED.

5:15!

Later than she'd intended. The inn was quiet. Darkness engulfed the window. Quickly she slipped into her embroidered blouse, suede-trimmed jeans, and sneakers. She tamed her hair into a French braid.

She made several trips to the supply closet, gathered what she needed, and deposited everything in her room, her base of operations. Justine's and Benny's voices wafted from the kitchen, Justine snapping orders and Benny responding dutifully, "Yes, Aunt Justine."

She heard the Povloski clan moving about, snippets of conversation, doors opening and closing, and then heavy footsteps on the stairs.

5:45.

Kelly darted to the first room, 201, to check out the master key. From below came the clatter of silverware and muffled conversations pierced by Justine's nervous snorts of laughter.

She turned the key. The door opened. She peeked inside. The sparse furnishings were similar to hers. Massive and ornate. A quick peek into 202 revealed a similar setup. The same for 203, 204, and 205. She would get to the third floor soon enough.

Kelly stepped back into the hallway. Someone was right behind her. She spun around. Luke.

"I'm glad you're here," Kelly said, grabbing him by the elbow and pulling him into her room. He was wearing jeans and a long-sleeved T-shirt, a sweatshirt draped across his shoulders, ready for bicycling, looking carefree. She closed the door, pushed him up against it, and clamped a hand over his mouth. "Don't speak above a whisper," she warned before she removed her hand.

"Do with me what you will," he whispered, stepping away from the door.

"Stop fooling around, Luke. I had too much scotch and wine last night. I was scared out of my wits by everything that's happened. I have no one else to turn to in Belvista, so I threw myself into your arms. I'm sorry if I gave you the wrong impression."

"I'm sorry that you're sorry. I'm not."

Kelly frowned. "Right now our relationship is going to be purely professional. We are going to find Meg. Distractions, like, well, you know what I mean, are unacceptable." She tucked tendrils of hair behind her ears. "For now, the important thing is that I have the master key."

"To my heart?"

"Cut it out, Luke. The key to Pruitt's Inn. We can go through every room and look for something of Meg's. I'll clean. You search."

"I'll clean. You search. You know best what you're looking for. I don't have a clue." Luke grinned. "Sorry. Police humor."

Kelly frowned, annoyed by his lighthearted mood during such a serious time. "Let's go, Luke. Every second counts. If we hear Justine, hide."

"And who will come seek? You or Justine?"

"Luke, this is serious business." She gathered up an armload of linens. "Please cooperate."

"Yes, ma'am." He scooped up the remaining linens and followed Kelly out the door.

Once inside 201, Luke became all business. In no time he had pulled the furniture away from the walls. While she looked everywhere, dusting and mopping as she went, he made the bed, laid out clean towels, and returned the furniture to its proper place.

"Justine wants the pillows plumped," Kelly said. She hated to appear bossy, but speed was important.

"Slave driver," Luke said playfully as he slapped two pillows together.

Kelly finished inspecting the contents of the chifferobe's drawers and shelves. "Nothing," she said. "Let's see what room 202 offers."

None of the other rooms on Kelly's floor revealed any trace of Meg. "I thought for sure we'd find something," Kelly said, closing the chifferobe doors.

"A lack of clues isn't necessarily bad," Luke said. "It means Meg wasn't held captive here." He walked toward the desk and stopped short. "What's this?" He ran his fingers along the windowsill.

Kelly rushed to his side. Luke was pointing at a roughened area. The wood looked as if it had been chewed or clawed.

"A cat or dog?"

"It's hard to say. A recent coat of paint covered the distressed area." He scrutinized the rest of the window trim. "Only the windowsill has been painted," he said. "To save money. Or it's a cover-up."

"The windowsill in my room is the same. Fresh paint over a distressed area." Kelly was annoyed with herself for having overlooked something significant.

"Let's check them all," Luke said, heading to the door.

The windowsill in every room they had cleaned had identical markings. They climbed the stairs to the third floor and let themselves into room 306, occupied by one of the Povloski couples. Luke poked his head out the window and looked up. "Do you remember anything about the police checking the attic?"

"No. This is important, isn't it?" Kelly asked, filled with hope.

"Could be."

Luke ran his fingers along the windowsill in 306. "I've seen this pattern before, but I can't remember where."

"Think hard, Luke."

"A shoulder massage would help."

"Sit down," Kelly said fiercely, pulling out the chair. "You're going to get the massage of a lifetime."

"Promise?"

Standing behind him, Kelly dug her fingers into his shoulders and kneaded as if she were making bread. He thought. She stiffened her hands and slammed them back and forth across his shoulders. He thought. She twisted her knuckles into the muscles along his spine.

Luke jumped to his feet.

"Did I hurt you?"

Luke shook his head and then winced as if he had dislocated something. "Children's swing sets, tree houses—that's where I've seen marks like these. We're looking at rope impressions. The wood is dry and splintery. A rope pulled across it cuts into the grain."

"Are you thinking what I'm thinking?" Kelly asked.

"That you have a sadistic nature? That you enjoyed letting out your pent-up hostility on me?"

"No!" Kelly huffed. "That the kidnapper shimmied down the side of the house on a rope and came in through the window."

Luke shook his head. "That's great for the movies, but it would make his getaway difficult. I'll read the reports and see if the officers searched the attic." He checked his watch. "Give me the master key. If it fits the attic door, I'll give it a quick look."

"I'll get a flashlight."

KELLY AND LUKE STOOD in the middle of the attic, surrounded by years of accumulated junk, wiping spiderwebs off their faces.

"There's no rope anywhere," Luke said, swinging the flashlight beam toward each of the walls and corners. "And it's obvious no one has been up here for a long time."

"Let's see about the windowsills," Kelly said. There were two windows, too small for most men to climb through, but no true windowsills and no paint, fresh or otherwise, on any loose wood in the entire attic.

"Luke, is it possible a man hid in Meg's room and carried her down by rope to avoid Justine and Benny?"

"How did he dispose of the rope afterward?"

"Justine might have found it and discarded it."

"But the kidnapper couldn't count on that."

"Unless they were in this together."

"Kelly, you—"

"I'm going to ask Justine." She realized Luke had considered the possibilities she brought up and rejected them. "Wait in my room."

There she was, bossing Luke around again. She just didn't have time to be nice. She was staying on track, searching for Meg.

"JUSTINE HAD AN EXPLANATION for the markings," Kelly said as she entered her room.

Luke was on his hands and knees, checking the baseboard and floor directly below the window. He looked up. "Fire away."

"Painters. Painters hung a rope ladder out the windows and painted the white trim that runs around the house just below each window."

"You're buying that?"

"According to Justine, they cut her a good deal. It was faster and cheaper than setting up scaffolding. She said some of the other houses in the neighborhood got wind of it and followed suit. She sees herself as a trendsetter."

"Nobody could make up that story," Luke said. "I'm buying it, too. But, just to make sure, I'll have my men check it out."

"WHEW!" KELLY EXCLAIMED. She glanced at her alarm clock on the nightstand in her room and checked it against her new watch. "It's eight o'clock." There was no time to check the rooms not rented to the Povloskis. Maybe tomorrow she'd find a way.

"We're only a few minutes behind your schedule," Luke said, stretching his back.

Kelly wished she could change clothes. She felt a mess. Moist tendrils of hair stuck to the back of her neck or spiraled around her face. He looked great. He was in really good shape. Guess that was part of the job description. Kelly stood in front of her vanity. Luke sat on the edge of the bed, watching her. She wanted to run a brush through her hair. Instead, she put on a beret.

"Planning a trip to France?" Luke asked, nodding at her beret.

"No, Mr. Smart-Aleck." Kelly grabbed a towel and snapped it at him. He grabbed the end of the towel and reeled her in. She landed in his arms, and they fell back on the bed. After a fumbled attempt, with interference from the beret, which slipped down over her eyes, Luke kissed her long and hard on the lips. Kelly's heart raced.

She rolled away from him and stood up. "Luke, you've got to promise you won't try that again."

He rose onto his elbows and looked her straight in the eye. "You don't enjoy a few stolen kisses after work?"

"No...well, maybe. All right, yes, I do... I'm certain you can tell that I do...but you and your kisses are keeping me from finding Meg."

"So, it's just a matter of bad timing on my part?"

"Yes," Kelly said. "And, speaking of timing, we need to go."

Kelly took the lead as they headed down the hallway.

"This isn't some private-eye show on TV," Luke whispered as they approached the top step. "Don't even think about saying 'The coast is clear.'"

Kelly sighed loudly and continued down the stairs, Luke

on her heels. They didn't see Justine or Benny, but they heard the clattering of dishes in the kitchen. Hand in hand, Kelly and Luke hurried across the porch, down the steps, along the path, and turned the corner.

"My car's on the next street," Luke said, setting a brisk pace. "I didn't want Justine losing sleep wondering about the Honda Accord with the bike rack parked near her inn."

"Everything is going according to plan," Kelly said.

"This secret operation was too easy." Luke pulled his car keys from his pocket. "I think Justine knew I was there and pretended not to notice. Nothing sneaks by that woman." As he unlocked his car, Kelly looked at the sturdy bikes, good for dirt roads. "But why would she break from her usual nastiness? I'm told it's kept bill collectors from her door for years."

Kelly hopped into Luke's car. "I had the crazy notion that Justine was letting me have the run of the house to look for clues. She got emotional telling me about her sister who died from pneumonia. Deep down, she's just an old softy."

"I wouldn't go that far," Luke said, turning the key in the ignition.

"Come to think of it, Benny can't keep secrets," Kelly said. "I'm sure he told Justine that I borrowed her phone to call you. It's as if we've fallen into her little plan."

"Justine killed two birds with one stone," Luke said. "She got her rooms cleaned and let you sleuth to your heart's content."

"Dead birds." Kelly shuddered. "What a lovely image."

NINETEEN

The Cattail Marshes

AS THEY PULLED AWAY from Pruitt's Inn, Luke said, "Let me bring you up to date on Meg's case."

"This sounds serious," Kelly said.

Luke slowed and turned left at the intersection. "I had Michael Duprey hauled down to the police station last night to answer more questions."

"Because he withheld the information that Tim Ramsey was the mystery man seen with Meg on the boardwalk?"

Luke picked up speed. "He needed to set things straight."

"I hope you didn't put pressure on him," Kelly said, sensing Luke's anger.

"I considered pistol-whipping his pretty face, but I held back. I had Detective Andy Quinn, our best interrogator, take charge. He couldn't crack Duprey's story. Quinn is like you. He believes Duprey."

"But you don't."

"I have my doubts." Luke braked as a car swerved in front of him. "However, we checked Duprey's alibis for the days when the other three women disappeared. They're solid. Two of the times he was at small gallery shows exhibiting his work and his friend Greg Saunders' work. He's more talented than I was led to believe. Gallery owners corroborated his alibi."

"Did he have an alibi when the third woman went missing?"

"Duprey was at his sister's in Connecticut. So he's not a serial kidnapper. But he could be responsible for Meg's disappearance. We're working on that. In my mind, he could be one of those smooth charmers in public who turns vicious in private. That's where things stand with Duprey. As for Saunders, he seems to have alibis too. Still, I asked him to drive down from Connecticut."

Luke braked for a dog running across the road. "The word in the artists' community is that Duprey and Saunders are cutthroat rivals. Duprey considers Saunders a second-rate artist and resents his financial success. Saunders calls Duprey old-fashioned, but deep down he's jealous of Duprey's ability to paint pretty women and settings. He's afraid Duprey will soon surpass him. But for now, let's forget them and concentrate on Meg, okay?"

Fifteen minutes from Pruitt's Inn, beyond Belvista's populated neighborhoods, Luke pulled into a parklike compound nestled among towering blue spruces. Kelly saw the sign Cattail Marshes Service Stop at the entrance. A smaller sign added Open Sunrise to Sunset. Only three cars were ahead of them in line, and Kelly couldn't wait to explore the area. The car ahead went through the gate, and Luke pulled forward. "I'm glad you invited me," he said.

"Me, too. You had the right idea coming this far by car. Now we'll have more time to poke around the marshes and maybe find clues to Meg's disappearance. Did you know that Michael Duprey and Meg came to the marshes by car that Saturday?"

"Yes." The next car pulled ahead, and Luke stepped on the gas. "Duprey can rattle off the days and hours when he and Meg were together. He's rehearsed it, probably in front of a mirror."

Kelly felt that Luke was overly critical of Michael. "They must have parked here," she said calmly. "Maybe somebody remembers them."

"Good morning, Willy," Luke said as he rolled down the window.

"Your usual shady spot's waiting," Willy said with a toothy grin. He hunched down and looked from the open window across to Kelly. "Good morning, uh… Well, now, good morning, ma'am," he said. Kelly figured from his surprised look that he was expecting someone else in the passenger seat.

"Have a fine day, sir," Willy said, straightening up. He rapped his knuckles against Luke's knuckles, then waved in the next car, a canary-yellow SUV.

Luke parked. He reached into the glove compartment, pulled out a Glock, and hooked it into a holster on his jeans. Kelly looked over her shoulder, half expecting a black Lexus to be lurking somewhere. She craned her neck. Not a black car anywhere in sight.

"Keep in mind, this isn't where Meg was last seen," Luke said as he and Kelly got out of the car.

"I know. But very early that next morning, Sunday morning, Meg could have left Pruitt's Inn on her bike without anyone seeing her. She could have stopped here for water or something."

"We'll ask around," Luke said, locking the car.

"Then we'll head to the marshes." Kelly took photos of Meg from her purse. She felt she was on the right track, even if Luke had doubts. He hammered away at who had seen her last: Michael Duprey. And where he had seen her: Pruitt's Inn.

"I don't think the marshes will give up any secrets after three weeks," Luke said, draping an arm across her shoulders, "but the atmosphere might help you relax. You're no good to Meg if you can't think straight."

"You're right. I'll try to relax." Kelly took in the peaceful setting. Nearby were racks with maybe thirty bikes for rent. At the far end was a stable with horses available for riding. Saddles were lined up. A magnificent white horse whinnied and flicked its tail.

"Not many people at this early hour," Kelly said, noticing a few joggers stretching their legs.

"It's more a weekend place."

"I'm going to start with the general store." Kelly pointed toward a sprawling log-cabin structure with rocking chairs on the porch. "Maybe Meg bought a disk for her camera." She held up photographs of Meg. "I'll ask the clerks if they remember her."

Luke took several photos. "I'll ask at the stables and check with Willy. We'll meet back here in ten minutes. Don't go wandering off, okay?"

LUKE HAD ALREADY LIFTED both bikes from his car rack and was testing the air in the tires when Kelly returned.

"The clerks don't remember Meg," she said dejectedly.

"Nobody at the stables saw her, either. Willy doesn't remember seeing Meg or anyone who fits Duprey's description here that Saturday or Sunday."

Kelly gritted her teeth. "This is so frustrating." She looked back at the general store. "They had an entire souvenir section devoted to cattails. Hand towels embroidered with cattails. Chairs with cattail-rush seats. Cattail-reed dolls."

"What are you getting at?" Luke asked. He checked the chain on her bike.

"Meg is a sucker for souvenirs. If she'd come here, she'd have bought something. A cashier would have remembered her."

"What did you buy?" Luke asked, nodding at the bag she was holding.

"A cattail cookbook for Justine. It might rev up her cuisine." Kelly pulled the slim book from the bag and held it up. "Did you know that cattail shoots can be peeled and eaten in salads?"

"Sure," Luke said. He wiped his hands on a towel. "They're good—taste like cucumbers. I've had cattail fried rice too."

"Are you teasing me?"

"No. Sliced cattail hearts sautéed in sesame oil, some ginger and wild rice. It's great. But you have to try the cattail soup. Some brown rice, soy… Hey, I just thought of something."

"About Meg?"

Luke nodded. "Could be Meg and Duprey didn't use this rest stop. Lots of people just park on the street near here and bike the rest of the way. We get complaints about that all the time."

Kelly felt better after hearing Luke's explanation. Luke could always cheer her up. And he was considerate. He'd put two bottles of chilled water into her bike basket.

"It's only four miles on the paved road," Luke said, steering her bike toward her. "But it's one lane, and traffic can be tricky, so be careful. Then it's a breeze. There won't be any cars once we enter the marshes."

"They're not allowed?" Kelly asked, gripping the handlebars.

"They're allowed, but the speed limit is ten miles an hour, and let's just say they're not well received by bikers and joggers. I'll lead the way, okay?"

"Let's go," Kelly said enthusiastically.

Luke leaned over the handlebars of his bike into the stiff breeze. Kelly took off awkwardly and couldn't work up any speed or momentum. Distracted by several joggers passing by, she nearly tumbled to the ground.

Luke called over his shoulder, "You okay back there?"

Two cars whipped by, unnerving Kelly. "I'm fine." She threaded her way among potholes. A horse and rider nearly ran her off the road. "I can keep up." She didn't want to lose precious time. They had ninety minutes to explore before Luke's appointment at the hospital, and Kelly intended to make the most of it.

"You must be tired after moving all that furniture," she called ahead.

"The massage whipped me back into shape," he called back, making her laugh. She enjoyed every minute with him and wished the circumstances were different.

Kelly was happy to see the fork in the road, which materialized as the cloud of dust kicked up by the passing cars settled. From her map, she knew that the hospital was a mile farther to the left, and the cattail marshes lay to the right. Picking up the pace, she turned right and pedaled around two sharp turns.

The reeds and plants rising among the cattails were visible after the third turn. Gazing at the vast area's vegetation, she visualized a kitchen with earth-tone tiles, wallpaper with flecks of mossy green, granite countertops in subtle browns and greens.

Oops! Sharp turn ahead. Kelly braked, going around the corner, then pedaled fast, catching up to Luke. No wonder they didn't allow people in here at night. The road was treacherous.

After a while Kelly got control of her bike, and she and Luke kept a comfortable pace. She admired the fuzzy brown cattail spikes that nodded in the breeze as if to welcome her. Turtles sunned themselves on logs. Chirps and warbles came from both sides of the road. She almost allowed herself to relax, as if Meg's disappearance had never happened, that she'd merely dreamed it. "I can picture Meg bike-riding along this path, enjoying herself."

"It's one of my favorite places in Belvista." Luke leaned toward Kelly and coasted. "Can you keep a secret?"

Kelly nodded, carefully watching the road, which twisted and turned along the edge of the marsh. She veered around the waist-high and shoulder-high cattail stalks, which leaned into the road, and coasted in the shade of ferns and rushes.

"I come here by bike to read poetry and bird-watch on my days off. The guys in Atlantic City would laugh if they knew." He had a faraway look in his eyes. "I'm enjoying small-town life. I might consider staying on here as a detective when my consulting work winds down."

"You're a man of many surprises," Kelly said. "What's that?" She turned toward the splashing sound.

"A red-winged blackbird." Luke pointed toward the middle of the marsh. "They like the deep areas out there."

Through a break in the cattails, Kelly spotted the water. Dark, glistening like polished stone, the smooth surface gave way to inky-black ripples that inched toward the edge of the marsh and disappeared into the thick tangle of roots and stalks.

Kelly heard the splash again. She saw a flash of red and black break the water's surface. The bird rose, flapping its wings, skimming above the cattails' long, narrow leaves. She sighed at the sheer beauty of the sight and knew Meg would have taken many photos here.

"Detective Campbell! Miss Madison!" Hal Dunbar hurried on horseback down the road, waving a riding crop. His silver mount snorted as he dismounted. Two other men, deep in conversation, sat on their horses, a chestnut-brown beauty and a black stallion.

"You're looking at the three worst blowhards in the Business Club," Luke warned. "Traskell has an insurance agency. Ferguson sells building supplies. It's rumored that Dunbar, who expects to win the mayoral race, has promised them contracts. Unless they have something to say that could help with Meg's case, we'll try to get rid of them. Subtlety probably won't work."

"I like your style," Kelly said, braking. She remembered the email Hazie had found from Traskell's son, Jeff, to his buddies. He'd bragged about how he'd gotten paid to hack into websites about the Cinderellas and the town council. She immediately disliked Mr. Traskell for lumping Meg in with the so-called Cinderellas. He had discouraged a serious investigation. And Mr. Ferguson was no sweetheart either. He received insider information from the Traskells on bidding contracts. He probably went along with the Cinderella story to stay on Traskell's good side.

Feelings of remorse nagged Kelly. She wondered if she should break her promise to Sam and tell Luke about the businessmen's interest in Meg and the Cinderellas. Keeping all this secret from Luke bothered Kelly. She felt she wasn't doing what was best for Meg.

"We meet again, Miss Madison!" Hal Dunbar exclaimed, tapping his riding crop against the palm of one hand.

Traskell and Ferguson trotted off. Good riddance, thought Kelly.

"What brings you here?" Luke asked Dunbar.

Luke didn't hide his impatience as he and Kelly got off their bicycles.

"Something that will benefit Belvista. I'm talking about economic progress, Detective Campbell. I saw you coming this way and decided it's time for us to have a little chat."

"About what?" Luke asked grudgingly.

"To encourage you to change your old-fashioned thinking and lend your support to the Belvista of tomorrow." Hal Dunbar spread out his arms as if to embrace the marshes. "I'm talking about a maxi-mall beyond your wildest dreams—major department stores and an entertainment mega-complex that will draw top-name entertainers and sports teams!"

"Apparently you haven't been listening to the town council," Luke said frostily. "A mall like that isn't feasible here. The road can barely handle local traffic."

"Detective Campbell, close your eyes, and imagine wide, paved roads. A superhighway. It's time for a change. For years tourists have been coming to Belvista for the seashore and Victorian ambience. Let's give them something more. They want to shop, to spend, to put money into our pockets. Let's help them."

"I've heard everything you've said dozens of times, but—"

"Haven't you heard, Detective Campbell?" Hal Dunbar batted a cattail stalk with his riding crop. "The council is finally considering our proposal to drain and fill the marsh. It's about time. They've been listening to my pleas for a mall for more than a year. My advice, Detective Campbell? Get on the bandwagon if you plan to stay on in Belvista."

Hal Dunbar's horse whinnied, distracting him. "Be right back," he said. "Silver needs me."

Luke leaned close to Kelly. "This marshland issue is something I care about. Cut me some slack with our time. I promise we'll come back if we run out of time today."

"It's only fair," Kelly said, glancing down the path at Dunbar, who was petting his horse. "You worked hard for me this morning."

"It wasn't all work," Luke said, gazing into her eyes.

"Knock Hal Dunbar off his stirrup before he even gets up on his high horse," Kelly said.

"You really do have a vicious streak," Luke said. He looked up as Dunbar returned.

"So, Mr. Dunbar," Luke said, "let me make it clear. I'm not opposed to malls, but Belvista has more suitable locations." He pointed a finger at Dunbar. "Of course, they aren't surrounded by land you own."

Dunbar waved away Luke's criticism with a flick of his riding crop. "I can see the twenty-one cineplex over there, the sports arena, the—"

"Many of us like things the way they are," Luke said.

"This?" Hal Dunbar scoffed. "All you have here are a few walking trails and a picnic spot." He pointed toward the high, grassy area dotted with maple trees that backed onto the marsh. "Picnickers eat grilled hot dogs on a stick and call them cattails. That's their idea of fun! There's so much more we can do for them."

Shielding her eyes, Kelly saw picnic tables and benches housed in a dozen wooden shelters with gingerbread-trimmed roofs. They looked inviting, a perfect spot to relax. Maybe someday.

"The Business Club, under my leadership—" Hal Dunbar sniffed "—will rid Belvista of this swamp. When it rains, the cattails look like slimy cigars. When the cattails burst, they look like wads of filthy cotton. In winter this place is a frozen mass of rotting vegetation. Bring on a beautiful mall, and get rid of this ugly marsh."

"Save your speech-making for the town council." Luke turned to Kelly. "There's an ongoing dispute in this town between—"

"Between progressives and bird-watchers," Hal Dunbar interrupted.

"We prefer the word *nature-lovers.*" Luke turned back to Kelly. "In my few weeks here, I've learned something important. Besides bird watchers, Belvista has many garden club members, photographers, and your average Joes, like me, who enjoy a quiet place. We want this area preserved. There's history here, and it should be respected."

"Please, Detective Campbell. Don't bore us with your tales of the Indians who wove reeds into floor coverings for their wigwams. Or how they taught the early settlers to grind cattail roots into meal. Next you'll be reminding me of the schoolchildren's pageant, with those outlandish costumes, to celebrate the blossoming of the cattails."

Luke chuckled. "Haven't you forgotten the frog-jumping contests?"

"Be prepared for big changes, Detective Campbell. We've suggested to the council that when they improve Hospital Road, they also tackle this drainage project. There's room for condos here. Belvista's real-estate boom could spill over to this area."

Kelly was struck by an odd coincidence. Hal Dunbar and the Povloskis shared an interest in real estate, and the Povloskis were staying at Pruitt's Inn, where Meg had disappeared from. Could there be any connection? Maybe she was grasping at straws. She would mention it to Luke and ask him do a background check on the Povloski brothers.

Dunbar was still ranting about a possible drainage project. "Some people will be unhappy," he said, "but they'll get over it. That artist, Michael Duprey, for instance." He waved his riding crop toward the cattails. "He's over there somewhere, painting away, oblivious to the muck that's creeping over his boots."

Luke snickered. "We'll warn him of the danger."

Kelly was delighted. Michael might remember something

Meg had said about the marshes, like maybe returning to see some particular area. But a nervous feeling nagged at Kelly. Would Michael Duprey mention that she had shared a drink with him? Danced with him? Kissed? She hoped he would keep all that to himself.

TWENTY

Confession

LUKE AND KELLY GOT BACK onto their bikes and pedaled away from Hal Dunbar. Rounding a bend in the road, Kelly jammed on her brakes. "Luke, please stop!" she called ahead. "There's something I have to tell you."

Luke squealed to a halt. He hopped off his bike, dropped the kickstand, and hurried toward her. "You sound upset. What's the matter?"

"It's about Meg," Kelly said, resting her bicycle against her hip. "I've kept some things from you."

"Tell me now." His voice was sharp.

"I promised Sam I wouldn't tell you."

"Forget Sam." Luke's eyes bored through her.

Kelly took a deep breath. She told Luke everything she knew about Olivia and Hazie Moon. She included the incident at Beach Park, where two men knocked Sam and her down shortly before the attack on Olivia. Kelly finished by saying that Olivia and Hazie distrusted the police and the Business Club and relied on their neighbors, Bill and Bob, who owned a gym, for protection.

Luke didn't say a word the entire time Kelly talked. He gripped the handlebars of her bicycle so hard that Kelly thought they would snap in two.

"You're angry, aren't you?" she said.

"You bet I am!" Luke exclaimed. "First, Duprey holds back about Tim Ramsey. Then Sam holds back about the email and the attacks. And now you admit to being a part of a cover-up because of a promise to Sam. You are the three people in Belvista who claim to be most interested in finding Meg. What were the three of you thinking?" He slammed his fists onto the handlebars. Kelly jumped back. The bike fell to the ground, and the bottles of water rolled onto the road.

"I'm sorry," Kelly said, fighting the lump in her throat. She reached down for her bicycle at the very same moment Luke did. Their hands touched. Together they pulled up the bicycle.

"Teamwork," Luke said gently. "See how it gets things done?"

"Yes," Kelly said, ashamed of herself for not trusting him.

"I'm always surprised by what family members and witnesses reveal and what they hide," Luke said. He retrieved the bottles of water and set them in her bike basket. "That's why we question them more than once. People are like onions... layers have to be peeled away to get to the heart of the matter. If only they would tell us everything the first time around."

"Sam doesn't want Olivia and Hazie to get hurt," Kelly said defensively, and she straddled her bicycle. "Olivia is afraid that Jeff Traskell or Jeff's father will come after Hazie. And she believes that Mr. Traskell and his friends in the Business Club will find bogus zoning rules to shut down her café. I think she has reason to be concerned. And I'm afraid I might be endangering her and Hazie by telling you all this behind their backs."

"Give Belvista's finest some credit for knowing how to be discreet." Luke pulled out his cell phone. "I'm going to call Andy Quinn, the detective I was telling you about who questioned Duprey. I'll have him look into everything you've told me—without tipping anyone off. That will slow him down a bit, but he'll get the job done."

A sense of purposefulness shone in Luke's eyes as he punched in numbers in his cell phone. He stopped and glanced at Kelly. "Are you holding anything else back?"

"There is one other thing," she said, and she saw the muscles in Luke's jaw twitch.

"Let's hear it." He snapped shut his cell phone.

"This is just a hunch," Kelly said. "The type of thing you notice. A coincidence. A suspicious coincidence."

Luke raised an eyebrow.

Kelly explained that the Povloskis had an interest in Belvista real estate, as did Hal Dunbar. That the Povloskis, who lived in New York City, as she and Meg did, were now staying at Pruitt's, the very inn that Meg had disappeared from. And that Hal Dunbar mentioned that he had spoken to Meg in his store about a box of chalk.

Kelly realized that her words had come out as random thoughts, like some crazy conspiracy theory. She wished she had presented her information more clearly.

Luke pressed the heels of his hands into his eyes as if he were too tired to speak or needed time to think things through. "I'll have Detective Quinn work that angle too," Luke finally said. "He can get the Povloski addresses from Justine Pruitt's files—discreetly, of course—and take it from there."

Luke made his call to Detective Quinn and ran everything by him. Kelly felt a burden lifted from her shoulders and knew she had done the right thing.

Luke cracked a smile. "I hesitate to ask, Sherlock, but is there anything else you noticed that escaped my eyes?"

"Elementary, my dear Watson," Kelly said, tapping her wristwatch. "Time is passing, and we need to start pedaling."

TWENTY-ONE

The Boat

MICHAEL DUPREY GLANCED UP when Kelly and Luke hopped off their bicycles. Then he continued blending blues and yellows on his palette. Kelly understood all too well Meg's attraction to Michael. He was tall and handsome. His broad shoulders, expressive hands, and sensual mouth reminded her of the heroes on romance-novel covers. His hair, which hung below his collar, glistened in the sunlight.

Kelly studied his canvas. She could almost feel the gentle pull of the rowboat in the ruffled water. Michael's broad brushstrokes had partially concealed the boat within the swaying cattails caught in a gusting wind.

"That's a powerful image, Michael," Kelly said, surveying the peaceful surroundings. There was no boat anywhere. "Do you see the rowboat that way in your mind's eye?"

"I see the rowboat with Meg sitting in it. She's my muse. She'll bring the work to life." He swished his brush in turpentine and pulled it through a paint-stained cloth.

Luke peered at the painting. "Tell me about the rowboat."

Michael added olive flecks to the water. "It intrigued me— the powdery gray where the wood is dry, the translucent greens below the waterline."

"Never mind the dry rot and slime," Luke said. "Where did the boat come from?"

"It was here one morning several months ago when I arrived." Michael chose a palette knife from his supply box.

"Very early, about five. I thought a bird-watcher wanted a close-up look at something."

"Did you see the owner?"

"No. I made some quick sketches, in case he showed up to cart the boat away. It was July. No, June. I remember the pale light of a June sunrise cutting through the mists. The cattails' slender stalks appeared almost fragile. It was mystical, almost—"

"In a word or two, where are the sketches?"

"In Greg Saunders' studio."

"I'll need to see them." Luke looked from the painting to the cattails. "From your squiggles, I'd say the boat was over there." He pointed toward a nearby thicket of cattails.

"My paintings are not bound by truth and reality," Michael said. "First of all, it isn't a rowboat. It's a clammer's dory. A boat with pointed—"

"I know what a clammer's dory is," Luke snapped.

"But I don't," Kelly said. "Go ahead, Michael. Finish what you were saying."

"Both its bow and stern are pointed," Michael said. "It can be rowed forward and backward with equal ease."

"Why don't you just paint what you see?" Luke asked, his voice edged with irritation.

Michael's eyes flashed. "I don't want the sharpness of the boat to detract from Meg's serene expression." Michael stroked the palette knife across his shirtsleeve. "You and I are different, Detective Campbell. I pick and choose, taking exactly what I want from life. I alter things to suit my tastes."

Luke's mouth contorted. "You were about to tell me the location of the boat."

Michael jabbed his palette knife toward the picnic area. "Over there. In front of the picnic tables."

"I assume it's still there?"

"I don't know. As I explained to Kelly, I've been caught up with my painting."

Kelly frowned. "Luke, why are you so curious about the dory?"

"It's one of those out-of-place details. They're like coincidences. They make me curious."

"Come by this evening," Michael said. "I'll be glad to show you the sketches. As Kelly can tell you, I'm quite hospitable." He smiled. "My guests are always welcome to share a bottle of wine…or scotch."

"I'll be there," Luke said, and he turned his bike around. "I always make time for my primary suspects."

Kelly hopped onto her bicycle and followed Luke toward the picnic tables. She didn't know which angered her more, Michael's insinuations or Luke's brusqueness.

"You didn't have to be so rough with Michael," Kelly said.

"I'm trying to solve a case, not win friends." He pedaled ahead of her in silence.

"Cut Michael some slack," she called to him. "He misses Meg."

Luke slammed on his brakes, skidding to a stop. "He entertains you, drinks with you. That's how he eases his loneliness?"

"Try to understand." Kelly stopped next to Luke. "Loneliness is very powerful." She thrust her bicycle against an embankment. "Believe me, loneliness makes you behave in unexpected ways. You say things you never would under normal circumstances."

Kelly remembered Michael's warm, hard body and felt ashamed for encouraging him and betraying Meg. Now she felt foolish lecturing Luke. He was trying to help her. She got back onto her bicycle. "We'll talk about this later," she said, and she pedaled away.

LUKE AND KELLY PARKED their bicycles near the picnic tables and walked along the edge of the marsh. "This is hopeless," Kelly said after poking through cattail stalks and sinking into the mud. "Why didn't you ask Michael to come with us and show us where he saw the boat?"

"I don't want him to know any more than necessary." Luke tramped over reeds and leaves. "We'll give it ten more minutes. Then we'd better head over to the hospital."

They walked the width of the picnic area, checking everywhere. They started to circle back. "I found it!" Luke exclaimed.

"Where?" Kelly rushed to his side.

"Right there. Dead center in front of the middle picnic shelter."

Kelly didn't see the boat at first and almost stepped on the oars. "It's a clammer's boat," she said, noticing the peeling paint and pointed bow and stern.

"The owner's clever," Luke said. "He's camouflaged the boat. Look at this blanket of reeds woven through chicken wire."

Kelly poked at the sturdy rope tied to a ring at one end of the boat.

"Don't disturb anything," Luke warned. "We didn't find exactly what we came for, but I think we're on the right track. We may have something important here." He turned to Kelly. "I'm going to call Duprey and cancel going to his place this evening. I've seen the boat. I don't need to see his sketches of it."

"He's a real stone in your shoe, isn't he?" Kelly said.

"You got that right." Luke scowled. As he backed away, the mud swallowed his footprints.

TWENTY-TWO

A Ghastly Surprise

LUKE FLASHED HIS ID at Belvista Hospital's security officer. He and Kelly went immediately to the records office.

"I have your information," Chuck Lazenby said. He shook hands with Luke and Kelly. "I know you want facts, so here goes. Six young women died here during the past year." He withdrew computer printouts from the folder on his desk.

Luke perused the highlighted information. "It seems that Sam's theory—that for every woman who dies at the hospital, a woman is kidnapped—is wrong." He spread the printouts on the desk. Next to them, he placed a list of the names of the missing women and the dates they disappeared. "We have four matchups," he said. "Stacy Deems disappeared three days after Lisa McFarland died. Kim Eberly disappeared four days after Sarah Lane died. Mary Waverly, three days after Anna Morales."

Kelly trailed her fingertips across Julia Newcomb's name. Her breath caught in her throat. She, Kelly Madison, was Julia's counterpart, living on borrowed time. "My sister, Meg, vanished four days after Elizabeth Brown died," she said.

"That leaves one name," Luke said. "Rose D'Amici. No young woman disappeared during the week immediately following her death."

"None that you know of," Kelly said. She peered over Luke's shoulder. "Rose D'Amici died February fifth. A visitor could have come to town at that time. It's possible no one noticed her arrive or leave."

"Belvista doesn't attract many winter visitors looking for work," Luke said. "She would have stood out."

There was a gentle rap at the door.

"Come in," Lazenby said.

A freckle-faced nurse with pale blue eyes and blond, sun-streaked hair opened the door. She was holding a large manila envelope sealed with black tape.

Kelly noticed the name tag on the pocket of her floral smock: Jeannie Wilkins.

"We found this at the nurses' station," Jeannie said. "It's addressed to you, Luke." She tapped a finger on the label and read it aloud. "To Detective Luke Campbell, in care of Mr. Lazenby."

"Thanks," Luke said. A dazzling smile followed.

"See you…soon?" Jeannie said, and she breezed out the door.

Luke set the envelope on the desk. "I have a feeling it's our anonymous admirer."

"What could it be this time?" Kelly wondered.

Luke whipped out his penknife and sliced through the tape. "A note and an envelope," he said, shaking the contents onto the desk. Block letters cut from newspaper headlines spelled out a message. "Kelly," he said, "please wait in the hallway."

"It's from the kidnapper, isn't it?" Kelly's voice trembled. "Is it about Meg?" She reached for the note.

"All right. You can stay. But I want you to sit down," Luke said. He nodded to Lazenby, who settled Kelly into a chair. "Mr. Lazenby, I'll need latex gloves and plastic bags."

Lazenby made a call, and the gloves and bags arrived in a flash.

Luke put the spare bags and gloves into his pocket. He pulled on the gloves, picked up the note, and read aloud, "Greetings from Stacy, Kim, Mary, and Meg." He reached into the envelope and removed several photographs. "My God!" he exclaimed. His hand jerked back as if it had touched a burning coal. "Kelly, you don't need to see this." He turned abruptly to Lazenby. "Call security. Don't let anyone leave the hospital or grounds." He whipped out his cell phone and punched in numbers.

"Get me Chief Clemmens," Luke said. "It's an emergency." He stepped outside the room.

Kelly gripped the sides of the chair, plunging her nails into the upholstery.

Luke spoke quickly, but Kelly caught key phrases: "re-open the case"…"taking over the investigation"…"no leaks to the press"…"request Officers Jones and Simpson"…"call Atlantic City"…"get forensics and officers here now."

Luke came back into the room and removed the rest of the photographs. He scrutinized them front and back. "Kelly, please, please wait in the hallway. This is too ghastly for you. Or anyone else."

"I need to know, Luke." Her voice shook. "Let me see the photos."

"We're dealing with a deranged individual."

Lazenby peered over Luke's shoulder. He recoiled. "A real whacko," he said.

Kelly rose slowly and stood next to Luke.

"Let me warn you, Kelly," Luke said. "These are photos of women's dead bodies."

Taking a deep breath, Kelly looked down. She sobbed, "Oh, my God. Meg?"

"No, Meg's not one of them. There are only three women."

"Thank God," Kelly said. Waves of nausea gripped her. "Those poor women," she sobbed.

Luke took Lazenby aside. "The women are all posed the same way," he whispered, studying the photos. "Each is lying on her back on a table, her hands folded in prayer."

Lazenby whispered back, "I'd say the table is a hospital gurney."

Kelly caught the gist of their conversation, but their words were muffled as if coming from far away. Her knees buckled.

Luke caught Kelly as she swayed back. "Easy does it," he

said, taking her in his arms. He held her tightly, until her crying subsided. "Meg's alive. I'm sure of it," he said finally.

Kelly blinked away her tears and looked into his eyes. "Please don't lie to me."

"Meg's alive, but I'm afraid she's a prisoner of a killer."

"Are you sure?" Kelly asked.

"Meg's hair is auburn, like yours. Am I right?"

"Yes." Kelly sniffled. "But what does—"

"A lock of hair is taped to the back of each photo. The lock of hair taped to the first photo is blond. The second photo, light brown hair. The third, dark brown. The fourth 'photo'— a blank—has auburn hair taped to the back."

Kelly looked intently at the hair. "It could be Meg's," she said, biting back her tears.

"The psycho is letting us know he's in charge." Luke hugged Kelly. "I'm sorry I didn't believe you. I needed proof, but I wasn't expecting anything like this." His voice caught in his throat. "I hope my doubts about a possible kidnapper didn't slow the case."

"Excuse me, Detective Campbell," Lazenby said. "About the hospital gurney. The killer could work here at Belvista Hospital."

The door flew open.

"Kelly, this is Officer Jones," Luke said, pointing to the jut-jawed taller man walking into the room. "And this," he said, patting the ruddy-faced, gray-haired man on the back, "is Officer Simpson. Two of Belvista's finest."

"The rest of the 'finest' are here with Chief Clemmens and hospital security," Officer Jones said. "The chief is counting on you to work with the forensic team when they've processed the evidence."

"Thanks for getting here so fast," Luke said. He tapped the envelope. "Some sick murderer has invaded this town."

Luke pulled off his gloves and tossed them into the wastebasket. "Simpson, Jones, let me fill you in before the forensic team arrives. I've asked Chief Clemmens to call my boss in Atlantic City. He's requesting that four detectives come to Belvista."

Luke held up a hand as if to discourage the men from speaking. "That's customary in crimes of this magnitude. It has nothing to do with your ability. I'm counting on your help, your personal knowledge of local matters, and your expertise. Do I have it?"

"You do," Officer Jones said.

"Absolutely," Officer Simpson said.

"Good," Luke said. "If we overplay our hand, the serial killer might skip town. He'll leave behind a victim stashed somewhere without food or water. You get the picture?"

"I do."

"Absolutely."

"For starters, check out Belvista Flowers," Luke said. "See who recently ordered white chrysanthemums with yellow centers. Samuel Chambers' aunt is a silent partner in that establishment. Make your questions seem routine, but keep your eyes open for a possible hidden room, a photograph of Kelly Madison and her sister, Meg, envelopes that size—" he pointed toward the desk "—anything that might be remotely connected to this case."

"You got it," Officer Jones said, scribbling furiously in his notepad.

"When you finish," Luke said, "come back to the hospital, and go through employee files." Luke looked at Lazenby, who nodded his permission. "Draw up a list of everyone who took a vacation the first week in February. Add the names of the people who missed work anytime from August eleventh to August fifteenth—that's when Kelly's sister, Meg, was in Belvista—and from this past Saturday until today—that's when Kelly's been here. Got all that?"

"Yep." *Scribble. Scribble.*

"Absolutely." *Scribble. Scribble.*

"I'll expect a full report on my desk asap. Mr. Lazenby will keep all this secret, and I know I can count on you to do the same. Get going!"

Kelly could see that Luke had developed camaraderie with these men. What a predicament he was in. As an outsider, a detective, his attempts to build new skills and inspire confidence in the Belvista police force without hurting the pride of the local officers required timing and tact.

Luke pulled out his cell phone. "Kelly, once I talk to the forensic team, I'll have an officer take us back to my car. I want to look into other aspects of this case. Mr. Lazenby, I'll have our bikes picked up later."

LUKE AND KELLY SETTLED into the backseat of a squad car. Officer Patty Esposito drove, belting out country songs, pretending not to overhear their conversation.

"The information Jones and Simpson dig up could help," Luke said. "It will keep them busy and out of danger. They're good men, but they're inexperienced. They could get killed if they try to confront this maniac. The Atlantic City detectives and I will investigate Michael Duprey and his friends, especially Greg Saunders. That's a good place to start."

"Michael Duprey isn't the killer," Kelly blurted out.

"Oh, and do you have proof?"

"Michael wouldn't send flowers in a rusty can."

"Perhaps it was an artistic message, meaning something like beauty surrounded by corruption." Luke spoke through thinned lips. "That would be Duprey's style."

"You are impossible," Kelly snapped, and the car took a sharp turn.

"Thorough, you mean." Luke flipped through his notepad, ticking off names. "Father Shaunassey's a long shot, but he may know something. I'll review the file on the Bradford family drownings. But I plan to hone in on the funeral homes, the morgue, and the cemeteries, including the potter's field. Have I missed anything?"

Kelly regretted her little spat with Luke. He was so helpful, but any mention of Michael Duprey set him off. She vowed to mention his name only when necessary and not to flatter him in any way. "I have a theory," she said, tightening her seat belt.

"I'm listening."

Kelly sensed that Luke's heated anger was cooling. "I think that possibly the morticians in Belvista are killing poor girls without families and collecting exorbitant fees from the town for their services." As the words flowed from Kelly's mouth, she knew they sounded crazy, but Luke didn't laugh.

"Anything else?" he asked matter-of-factly.

"I don't trust Hal Dunbar," Kelly said, confident that Luke would hear her out. "He gave me a scare the day I went to the Mariners' Museum. He came out of nowhere and admitted having talked to Meg in his store. Then he passed a note to the guard, a Mr. James Ritter, at the museum. I saw only the word *trouble*, but shortly after that, the suspended boat I told you about started to fall, and I tried to get out of the way and ended up with a wound to my head. I wonder if that boat's falling near me was an accident or if it was intentional. Maybe Hal Dunbar told James Ritter something like 'Keep an eye on her. She's trouble.'"

"I trust your woman's intuition. I'll add Dunbar and Ritter to the list." Luke closed his notepad and dropped it into his pocket. "I'm not letting you out of my sight. There's plenty of investigative stuff I need to do, and you can come along. Who knows? You may see something I miss."

"What's first on your agenda?" Kelly asked, happy to be doing something that might help Meg.

"Here's the plan. A quick lunch at my house. Then I'll question Bill Kalinsky at his funeral home." He glanced at his watch. "We'll arrive in time for Julia Newcomb's wake. Then, on to Preston's Funeral Home. I wanted to meet Greg Saunders at his studio, but that will have to wait. He agreed to return to Belvista tomorrow."

Luke looked directly at Kelly. "We'll try to get through all this. I'll work at not losing my temper."

"And I won't mention you-know-who unless it's an absolute necessity," Kelly said. She caught a hint of satisfaction on Luke's face. "Do you mind passing by Pruitt's Inn first? I need to change into something more appropriate for the wake."

"Okay," Luke said. "And while you're there, pack a few things. You'll be staying with me until the killer is behind bars."

TWENTY-THREE

The Service Stop

OFFICER ESPOSITO LOOKED quickly over her shoulder at Luke and Kelly. "Stay out of trouble," she said as she approached the Cattail Marshes Service Stop.

"You, too," Luke said. "I need good officers like you. I heard about your commendations for working with neighborhood kids."

She shrugged off his compliment. "Just doing my job."

"Hey, stop right here," Luke said near the entrance. "There's Detective Quinn, leaning against his car. Looks like he's waiting for me."

Kelly hopped out.

"You must be Kelly Madison," the detective said with a lopsided smile. His red hair and freckled face added to his youthful appearance.

"And you're Andy Quinn. Thanks for helping with Meg's case."

"This must be important, since you came in person," Luke said.

"You need to see this." Quinn handed Luke a folded sheet of paper. "That guy Lazenby you talked to at the hospital was the main speaker at last month's Business Club luncheon. Take a look at his speech." Quinn lowered his sunglasses. "It's called 'Building a Better Community.'"

Luke unfolded the paper and studied the words.

"Looks like Lazenby's on their side," Quinn said.

"You mean, *Build! Build! Build! And destroy the marsh-*

lands! Thanks, Andy. It's safe to say we won't trust Lazenby. Anything else?"

"I've been on the email trail about the Cinderellas," Quinn said, and Kelly held her breath. "Seems the Business Club is concerned about Belvista's reputation as a peaceful resort. I didn't pick up any murderous intent, but I'm still looking. There's plenty about graft and bribes, but I'll can that until Meg is found."

"Keep up the good work," Luke said as Quinn got into his beat-up Chevy.

"I see why you like Detective Quinn," Kelly said. "I feel he's going to be a big help in finding Meg."

LUKE WAVED TO WILLY, who was working the entrance gate, and walked by Kelly's side toward his Honda Accord. "What happened here?" he said.

Kelly saw that the rear window on the driver's side was smashed. Glass crunched beneath their sneakers as they neared the car. Luke peered into the backseat. "Somebody messed with my folders. That one wasn't on top."

Kelly went around to the passenger side. "The killer must have followed us here. Before or after he delivered those gruesome photos to the hospital, he must have broken into your car. Are the files about Meg's case?"

"No, just administrative stuff. But I'll bet the creep was trying to find out how much the police know." He raked his fingers through his hair. "He's everywhere, and he's really starting to annoy me." He opened his door. "I'll check with Willy on the way out, but I doubt he saw anything. If he had, he'd have told me."

Luke's eyes scanned the line of trees. "Come on. We'd better go to Pruitt's and get your clothes. The sooner the better."

Before getting into the car, Kelly looked around. She didn't see anything suspicious. But there was an eerie calm, like in a horror movie just before someone screams.

TWENTY-FOUR

Benny Pruitt

KELLY STARTED UP THE STAIRS of Pruitt's Inn while Luke waited at the reception desk. At the landing, Kelly gasped. Benny was lying in the corridor near her room. He was moaning.

"Luke! Hurry!" Kelly cried. "Benny's hurt!"

Luke raced up the stairs. "I'll take it from here," he said to Kelly, who was kneeling beside Benny. He quickly checked Benny for cuts or broken bones. "He's hurt on the back of the head. What happened, Benny?"

Benny pointed to Kelly's room.

"Does it hurt much?" Kelly asked tenderly.

"Kiss it and make it better," Benny pleaded, and Kelly kissed his head.

Luke's face was etched with concern. He helped Benny sit up. "Benny, can you tell us what happened?"

"I moved the flowers and pink thing to Kelly's room." He held up a key and grinned. "I wanted Kelly to be surprised by the gifts."

"I think the kidnapper was here," Kelly said, startled.

Luke drew his gun. "Stay against that wall," he warned, and he entered Kelly's room. "No one's here," he said, and Kelly rushed in.

"Look! That's Meg's pink shawl on my bed. The one Rita Duprey gave her."

"Slow down," Luke said. "What's this about a shawl?"

"Rita gave it to Meg so Meg could pose for Michael's paintings. His work shows a passion for pink."

"Duprey again. Pink shawls. Jeeze, what next?" Luke muttered.

"White chrysanthemums with yellow centers," Kelly said, nudging the can by the doorway.

Luke returned to the hallway. "Benny, tell me about the flowers and shawl."

"I moved the flowers away from the door so Kelly wouldn't trip," Benny said. "The shawl was hanging on the doorknob. I touched it and closed my eyes, thinking about Meg. She was so pretty, so nice to me. Then *ba-ba-bam!* My head hurt, and I fell down." He rubbed the back of his head. "Somebody hit me hard."

"Did you get a look at him?" Luke asked.

"No. He's a very sneaky man."

"Benny almost caught the kidnapper in the act," Kelly said, stroking Benny's hair. "He must have heard Benny coming and ducked into one of these rooms. That's how he sneaked up on Benny."

"Don't touch anything. I'll have forensics check this out." Luke made a quick call to the lab, then turned to Kelly. "The kidnapper must have a master key."

"Justine is free with that key," Kelly whispered. "Apparently Benny has a key too."

Luke scooped up the shawl.

"Wait," Kelly said. "There's a note pinned to the fringe." She reached out to unfasten it, but Luke stepped into her way. "There might be prints," he said. He put on latex gloves left over from the hospital, then unfastened the paper and slipped it into one of the plastic bags.

"It's a poem," Kelly said. She began to read aloud:

I've trapped only four.
I still need more.

Luke read the remainder:

Number five had best beware.
She's one-half of a pretty pair.

"Miss Pruitt!" Luke bellowed over the banister. "Come up here! Benny's been hurt!" He turned to Kelly. "Pack everything. I need to speak with Benny and his aunt."

"About the master key?" Kelly asked.

Luke nodded. "And about people roaming around as they please. We've missed the obvious. The kidnapper could have come in, kidnapped Meg, and carried her out the front door, and nobody, not even Justine Pruitt, would have noticed." He gritted his teeth. "Stay put, Benny, and ask Aunt Justine for a glass of water. You've had quite a scare."

When they heard Justine approaching, Luke followed Kelly into her room. "Start packing," he said. "Then we'll go to my house."

"Do you suppose that Benny...?"

"Benny had no part in this, other than being in the wrong place at the wrong time. He'll need to be fingerprinted, but that's about it."

"They won't suspect Benny, will they?"

"No," Luke said. "When Benny helped me clean up my yard, I left him written instructions. I quickly found out he had never learned to read or write. We've learned this much: our guy takes chances. Our guy's daring. He likes danger. He's calculating. He has a thing for poetry. My men will agree that that's not Benny."

A startled look crossed Kelly's face.

"What's the matter?" Luke asked.

"You've just described yourself."

"I'm not a murderer," Luke said, backing away. "How could you even think such a thing?"

"I demand an explanation." Justine Pruitt stood in the doorway, fists on hips. "Why is my nephew cowering like a frightened puppy? He's practically begging for water!"

"Someone attacked him in the hallway."

Justine rushed to Benny. "Are you hurt? What happened?"

"I got beaned," Benny said.

Justine turned on Luke, finger wagging. "Police brutality?" she asked, her beady eyes flinty.

"No, ma'am," Luke said. "Someone sneaked in here and did this. But Benny seems okay except for a bump on his head."

Justine poked her fingers through Benny's hair. "Not too bad," she said. "Benny, you gave me a scare."

"Forensics people will be here to dust for prints. Benny touched the plant and shawl, so they'll want his fingerprints for comparison purposes. From now on, an officer will assist you 24/7, watching who comes and goes." He brushed past Justine into the hallway. "Kelly is moving out. Don't rent the room. Don't touch anything in it. Understand?"

"Why are you picking on me and my Benny?" Justine glowered at Luke, then followed him.

Kelly left her door ajar while she packed so she could hear their conversation.

"We're good people," Justine said. "It's our guests who bring trouble to our door." She gave Luke a worried look. "They won't be questioning my Benny about Meg again, will they?" Her voice trembled.

"If you know anything about Meg's disappearance, tell me now."

"The bicycle," Benny whimpered.

"Don't say another word!" Justine cried.

Kelly rushed from her room. "What about the bicycle?"

Benny hung his head. "I was supposed to return her bicycle."

"I didn't want trouble," Justine said. "Meg told me she planned to go for a ride that Sunday morning, but she didn't say where. That bicycle sat by the shed all day. On Monday, before I called the police, I told Benny to take the bicycle to Michael Duprey's studio and leave it there. That's where it belonged. Michael and Meg were sneaking around here, thinking I didn't see anything. The police came back, after talking to Michael, asking over and over again about that bicycle."

"Benny," Luke said, "did you return the bicycle?"

"No. I hid it in our cellar."

Kelly's anger exploded. "You interfered with the investigation, Benny! Didn't you realize—?"

Luke tugged at Kelly's sleeve. "Calm down," he whispered. "Benny will clam up if you holler at him."

"I kept the bicycle." Benny squeezed his thumbs and index fingers together. "I like to ring the bell. It's real pretty, like Meg."

"He meant no harm," Justine said. "I'll show you where he keeps the bicycle."

Luke glared at Justine. "You knew about this and didn't tell us." His eyes flashed with anger. "I'll want to search the entire cellar."

"I'll go with you," Kelly said.

At the top of the cellar stairs, Kelly stopped short. "Justine, did you see Meg leave here that Saturday night?"

Justine hesitated, biting her lip. "No. I don't know. I fell asleep at the front desk. I'm only human."

"Stay right here by the stairs," Luke warned Justine. "And stay awake. If anyone comes, call down to me. Do I make myself clear?"

"Benny will help me," Justine said, her voice more timid than Kelly would have expected. "This will help," Justine said, taking a flashlight from a shelf at the top of the stairs and handing it to Luke. She flipped the switch on the wall. "The light down there is dim."

Luke and Kelly made their way down the rickety steps from the kitchen to the cellar. It was much like the attic. Same musty smell. Junk everywhere.

"Over there," Luke said, directing the flashlight beam.

The bicycle was barely hidden beneath a tarp. Kelly ran her fingertips along the handlebars where Meg's fingers had once rested. She remembered Meg, so young and beautiful, riding along in the sunshine in Central Park, enjoying life. And then she'd come to Belvista and disappeared. Gone. "Luke," she said, "I'm sorry to be a wimp, but I feel faint."

"Sit right here," he said, leading her to the bottom step. "Take a few deep breaths." He sat next to her and put an arm across her shoulders. "We'll find Meg," he said reassuringly.

"I'm all right. I don't want to slow down the progress we're making."

"I'll search the cellar," Luke said. "It's small. If Meg's here, we'll find her."

Kelly knew they wouldn't find Meg. Luke was right. Benny didn't kidnap her. Someone much more clever than Benny was responsible.

A thorough search revealed no signs of Meg.

Luke moved the bicycle toward the stairs. "I'll see if forensics turns up anything."

Kelly knew he was trying to keep up her spirits about finding Meg alive. "Thank you," she said, her voice filled with gratitude.

"We're coming down," Justine called from the top of the stairs. She came first, Benny in tow. "Benny has something else to say."

"Tell me," Luke said gently. "Don't be afraid."

"Behind the paint," Benny said, pointing at the ledge of the low cement wall that separated the root cellar from the main room.

"Show me," Luke said.

As Luke held his flashlight high, Benny stood on tiptoe and lifted two cans of paint. He set them by his feet, reached up again, and pulled out an old shoebox.

"Thanks, Benny," Luke said as Benny returned the paint cans to the ledge. Luke opened the box carefully. Kelly peered over his shoulder. She saw rings, bracelets, a silver belt, and a pair of pink panties.

Luke moved the panties aside, and Kelly gasped. "Meg's scarf!" The silky gray and yellow scarf slithered through Luke's fingers, and Kelly grabbed it. "Meg was here?" Tears streamed down her face. "Here in this awful place?"

"It's not what you think," Justine insisted. "It's a box of

keepsakes. Benny just admitted to me that he'd collected them from women guests who've stayed at the inn over the years. I swear, he never hurt any of those women."

Benny whimpered. "The scarf was pretty, like Meg."

"I believe you, Benny," Luke said, and he slid the scarf into a plastic bag.

"But, Luke, think of the coincidence," Kelly said. "Sam Chambers claims that serial killers keep mementos of their victims."

"This is different, Kelly," Luke said sharply. "I'll explain later. Benny, tell me where you found Meg's scarf."

"In the yard by the back porch. I put it in my box of pretties."

"Did you see Meg drop it in the yard?" Luke asked.

"No. But it was her secret place."

"Tell me what you mean," Luke said encouragingly.

"Every night, past my bedtime, Meg went out the back door and stood in the dark."

"Why did she do that, Benny?"

"To smoke a cigarette." He leaned close to Luke, and Kelly strained to hear. "Aunt Justine doesn't let people smoke in our inn. Or on the porch."

"Did you ever go out there and talk to Meg?"

"No." Benny's eyes grew big. "It was dark and scary. Every night the back door creaked open. I looked out my bedroom window and watched. Meg, so pretty. She walked away from the porch into the dark, but I could see her."

"How, Benny?"

"The end of her cigarette glowed like a firefly. It moved this way and that."

"Then what?"

"The little red light on her cigarette went out. Then I'd hear the back door shut. She'd go up to her room. *Squeak! Squeak!* The stairs squeaked." He grinned.

Luke pressed on. "Did anyone ever meet Meg in her secret place?"

"No."

"Are you sure?"

Benny blinked fast. "I squished my face against the window, but I couldn't see everything. Shrubs and trees got in the way."

"Think, Benny. Did you hear the door shut on that Saturday night, Meg's last night here? Did you hear the stairs squeak?"

"No."

"Did you worry about Meg, that something might have happened?"

"No. I fell asleep." He rubbed his eyes. "I was tired."

"Did you ever tell Aunt Justine?"

"Just did tell her now."

"Why did you wait so long?"

Benny hunched his shoulders. "Aunt Justine doesn't like smokers. I like Meg. I wanted her to stay a long time."

Kelly exhaled. She hadn't dared breathe, let alone speak, for fear of breaking the rapport between Luke and Benny.

"Let's get out of this cellar," Luke said, batting a cobweb from his neck.

As they climbed the stairs, Luke and Kelly put the scene together. The kidnapper must have stalked Meg and thus had known her nightly routine. That Saturday night, he parked in the alley, hid in the shrubbery, and waited until she came outside for her nightly cigarette. Under cover of darkness, he captured her and carried her to his car. Possibly Michael Duprey, who had stood in the side yard, tossing pebbles at Meg's window, was unaware of what was happening in the backyard. Or, even more likely, the incident had occurred after Michael Duprey gave up and left.

"Lunch at my house will give us time to make sense of all this," Luke said. "Then we'll go ahead with our plans to visit the funeral homes. Get your suitcase, and we'll be on our way."

"I don't know what I would have done without you," Kelly said, and deep in her heart she believed those words. But did anyone, even an experienced detective like Luke Campbell, stand a chance against a serial killer determined to unleash his vicious plans? She'd read news accounts about how some of these monsters eluded the police for decades.

TWENTY-FIVE

A Puzzling Poem

"I'LL WORK ON THE SANDWICHES," Luke said, when they arrived at his house. He took tomatoes from the windowsill, pumpernickel bread and ham and cheese slices from the refrigerator, and set them on the counter.

"What were you going to tell me about Benny's box of treasures?" Kelly asked, taking paper napkins from the holder.

Luke finished slicing the tomatoes. "It's a lonely-guy thing. Benny fantasizes about women. He touches silky things, sexy stuff, like—"

"Scarves."

Luke nodded and set out the sandwiches. "Intimate items bring lonely men like Benny closer to the woman's world, a world they fear they'll never know."

"You are quite the detective, tracking clues and the human heart." Kelly found two matching plates in the cabinet.

Luke patted his stomach. "Ripping apart Pruitt's cellar sure worked up my appetite."

"Mine, too," Kelly admitted, taking a pitcher of tea from the refrigerator and filling two glasses.

"Come on, let's eat." Luke held out a chair for her. "Justine surprised me. Coming up with that story about falling asleep at the front desk."

"You don't believe her?"

Luke shook his head. "I always imagined her keeping a vampire's schedule. You know, sleeping by day, roaming around at night."

Kelly realized that much of Luke's humor was meant to keep her from falling apart. The lines between his eyes revealed that he was worried, too. The kidnapper was taking more chances, ready to strike at any moment.

"I'll slice a lemon," Kelly said, and she got up from the table.

"I'll do it," Luke said, and he went to the counter.

Handing him the knife, Kelly stopped as if she'd walked into a brick wall. "Luke, did you change knives? This one doesn't have the carved initials."

Luke examined the knife. "The creep!" Luke exclaimed. "He comes and goes in my house as he pleases, just as he did at Pruitt's Inn."

"No one is safe anywhere," Kelly said.

Luke pulled his gun from its holster. "I doubt the kidnapper is hanging around, but I need to make sure. Stay close, and do exactly what I say."

In ten minutes, they finished searching the house and were satisfied that the kidnapper was gone. Back in the kitchen, Luke grabbed the knife holder. "Look at this," he said, and he extracted a slip of paper protruding from the opening where the knife had been. "It's another poem."

Kelly read over his shoulder:

One slipped away
On a snowy day.
Double's my due
One white, one blue.

"He must have found an unlocked window and switched knives. He's added another keepsake to his collection."

Kelly choked back her tears. "He's taking away bits and pieces of us."

Luke pulled Kelly toward him. "He won't harm you. I swear it." His arms slid down to the small of her back, his touch firm and soothing. Cautiously, hesitantly, their lips met and lingered. Kelly enjoyed the moment. She wasn't going to stick to her silly notion that she and Luke should forego their feelings for each other until Meg was found. No one could possibly know what sorrow the next day could bring. Here was a moment's happiness. Why should she deny herself?

"Luke, what I said about your romantic—"

"I know," he said. "Bad timing. I promised to keep my distance until we find Meg." He pulled away. "Sorry."

She kissed him. "I spoke without thinking. I enjoy being with you. A kiss every now and then isn't going to hurt the investigation."

"Sounds good to me," he said.

They kissed, and Kelly melted into his arms with that warm, comfortable feeling that comes when you walk into your home after having been away for a long time.

"I'm glad we had this little talk," Kelly said. "I just wanted you to know, it's not you or your kisses that I object to. It's just that I'm so fidgety, thinking about what's happening to Meg, what could happen to me, too."

Luke cradled Kelly's face in his hands. "He'll never get near you—not if I can help it."

"I think he's been spying on us," Kelly said, her eyes darting from the window to the door. "He chose the Jamisons' initialed knife, something we'd talked about. I think he was outside listening. He wants us to know he's stalking us."

Kelly closed her eyes as Luke kissed her again. There was tenderness to his passionate embrace, an acceptance that he would proceed slowly.

"I'm sorry for what I said earlier," she murmured, and she rested her head on his shoulder. "I practically accused you of being the kidnapper."

"We won't let him destroy us," Luke said, stroking her cheek with the back of his hand. "Together, we'll figure this out and find Meg." He kissed her again. "I now have a really good reason to find Meg."

"And what's that?"

"The sooner she's reunited with Michael Duprey, the sooner he'll take his eyes off you."

"Why, Luke Campbell, you sound jealous."

"Men like me don't stand a chance against the smooth, romantic types like Duprey."

"Yes, you do," Kelly protested. "You're a fighter. You won't give up. You'll find Meg. Michael is keeping Meg alive through his paintings, but that's just romantic dreaming that makes him feel good about himself." She kissed Luke, happy that this discussion of Michael Duprey had cleared the air.

"If we keep this up, we'll never find Meg," Luke said. "Let's eat while we dig into the poems."

"I understand the first half," Kelly said several minutes later. "One slipped away on a snowy day. He's talking about Rose D'Amici. She died last winter at the hospital."

"Double's my due," Luke quoted, finishing the first half of his sandwich. "He believes he deserves to abduct two women. In his sick logic, they balance with Rose D'Amici, from last February, and Julia Newcomb, who died Saturday. But why didn't he match up someone with Rose D'Amici before now? Why wait? And what does he mean by one white, one blue? You're the expert on color, Kelly. What do you think?"

She read the lines again. "He wants two women. A woman in white and a woman in blue."

"You're the woman in blue. You were wearing a blue skirt when you arrived in Belvista."

"White?" Kelly asked, puzzled. "He could mean a bride. Is there going to be a wedding in Belvista?"

"I'll check with the *Bugle* and see what they know." While Luke called and talked to an editor, Kelly thought about the poems. Luke flipped shut his cell phone. "Our idea didn't pan out."

Kelly snapped her fingers. "In the last poem, the kidnapper referred to capturing a pretty pair. I thought he meant Meg and me. Now I'm not so sure. Meg never wore white in Belvista."

Luke's phone rang. He answered. "She's here." He passed the phone to Kelly and mouthed the word *Justine*.

"Hello, Justine," Kelly said.

"If you know what's good for you and your purse, you'll hurry back to the inn."

"What's this all about?"

"I have six Povloskis here, dying to spend their good money on your creations. I know you must be running out of money while you search for Meg. It's now or never, missy. They won't wait."

"I'm on my way."

"What did Justine want?" Luke asked.

"A business opportunity with six Povloskis." She checked her watch. "Could we stop there on our way to the funeral home? I'll be real fast."

"We don't have much time, but tell you what. You work with the Povloskis, and I'll talk to Justine's neighbors about Meg. They might remember something they forgot to tell the officers."

"Teamwork," Kelly said. "It's becoming a habit."

TWENTY-SIX

The Povloskis

"THE POVLOSKIS, I PRESUME?" Kelly said, glancing at Justine's parlor, where six women sat, smiling, beckoning her to join them.

Justine nodded. "They mentioned they might like some help with kitchens and baths for their inns. They're nice people. They stayed here about a month ago."

"While Meg was here?"

Justine's eyes narrowed. "Before Meg came to town. Let's stick to business. I said you might be interested."

"Justine, why are you being so kind to me?"

"You could have accused my Benny of hurting Meg because of the bicycle." Justine's tightly clenched lips relaxed. "I figure an understanding heart beats under those artsy-smartsy clothes."

"Thanks," Kelly said. "I'm curious about the Povloski brothers." She was hoping to allay her fears that they were somehow involved in the disappearance of Meg and the other women. "What are they like?"

"Big strong guys, like the stevedores I used to go for. Good husband material. They don't say much—let the wives run the show and the finances."

Kelly walked into the parlor, trying to imagine Justine in the arms of a stevedore. The oldest of the women—Kelly guessed they ranged in age from about thirty to forty-five—stood up and shook Kelly's hand.

"I am Mrs. Stanislaus Povloski, but please call me Rosalie."

Her Polish accent rolled over the syllables. "I speak for all Povloski wives."

After quick introductions all around, Kelly sat down.

"We hear you are expert in renovations," Rosalie began. "We buy twelve inns, two inns each couple. Need to remodel twelve kitchens and one hundred baths."

Kelly smiled as dollar signs danced before her eyes.

"Some inns have baths in every room," Rosalie said. "Some rooms share bath. Some baths only in hallways. Many baths. Kitchens very bad. You have friends, contacts in business. You buy in bulk, get good prices, yah?"

Kelly rattled off cost-saving ideas. "Formica counters. Tile overruns. Scratch-and-dent appliances."

"Good," Rosalie said. "Big bang for buck, yah?"

"Yah." Kelly flustered. "I mean, yes."

"We need help with colors too," Rosalie said. "You say what color walls, our husbands do painting. You say what color fabric, we make drapes and bedspreads. You work for us, yah?"

"I was hoping you'd ask," Kelly said. They agreed on her fee, and she shook hands all around. "Let's get down to business," she said cheerfully. The women cackled like hens as they wrote down all the basic information about themselves and their inns. A feeling of excitement filled the room as Kelly came up with good ideas on their tight budgets. Justine was bustling about, acting like the broker in a major corporate takeover.

The grandfather clock struck three-thirty. "Like you, we're pressed for time," Rosalie said. "Our husbands are at Town Hall to see about building permits, code enforcement, such things they need. They return soon, and we must have this planned."

"I'll need to visit each inn and take measurements. Are you sure they will accept these ideas?" Kelly asked.

"Yah. They are strong workers but have no eye for style. You know men. They move fast like rabbits on practical things, slow like tortoises on pretty things. The woman must take the lead but let him think the ideas are his."

"Does that really work?" Kelly asked.

"We have our ways." Rosalie laughed.

The women laughed along with her, and Kelly wondered if maybe she and her friends could learn from these Old-World wives.

Kelly was thrilled by this unexpected opportunity. She had one high-paying client, but these twelve inns could keep her going until more wealthy clients lined up. The Povloskis could be the tip of the iceberg. Who knew how many prospective re-habbers were out there? If Luke and the Belvista police couldn't find Meg in the next few days, she would use the Povloskis' down payment to hire a private detective.

A crash, followed by the tinkling of broken glass, shattered Kelly's thoughts. The women jumped up. A red apple rolled across the floor and landed at Kelly's feet.

The women all talked at once.

"What's going on?"

"Who threw apple?"

"Why at us?"

Justine charged in. "What was that?"

"An apple," Kelly said.

"My computer?" Justine asked, dumbfounded.

"The fruit," Kelly said, "and a note taped to it." She read the message out loud. "Go back to The Big Apple."

"Big Apple," Rosalie shouted. "Is New York, no?"

WHUMP! A noise at the front porch.

Justine ran and opened the door. "Another apple," she said, picking it up.

The Povloskis clamored around, noisily asking what was happening.

"This one has cattail leaves wrapped around it," Justine said. "And a note." She read aloud, "Go home, Povloskis. Stay away from our marshlands."

"What's going on?" Rosalie asked. "They fight us?"

Luke rushed into the foyer, brushing grass clippings from his T-shirt. "It's a practical joke," he said. "I tackled the culprit. Ladies, go right back to what you were doing."

Justine turned to Kelly. "Shatterproof glass and good insurance—that's what your remodeled inns need. You want more ideas, come to me."

"Who threw the apples?" Kelly whispered to Luke as Justine whistled her way toward the reception counter.

"An overzealous environmentalist. They don't want Belvista to trade its parks and picnic areas for a mall. I got the guy's name. I'll find out if he did this on his own or was set up."

"I don't see what this debate about the cattail marshlands has to do with the Povloskis," Kelly said.

"The Povloski men were overheard down at the town hall talking about the cattail marshes. There's a rumor they were looking for property to buy near the proposed maxi-mall. This was a crude attempt to stop them."

"If the Povloski men are as practical-minded as their wives, it will take more than an apple and an anonymous threat to stop them," Kelly said.

"I'll keep these for now," Luke said, and he picked up both apples. "Next week there's a meeting to air all these grievances, and the fate of the cattail marshes could very well be decided. The maxi-mall is coming. We just don't know where."

"I dislike that maxi-mall already," Justine snapped as she walked by with a dustpan in hand, headed toward the shards of glass. "It just brought trouble to my inn." She rattled the dustpan and brush in Luke's face.

"Kelly, we'll finish our business later," Rosalie said, smiling broadly. "My family and I say we go ahead full-blast-please with you." She bustled toward the stairs, where her sisters-in-law were chattering away. "No one stops this family," she said to the group.

"We might be missing something," Kelly said to Luke once they were alone. "Is it possible that Meg walked into the middle of some kind of maxi-mall dispute? Could the kidnapper somehow be involved in one side or the other?"

From the look on Luke's face, she knew that he had already considered the possibility.

TWENTY-SEVEN

Kalinsky's Funeral Home

KELLY AND LUKE CROSSED the threshold of Kalinsky's Funeral Home, where the wake for Julia Newcomb was in progress. They glanced around the three large rooms where grieving friends and family had gathered to pay their respects.

"Everything is the color of ashes," Kelly whispered to Luke, observing the grayish-white upholstery, wallpaper, and carpet. The pewter candlesticks and picture frames assumed a deathly pallor that chilled Kelly to the bone.

Bill Kalinsky greeted them in hushed tones, tugging at the lapels of his black suit. "Please sign the guest book," he said.

Luke ran a finger down the names on the pages and recorded several in his notepad. As Kelly signed her name, Luke whispered, "There are some names I'm not familiar with. I'll have Officers Jones and Simpson check on them."

Kelly and Luke passed among the mourners, who stood in small groups or sat on tufted chairs. Kelly overheard their murmured grief.

"I can't believe she's gone."

"She was so young."

Tears welled in Kelly's eyes. Every word about Julia might soon be true of Meg.

Kelly and Luke moved to the middle room and joined the line of mourners who passed by the open casket. Julia Newcomb's interlaced fingers, pale against her maroon dress, held an amber rosary. Her frail body seemed to float on the bed of white satin in the dove-gray casket. Surrounding Julia, baskets brimming with white roses and sprigs of baby's breath filled the room with a heady fragrance. Kelly read the cards nestled among the flowers. All were from Belvista Flowers.

"That's Alex Bradford at the door," Kelly whispered to Luke. "He's standing in for Bill Kalinsky, greeting people. He told me he worked at Preston's Funeral Home. I wonder why he's here."

"Let's find out." Luke cornered Bill Kalinsky. "We need to speak in private."

"Of course." He led them to his office and motioned them toward the leather-cushioned chairs that surrounded the desk.

"What can you tell me about your employee, Alex Bradford?" Luke asked as he sat down next to Kelly.

"I couldn't ask for a better worker. I need an assistant." Bill Kalinsky leaned back in his chair and tugged at his lapels. "Alex is my first choice. I borrow him from Preston's every chance I get. I wish he'd agree to work for me exclusively."

"What's holding him back?"

"He feels an allegiance to Preston's. Walt Preston handled the funeral arrangements for Alex's family. Alex was his helper at that time." He straightened his tie. "He's good at his job. He treats the dearly departed with respect. He spends hours helping relatives choose the casket and the clothing. He even helps the groundskeepers at St. Anne's Cemetery, on his own time."

"Sounds too good to be true," Luke said. "What does he do there?"

"He rakes leaves, waters the flowers, and washes the tombstones too. He's got hoses everywhere. And he keeps the mausoleum area immaculate. He stores articles left behind by the family and visitors. You know how it is, grieving people—"

"What kind of articles?" Luke asked.

"Personal stuff, like—"

"Eyeglass cases, teddy bears," Kelly said.

Luke shot her a curious glance. She returned a stern expression that meant, *I'll explain later.*

"He finds expensive things left behind, too," Bill Kalinsky said. "Would you believe a fur stole? That happened last winter."

"Where does he store these treasures?" Luke asked.

"At the cemetery storage shed. Or, if it's something valuable, at his house."

Luke whipped out his notepad, jotted down several words, and added a furious exclamation point.

"Mr. Kalinsky, I'm going to confide in you." Luke leaned forward. "I don't want you to discuss this with your staff, including part-time employees. Do I make myself clear?"

Bill Kalinsky frowned. "Is Alex in trouble?"

"Let's just answer my questions." Luke flipped through his notepad. "In the past year, five young women, in addition to Julia Newcomb, died at Belvista Hospital. I want to know if your funeral home handled the arrangements. Would you please check your records?"

"That's not necessary." Bill Kalinsky tugged down the sleeves of his jacket. "I never forget a client's name. If you're referring to Elizabeth Brown, Anna Morales, and Sarah Lane, the answer's yes. I handled those arrangements."

Luke flipped through several pages in his notepad. "What about Lisa McFarland and Rose D'Amici?"

"No. Preston's handled those."

"Did Alex Bradford prepare Elizabeth Brown, Anna Morales, and Sarah Lane?"

"Miss Brown, yes." Bill Kalinsky frowned. "Miss Morales, yes. Miss Lane, hmm…"

Luke snapped his notepad shut. "Come on, Mr. Kalinsky. A life is at stake here."

"Yes, Miss Lane as well."

"Is it possible that Alex Bradford prepared Lisa McFarland and Rose D'Amici for Walt Preston?"

"It's possible. I could find out. Discreetly, of course."

"Call me as soon as possible." He handed Bill Kalinsky his card.

Someone knocked on the door.

"Bill…" Alex Bradford entered the room. His expression turned from a faint smile to an iron-stern scowl. Dark circles beneath his eyes accentuated his pale complexion. "Pardon the interruption," he said coldly. "Officer Jones wants to see Detective Campbell. He's waiting at the back door. He says it's an emergency."

As soon as they stepped outside Bill Kalinsky's office, Luke said, "Kelly, how did you know what Bradford had picked up at the cemetery?"

"He had a lost-and-found basket in his truck. The eyeglass case and teddy bear were in it."

As they hurried toward the back door, Luke made a quick call. "Quinn, this is Campbell. Get over to St. Anne's Cemetery right away. Take two officers with you. Look in every storage area and see if there's any clothing or anything else connected to the missing women." There was a pause while Quinn spoke, then Luke said, "Meg Madison's pajamas and camera could be there. And, Quinn, check the mausoleum and the area around it. Any place you see hoses." Another pause. "You're looking for a possible entrance to a crypt."

"Officer Jones, what's wrong?" Luke asked when they reached the back door.

"Sam Chambers is in the hospital," Jones said. "He's asking for you and Kelly. He's been stabbed."

TWENTY-EIGHT

The Woman in White

PALE BUT ABLE TO SIT UP, Sam greeted Luke and Kelly. His right arm was splinted and hung in a sling. "He's a coward," Sam blurted out. "He got into my room at my aunt's inn and hid behind the door. He grabbed me from behind."

"Did you see him?" Luke asked.

"No. But I know he's taller than I am and strong. I was squashed like a bug against his chest. He's lean."

"'Lean' lets the Povloski brothers off the hook," Kelly said. "Justine mentioned they were built like stevedores."

"Did he say anything?" Luke asked.

"No. He shoved a needle into my arm. I came to in searing pain, a knife in my shoulder."

"The sadistic creep," Luke said angrily. "He wanted to hurt you just badly enough to scare you away."

Sam winced with pain. "A guy named Jim from forensics came and took the knife to the crime lab."

"The rest of the team is at your place, dusting for prints and looking for evidence."

"An interesting knife," Sam said. "It had initials carved into the handle. *MJ* and *KJ.*"

Kelly gasped. "The knife stolen from your house, Luke."

Fury raged in Luke's eyes. "This is becoming personal. I can't wait to kick his—"

"The kidnapper made a statement," Sam said. "He said he'll hurt anyone who tries to help Kelly."

"It's just like you said, Sam." Kelly approached the bed.

"The kidnapper wants to show us that he's in control. I'm so sorry he attacked you."

"We'll get him." Luke gripped the bottom rail of the bed.

"Sam—" Kelly plumped his pillow "—there's something I have to ask." She hesitated, not wanting to believe her own suspicions. "Do you think Michael Duprey could have done this to you?"

"Michael? That seems a long shot."

"I know," Kelly said. "I don't like to think that an artist could use his hands for something vicious. But—"

"Kelly?" A stunned expression crossed Luke's face. "I can't believe you're saying this. What brought about this sudden change of heart?"

"Something Michael said the day I met him." Kelly turned to Sam. "Michael said you came to his studio your first week in town, hoping to uncover something scandalous about Meg's past. He said you wanted to write a sensationalized story."

"He's lying!" Sam rose from his pillow and rested on his good arm. "I was looking for something, anything, to support my kidnapper theory. I asked Michael if he believed the rumor that Meg had run off with a man. He went nuts! He said he was the only man in Meg's life. He shoved me out the door. Told me to stay away. Then he slammed the door in my face."

"Tell me, Sam. Do you think Michael loves my sister?"

Sam shook his head. "Michael Duprey loves only one person. Himself."

"Thanks, Sam," Kelly said.

Luke waited while Kelly plumped Sam's pillows. "Sam, let's come back to the stabbing. It happened at your aunt's. Did she see anyone entering or leaving your room around the time you were stabbed?"

"Unfortunately, no. Aunt Grace was making fish chowder in the kitchen, probably singing away." Sam reached under his pillow and pulled out a piece of notepaper. "I'll show you a sample of the sicko's thinking. There was a poem attached to the knife. Your guy, Jim, from forensics took that back to the lab too. I memorized the words and wrote them down."

Luke sat on the edge of the bed and read:

Soon will come the destined date,
Can't be early, can't be late.
Both damsels will come to me,
Easy as pie, you shall see.

"Quite a mix of vocabulary," Sam commented. "A dramatic expression like 'destined date,' the antiquated 'damsels,' and the homespun 'easy as pie.' He could be a mixture himself— say, an English lit major who does manual labor."

"That doesn't fit the Povloski brothers either," Kelly said. "From what Justine said, they wouldn't use fancy words."

"I'll drop them to the bottom of my list of possible suspects," Luke said. "And be glad of it. The six of them look enough alike to create problems for my officers."

Luke pulled the other poems from his pocket. "You're good with words, Sam. We're stumped. See if you can interpret these."

Sam read them aloud. His expressions ranged from confusion to disgust.

"What do you make of 'a woman in white and a woman in blue'?" Luke asked.

"This could be way off." Sweat beaded on Sam's face. "Right now, I'm in a world of white. White sheets, pillowcases, and bandages. Many of the women in my life right now are wearing white."

"Nurses!" Kelly exclaimed.

"Jeannie Wilkins," Luke said. "I know for a fact that she's the only nurse in the hospital in the right age group." He looked sheepishly at Kelly.

"She's pretty, like the others," Kelly admitted.

"I can't figure out why he waited so long to match up a victim with Rose D'Amici, the young woman who died in the hospital last February," Sam said. "But one thing's for sure. He's thumbing his nose at the police now. And he's doing it through you, Luke. He's showing off. You're the new guy in town. The expert. If he can get away with murder while you're working the case, he's won some kind of personal battle."

Luke gritted his teeth. "He won't get away with anything else!" He poked his head into the hallway. "Please send in Jeannie Wilkins immediately."

"The murderer's coming for Jeannie and me." Kelly shuddered at the thought.

"And when he does, we'll be ready," Luke said through clenched teeth.

"I think I'm getting inside his sick mind." Sam sat up straighter. "He'll try to abduct two women at the same time, or at least on the same night. That will be a grand coup for him. He'll show everyone that he's smarter than the police, including you, Luke, the expert in modern ways to track criminals."

Jeannie Wilkins came into the room. "Am I needed here?" she asked, a puzzled look on her face.

"Jeannie, you'll be taking some time off from work," Luke said. "Your life has been threatened by a very dangerous man."

Jeannie backed toward the door. "Who?"

"We don't know his name yet," Luke replied. "Officer Simpson, Kelly, and I will go with you to your apartment while you pack some clothes. Then we'll all go to my house. Officer Jones will meet us there. Four detectives I would trust with my life are on their way from Atlantic City. Once they arrive, you'll be completely safe."

"Do I have your personal assurance?" Jeannie asked.

Jeannie's flirtatious manner annoyed Kelly.

"Of course," Luke replied. A warm, friendly smile followed his reassuring comment.

Kelly didn't like the situation. The murderer had thrown her and Jeannie Wilkins together, bringing them under one roof. Luke's roof. She was concerned about Jeannie's safety, but jealousy nagged at her. She caught Luke and Jeannie's affectionate glances, their playful expressions. Kelly had no idea what to say or do around them. Worst of all, this obsession was distracting her from her main concern, rescuing Meg.

TWENTY-NINE

Kelly and Jeannie

WHEN OFFICER SIMPSON OFFERED TO DRIVE, Jeannie opened the passenger door and waved Kelly inside. "Here, Kelly, you take the front. There's more space for those long legs of yours." Jeannie then hopped into the backseat behind the driver. "Come on, Luke," Jeannie said playfully. "Sit next to me. I won't bite."

Without saying a word, Luke ducked into the backseat.

Annoyed, Kelly felt like a chaperone.

All the way to her apartment, Jeannie swung the conversation around to her work at the hospital. A string of harrowing heroic experiences flowed from her lips.

Kelly noticed the trembling in Jeannie's voice. Obviously, Jeannie was frightened by thoughts of being kidnapped by a killer. That was understandable and accounted in part for her nervous chatter. But Jeannie did everything possible to call attention to herself and impress Luke.

Jeannie stopped in midsentence. "Now, that's enough about me. Kelly, tell us about your work. Luke mentioned that you do something with bathrooms."

"Yes," Kelly said. "I mix grout while you pull patients from the jaws of death."

Jeannie sighed dramatically. "Luke, am I exaggerating my nursing experiences?"

"No," Luke admitted as the car veered sharply, tossing him against Jeannie. "Your day is filled with more—"

Luke's phone rang. He picked up, listened for what seemed like hours to Kelly, and said, "Thanks, Quinn."

Fighting back her fear, Kelly turned to Luke. "Did Quinn find anything of Meg's at the cemetery?"

"No," Luke said. "Nothing suspicious at all."

Kelly drew an uneasy breath and tried to think positive thoughts. She wasn't very successful.

OFFICER SIMPSON STOOD GUARD outside Jeannie's apartment. Inside, Luke paced back and forth in the kitchen. "We need to hurry!" he called out.

Jeannie was busily choosing clothes for her overnight bag. Kelly, who was helping her pack, stopped short in front of the mirror above Jeannie's dresser. Several photographs poked from the frame. Luke and Jeannie riding bicycles. Luke and Jeannie walking along the seashore. Luke and Jeannie here, there, and everywhere! Kelly wanted to rip the photos to shreds.

Jeannie looked up and chuckled. "Kelly, would you like to hear a funny story about Luke and me and poison ivy?"

"Tell her no!" Luke called, rushing into the bedroom.

Before Kelly could reply, Jeannie said, "A few weeks ago, when Luke and I went bike riding, I veered away from a rabbit and tumbled into the grass."

"Kelly isn't interested in this," Luke said, stepping gingerly over the shoes Jeannie had set out.

"Of course she is." Jeannie turned toward Kelly. "Luke turned around to see what had happened, and he fell too. We rolled down an embankment, and he landed on top of me in a poison-ivy patch. We tried to stand up, but we kept rolling like one big snowball." She laughed and her blue eyes twinkled behind her pale lashes. "Tell her, Luke. Wasn't that a riot?"

"Are we finished here?" Luke said impatiently. "In case you've forgotten, there's a murderer lurking around here somewhere."

AT LUKE'S URGING, Officer Simpson drove like crazy, taking corners sharply. When they stopped for a quick supper at the

Barnacle Café, Jeannie squeezed in next to Luke. As they drove to Luke's house, Jeannie snuggled against Luke's shoulder. It was nearly dark when they arrived at Luke's house. Kelly and Jeannie waited in the dining room while the men, guns drawn, searched the house. The danger of a madman on the loose, possibly in this very house, overwhelmed Kelly. Seeing Jeannie's hands tremble, she regretted her jealous thoughts. This was the time to stick together.

"Jeannie, let's agree to be friends," Kelly said.

"Good idea," Jeannie said. "I've been acting like an idiot. Luke needs to concentrate on finding the killer. We can't sidetrack him with our personal feelings."

"Clear on the first floor!" Officer Jones called out.

"Clear on the second, including the attic!" Officer Simpson shouted.

"No one's in the basement," Luke said, slapping the dust from the shoulders of his jacket. "First job, let's hang blankets over the first-floor windows so no one can see in. The previous owners left plenty. One of these days I'll get blinds." He turned to Kelly and Jeannie. "You two should get some rest. At the top of the stairs, turn left. You'll be sleeping in my room, at the end of the hall. I hope you don't mind sharing. The guest rooms don't have any furniture yet. I'll be in the dining room, working out strategies."

Kelly followed Jeannie up the stairs. At the top step, she looked back at the dining room and living room. The other rooms were only partially visible. Kelly saw Luke and the officers huddled over the dining room table, talking and making notes. She watched while Jeannie went on ahead.

Luke turned to his computer, and his fingers raced across the keys. He looked up when the banister creaked. The light from the ceiling fixture shone on his handsome face. His dark eyes bored through Kelly. She remembered the thrilling kisses they had shared in this house. She wouldn't give him up without a fight.

"Good night," Kelly said.

"Good night," Luke said, and he filled the printer tray with paper. "If there's anything you need, just ask."

Kelly fought the urge to run down the stairs and into his arms. She turned and hurried to Luke's bedroom. She and Jeannie began unpacking. Tired of Jeannie's chatter about handsome doctors, Kelly began arranging her clothes in the closet. She came upon Luke's tweed jacket and hung her flouncy blue skirt alongside it. The intimacy of the moment, of seeing, side by side, the clothing they had worn when they first met, caught Kelly by surprise. Closing her eyes, she brushed Luke's sleeve against her cheek, and a warm feeling coursed through her body.

"Can you help with these sheets?" Jeannie asked. "The mattress won't cooperate."

"Okay," Kelly said.

As they wrestled the fitted sheet over the mattress, Kelly studied Jeannie's face. Fear showed in the worry lines between her eyes.

"You don't have to be brave on my account," Kelly said, stretching the last corner of the sheet over the mattress.

Jeannie's lips trembled. "I keep imagining him sneaking up behind me and dragging me away."

"I know," Kelly said, spreading the top sheet. "I've almost forgotten what it's like to sleep the whole night through. I wake up in a panic, thinking someone's creeping into the room. I check under the bed and behind the door."

Jeannie slipped a pillow into a case. "I'd like to clear the air."

"About Luke, you mean."

"I'm fond of Luke. I've been throwing myself at him. But any fool can see he's crazy about you. And unless my eyes deceive me, you feel the same about him." She folded back the top sheet. "Today I tried to make Luke choose me over you. But I'm fighting a losing cause."

Kelly swallowed her words. She didn't want to say anything that would encourage Jeannie to chase after Luke.

"It's all right," Jeannie said. "No sparks flew between us. We both enjoyed bike riding, but the relationship wasn't going anywhere. We just didn't connect."

Kelly smoothed the blanket, glad to hear Jeannie's words.

"I'm the old-fashioned type," Jeannie admitted. "I need a man in my life. The minute one guy leaves, I look for another. So with Luke out of the picture, I'm looking. I know how dependent that makes me sound, but—"

There was a soft rap at the door.

"Come in," Jeannie said.

"Just checking." Luke stepped into the room. "Are you finding everything you need?" He walked across the room and tested the window latches. "Keep them locked," he cautioned. "Officer Jones is stationed outside. He's keeping an eye on the roof, in case the kidnapper tries to enter from the second floor."

Kelly and Jeannie looked cautiously from one window to the other.

"I'm sorry about the mess," Luke said. He picked up a hammer and several sacks of nails scattered beneath a stepladder, which leaned against a wall. "Squirrels chewed through the slats on the attic vents. I got up there the other day and made some repairs." He nodded toward the attic entrance in the closet ceiling. "You two would have a ball up there. Mrs. Jamison left trunks filled with clothes from her heyday in the sixties." He smiled. "When this is over, I'll haul the trunk down, and you can help yourselves. They're your kind of clothes, Kelly."

"Yeah, hippie chic," Jeannie teased, patting Kelly affectionately on the back. Kelly sensed their rivalry was over.

"If you don't need anything," Luke said, backing out of the room, "I'll go downstairs. Officer Simpson is guarding the front door. I'm watching the back. Lock yourselves in, and don't come out unless Jones, Simpson, or I say so. The detectives from Atlantic City will be here in about an hour." He grabbed hold of the doorknob. "By the way, Detective Quinn just called in his report on the Povloskis. They work for a construction company in Queens. Their boss can account for the time when the women went missing. They are no longer suspects."

"I HOPE THIS NEXT HOUR until the detectives get here flies by," Jeannie said, arranging her lipsticks on top of the bureau. "Every little noise sends shivers up my spine."

"We can't just hide here like scared rabbits," Kelly said.

Jeannie kicked off her shoes. "Let's do some yoga stretches and meditation. That's how I get through stressful times."

Kelly placed herself opposite Jeannie, between the bed and dresser, where there was room to move. "Meg and I like to warm up with the Salute to the Sun."

"Me, too," Jeannie said, and she closed her eyes.

Kelly stood tall with her feet together, her palms pressed together in front of her chest. She relaxed her whole body. Slowly she worked her way through the raised-arms pose and the hand-to-foot pose. In the downward-dog pose, she tilted her head backward, arched her back, and gazed at the ceiling. She felt the tension of the day melt away. By the time she completed the twelfth and final position, she was refreshed, her mind clear, her attitude positive. She opened her eyes and saw Jeannie already sitting cross-legged on the floor, meditating.

"I feel better already," Jeannie said, rolling her shoulders.

"You sound like Meg," Kelly said.

"Kelly, have you considered—" Jeannie bit her lip. "What if—"

"What if Meg's dead?" Kelly sat on her side of the bed. "I believe Meg's alive. I'll never give up hope. Never."

"But, Kelly, more than three weeks have passed."

Tears filled Kelly's eyes. "She's all I have in this world. We had a stupid argument about money. I started it. If only—"

"Kelly, I'm sorry. I didn't mean to upset you." Jeannie came and put her arms around Kelly and hugged her tightly. "Please promise me you'll try to face things realistically. That's—"

Meeeeeeoooowwwwww! Yooooowlllll! Meeeeeeoooowww-www!

Jeannie sat bolt upright. "What was that?"

"Rusty!"

"I'm scared," Jeannie said.

"Shhh!"

Meeeeeeoooowwwwww! Yooooowlllll!

The back door opened and slammed shut.

"Rusty?" Luke's voice came from far away.

Yooooowwwwwww! Rusty's long, shrill wail was racked with pain.

Then silence.

Kelly turned out the light and peered out the bedroom window into the darkness.

"Do you see anything?" Jeannie cowered against the headboard, a blanket hastily pulled to her chin.

"Officer Jones is hurt! He's lying near the bushes." Panic rose in Kelly's voice. "I don't see Luke anywhere." She ran to the door. "Stay here and keep quiet." Kelly unlocked the door and tiptoed down the hallway. Holding her breath, she peered over the banister into the living room. Officer Simpson lay motionless, spread-eagled on his back.

Kelly gasped and fled back to the bedroom. She closed and locked the door behind her. "He's in the house," she whispered.

"Who?" Jeannie asked, wide-eyed.

"The murderer," Kelly said, frozen with terror.

THIRTY

A Terrifying Night

"I'M SCARED. He's going to kill us!" Jeannie cried.

"Not without a fight." Kelly clenched her hands into fists, trying to conquer the panic rising within her. She had to act. What could she do? Hide. Get away from him.

Kelly shoved the ladder into the closet, yanked it open, and climbed up the steps. "Come on, Jeannie. Together, we can do this."

Kelly reached up, shoved aside the wood panel leading to the attic, and hoisted herself through the opening. She fell forward, scraping her hands on the rough floorboards.

The doorknob rattled.

"Hurry." Kelly helped Jeannie scramble up beside her.

A fist pounded the bedroom door.

"He'll break through!" Jeannie sobbed.

Silence.

"He's gone, but he'll be back." Kelly reached down and gripped the ladder's top step. "Help me," she whispered.

Jeannie grabbed hold.

"Ready, yank!"

"It's slipping away!" Jeannie said.

"Shhh! Pull!"

The ladder rose slowly, swayed, and stopped. "Work with me," Kelly whispered. She steadied the ladder, and Jeannie worked her hands down to the third step.

Footsteps sounded in the hall.

Coming to their knees, Kelly and Jeannie lifted the ladder to eye level.

The footsteps were at the bedroom door.

Kelly and Jeannie stood up, collapsed the ladder, and pulled it through the opening.

"Hurry," Kelly said, shoving the ladder aside.

They slid the panel into place.

"Ouch! I tripped on something." Jeannie steadied herself and ran her hands along the object. "It's a trunk."

CRAAAAACK! Below them, wood splintered.

"He's breaking down the door," Kelly rasped. She and Jeannie pushed and heaved until the trunk slid over the panel.

CRAAAAACK! More wood splintered. The door banged open. Footsteps stormed across the bedroom below.

"He's got an axe," Jeannie said. She squeezed Kelly's hand.

Footsteps. Grunts. Ripping noises.

"I think he's slashing the bedding."

Boxes slammed against the closet wall.

Crashing. Thrashing.

"He's right beneath us." They clung to each other, stifling their sobs. Kelly wondered what had happened to Luke. She hadn't seen him in the hall or stairway. He wasn't in the dining room or living room when she looked down. She would never forgive herself if the kidnapper had harmed him.

Thin bands of moonlight shone faintly through the slatted vents at either end of the attic. Jeannie began to whimper, and Kelly hugged her. They were trapped. They were at the kidnapper's mercy. His fists pounded the panel as he tried to lift it.

"Hush," Kelly said, straightening up. "Hush."

A steady humming rose above the sound of the kidnapper's fists. Faint at first, the humming grew louder, coming faster now, as fast as the beating of their hearts.

"Cars," Jeannie whispered. "Two cars."

The slamming of car doors. An unfamiliar man's voice.

"Campbell?" The voice called out.

"Jones? Simpson? Where are you?" came other voices.

"It's the detectives," Kelly said, and she exhaled in relief.

"Thank God!" Jeannie sobbed. She hugged Kelly, and tears rolled down their cheeks.

Footsteps hurried to the bedroom window. The window lock clicked. The sash creaked.

"I pray he's leaving," Kelly said.

Voices boomed up the stairwell. "Kelly Madison? Jeannie Wilkins?"

Footsteps. "Luke! What the hell happened to you?"

"The maniac tried to rearrange my face. Officers Jones and Simpson are hurt pretty bad. Ryan, call 911." Luke raced up the steps two at a time. "Kelly and Jeannie, are you up there?"

Kelly heard the panic in his voice.

"We're here!" Jeannie shouted.

"We're stuck!" Kelly cried, realizing the trunk was wedged between the floorboards. "The trunk won't budge. We'll have to unpack it."

Kelly and Jeannie frantically tossed clothes from the trunk. Bell-bottoms and T-shirts in psychedelic colors flew everywhere. Then they worked to push the trunk aside. Struggling, they pulled up the panel and moved the ladder down through the opening.

Luke snapped open the ladder and climbed up several steps. "Come on down," he said, holding out his arms.

"Did you catch the murderer?" Kelly asked, climbing onto the ladder. "He left by the window."

"He got away," Luke said.

Sobbing, Jeannie followed Kelly down the ladder.

Sirens screamed. Ambulances pulled up. Medics raced to the house.

Men's and women's voices. "Two stretchers," said a man's deep voice. "Louise, call it in."

"We'll be bringing in two officers," came a woman's strong voice. "Conscious now, but should be checked out."

One of the medics called out, "Hey, Detective Campbell, the officers are dazed, but they're going to make it!"

"Thank God," Luke said, helping Kelly and Jeannie to the bed. "Everyone's safe." He cupped his hands to his mouth and called out, "Ask if they saw the killer!"

Mumbled voices.

"No," came the answer.

"He's out of control," Luke said.

Kelly saw feathers lying everywhere in the bedroom. Both pillows were slashed. The sheets and blankets were tossed in a heap on the floor.

Jeannie picked up a handful of feathers and watched them slip between her fingers. She sobbed uncontrollably. "It looks like we had a pillow fight," she said, sobbing and laughing.

"And we won," Kelly said through her tears.

THIRTY-ONE

Victims and Suspects

AT SIX THE NEXT MORNING, Kelly, Jeannie, Luke, and the Atlantic City detectives arrived at the police station. Simpson and Jones, released from the hospital and in pretty good condition, met them there. Everyone was jumpy, remembering the maniac's reign of terror. Dark half-moons hung below their sleep-deprived eyes.

Awed, Kelly watched Luke's office swarm with energy. Within minutes Luke and the detectives had dragged in boxes of computer information they had gathered, working through the night. Kelly recognized Luke's handwriting on the labels: *School, Boating Records, Drownings, Funeral Homes.* On and on. Luke had thought of everything.

The detectives covered the walls with maps and charts. An *X,* pinned to Pruitt's Inn, marked the last place where Meg had been seen. Three other *X*'s dotted the map. The detectives posted a separate chart of information for each of the ten women, the four missing and the six deceased.

Kelly frowned. "Luke, did you notice that none of the missing women weighed more than one hundred thirty pounds?"

"The kidnapper is practical," Luke said. He was reviewing eyewitness accounts. "Sam Chambers figures he most likely injected his victims with a sedative. Too much, he could kill them. He doesn't want that. Too little, they could regain consciousness. He has to move quickly, carrying his victim, and get where he's going before she regains consciousness. If she were groggy but capable of struggling, scratch marks on his face would be hard to explain to friends and coworkers. Sam has lots of data. He knows his stuff. I agree with him on this. So do the detectives."

Kelly felt foolish for not having figured out such an obvious thing. She left Luke alone and studied the description of the clothing the missing women were wearing when last seen.

The detectives gathered around Luke's desk to discuss the suspects. Jones and Simpson, bandages and bruises dotting their faces, sat near Luke. Kelly thought they would burst with pride at being involved in a big-time investigation.

Luke stood beside his desk and addressed his men. "As you know, we're waiting for County Chief Prosecutor Attenborough to bring in search warrants for Duprey's and Saunders' studios and Bradford's house. Judge Pugliesi may refuse to sign the warrants. What we've got is sketchy." He checked his watch. "Let's review plans and then crack those files. Attenborough wants a case built on facts, with motive, opportunity, and method spelled out. Especially motive. He eats motive for breakfast, lunch, and dinner."

"Attenborough got stung early in his career," Officer Jones said. "He made a case against the wrong man. The media crucified Attenborough and claimed the real killer nearly got away. Attenborough got real cautious after that. He hasn't lost a case since then."

Luke ran his fingers through his hair. "We'll do this Attenborough's way. But my gut says Alex Bradford is our man. Bill Kalinsky, the funeral director, just called in that Alex Bradford prepared the bodies of all six women who died this year. Lisa McFarland and Rose D'Amici, whose burials Preston's Funeral Home arranged, and the four women in the care of Kalinsky's Funeral Home. That's a whopping coincidence." His eyes narrowed. "The files show that the camouflaged boat in the cattail marshes belongs to Bradford. His entire family drowned while he was conveniently absent." He cocked an eyebrow. "I'm not buying that. That needs further investigation."

Luke sat on the edge of his desk. "Living alone, Bradford

comes and goes as he wants, with plenty of opportunity to kidnap unsuspecting women. Kelly tells me that Bradford encouraged her to go for a drive with him...twice. Sometimes when she saw Bradford, a black Lexus was in the vicinity. There's no Lexus registered in Bradford's name, so could be he borrows it from a friend. That's a loose end we still need to straighten out."

Kelly sat silently listening, glad that she was privileged to learn all these details. She knew from the determined look on Luke's face that the skills of every police officer would be used. But was it enough? Would Meg be found alive?

Luke held up a report. "There's some bad news from forensics. There were no fingerprints on the envelope, note, and photos delivered to the hospital. The kidnapper must have worn gloves. Speaking of fingerprints, we didn't get anything helpful from Kelly's room at Pruitt's Inn or from Meg's bicycle. Benny had wiped the bicycle clean, trying to keep it in good condition."

Luke tossed aside the report. "I don't know what Bradford's motive is, so we'll bring in anybody who can tell us something about him. We don't want to ruffle the county chief prosecutor's feathers, so we'll consider other suspects. We'll hone in on every possible place where the women might be kept."

Luke turned to Officer Jones. "Jones, get on the phone. Check on Duprey's artist friends in Connecticut. See if they back up his story. Find out when Greg Saunders arrived there. It's possible Duprey and Saunders know something they didn't tell. Waters, bring in Duprey and grill him. Turn up the heat, and see what he spits out about Saunders, his rival."

Luke went over to the map and tapped his pencil on the artists' quarter. "Abbott, if we get the warrants, I'd like you to go through Duprey's and Saunders' studios. They're side by side. Don't miss anything. Secret room, connecting passage—you know the drill. This Saunders guy is a mystery man. Get specifics, facts. Simpson, you'll go with Abbott. Remember, forty-five minutes, in and out. Get to St. Anne's Cemetery by ten, and don't let Bradford out of your sight. All right, shall we review?"

Detective Jessup ran a stubby finger across the cattail marshes. "I'll search near the clam boat and picnic areas. I'm looking for graves and the kidnapper's hiding place."

"I'm with Detective Jessup," Officer Jones said.

"I'll keep Bradford in view at the church and cemetery," Detective Abbott said. "Bill Kalinsky says Bradford never misses a funeral. He insists on driving the hearse." He shrugged. "Some of us like SUVs. Some like hearses."

"I'm shadowing Detective Abbott," Officer Simpson said. "I'll also check suspicious areas in the cemetery. Could be Bradford's digging extra graves."

"Jeannie and I will be among the mourners at the church and cemetery," Detective Ryan said. "I'm her kissin' cousin from Atlantic City. We'll see that Bradford doesn't bolt for home."

Jeannie gave the detective a flirty smile. Kelly saw that Jeannie was taken with brawny Patrick Ryan and his roguish personality.

Luke slapped Bradford's house, circled in red on the map. "That gives me two hours—if we get the warrants—to search Bradford's place while he's at the nine o'clock Mass and ten o'clock burial. Kelly, you'll come with me. You did a good job rifling through Duprey's studio."

Chief Clemmens cleared his throat. "That leaves the police station to me. I'll have the pleasure of handling any reporters who show up." He guffawed.

"One last thing." Luke patted his holster. "Shoot, if you have to. But do not, under any circumstances, kill the kidnapper. He's the only one who knows where Meg is."

Luke went to his desk and rolled up his sleeves. "Let's hit these files. The more eyes on them the better."

Folders were opened. Folders were closed. The clock ticked. A feeling of excitement hovered over the team as if at any moment one of them would discover the telling detail and shout it out.

Luke removed his glasses and rubbed his bloodshot eyes. Bruises had started to appear on his cheeks. "It's seven-forty. Let's stop and review what we have. I'm counting on officers Jones and Simpson to divulge any local hearsay." He winked. "Don't worry about shocking us."

Detective Ryan flipped through his notes. "Bradford had two disciplinary reports from school. Third and fifth grade. Both times, he struck a fellow student hard enough to require medical attention. He has no police record. He took a two-week vacation starting January twenty-sixth and was away from Belvista when Rose D'Amici died on February fifth. There are no purchase slips showing he bought building supplies for a secret room."

Luke leaned back in his chair. "Jones, Simpson? Anything else?"

"I'm thinking back to the day Bradford's family drowned," Officer Simpson said. "This may be nothing...."

"It could be crucial," Luke encouraged. "Talk to us."

"Rumor has it that Bradford went to the animal pound the day of the drownings and took home eight kittens. Nobody ever saw those kittens again. Sort of weird, don't you think?"

"Thanks," Luke said. "Weird could be what we're looking for. I'll follow up on that."

"James Ritter, the watchman at the Mariners' Museum, has a police record. Petty theft," Detective Abbott added.

Chief Clemmens gulped down the last of his coffee. "Hal Dunbar pushed the museum director to overlook Ritter's past and hire him."

"I'll talk to Dunbar and see what his connection is with Ritter," Luke said.

Officer Abbott slapped his knee. "Hal Dunbar pulled in for questioning. That warms my heart."

Luke leaned across his desk. "Do you have something against Dunbar?"

"Him and his highfalutin ideas! Just because he rubs shoulders with Henry Erdlinger, he thinks he's better than the rest of us."

Kelly's eyes widened. "Henry Erdlinger! Don't you remember, Luke? He and his wife were supposed to interview Meg for a job on Monday, the day after she disappeared."

"Officer Jones," Luke said, "are you saying Dunbar and Erdlinger are friends?"

"More like business partners. A land deal. Something to do with the cattail marshes."

Luke stacked his folders. "Chief Clemmens, have Dunbar meet me here at noon. And I'll want to look through the town council minutes. What else do we have?"

"We didn't find much on Duprey," Detective Waters said. "He came here from Dijon, France, five years ago. No police record in Belvista. No boat. No buying building supplies."

Luke set aside the folders. "Simpson, Jones. Do you know anything about Duprey?"

"He's a real lady's man," Officer Simpson said. "He milks the old starving-artist routine to charm rich women—or poor ones, if they're pretty."

Kelly wanted to run from the room. What a fool she had been to fall for Michael's phony charm.

"Michael Duprey's guilty of pursuing women, but I doubt he's kidnapping them," Luke said. "Women are practically knocking down his door. They're taken in by his looks and—" he gritted his teeth "—artistic temperament. Kidnapping? That's not his style." Luke paused, composing himself. "Officer Browning, you'll tail him until Meg is free. Just in case." Luke's eyes narrowed. "Some of Belvista's business owners are cooking up shady deals, but kidnappings are not on their agenda. Bradford is our man."

The police station door banged open.

"Welcome, County Chief Prosecutor Attenborough," Luke called out. "Looks like you had a successful visit with Judge Pugliesi."

Attenborough—tall, dapper, hawk nose, shaved head—

strode into the police station, clutching the search warrants. Everyone stopped talking. The tension in the room was palpable.

"Okay, Campbell, here are your no-knock warrants," Attenborough said in his barking voice, and he dropped them onto Luke's desk. "I owe the judge for this. Deliver me the kidnapper. My career is on the line."

Attenborough blew through the police station like a tornado, and everyone cleared a path.

Luke held up the search warrants and pumped an arm in victory. Everyone cheered. "Okay, let's man our battle stations and win this war. I think we all picked up on Attenborough's subtle message." Laughter filled the room. "We need something that will stand up in court. What are we waiting for? Let's go get it!"

THIRTY-TWO

The Hiding Place

KELLY WAS SURPRISED that everything appeared normal. Alex Bradford's house sat on a quiet, maple-shaded street behind the library. Luke had told her that after the drownings and funerals, Alex had sold the family home and moved to this blue-collar neighborhood. Small, unobtrusive, the one-story house with a garage at the rear held secrets and answers—Kelly was certain of that. Luke drove by to make sure there wasn't anyone around, then parked his car in the library parking area.

Luke and Kelly ducked beneath the branches of a maple tree. Shielded by a high privet hedge, they walked onto the property. Luke headed toward the garage.

"Let's go into the house," Kelly said, and she looked over her shoulder. She had the creepy feeling that Alex was lurking somewhere, watching them. She knew that was crazy, because Alex was busy with Julia Newcomb's funeral.

"We'll check the garage first," Luke said. "It often reveals more about a man than his house does."

"UNBELIEVABLY NEAT," Luke commented as he peered through the garage window. He broke the lock on the door, and they entered. "No possibility of a hidden room," he added, inspecting the thin walls. He climbed a ladder and checked the storage area. "Nothing up here."

"What should I be looking for?" Kelly asked. She poked through the rakes and shovels.

"The unusual. Something out of place." He rummaged through the jeans and jackets hanging on a peg. "Hey, what's this?" He crouched in front of a line of gallon-size water jugs. "They're clean as a whistle." Touching only the cork, he tipped one jug. "There are a few drops of water inside. Looks pretty fresh."

Kelly knelt next to Luke. "He's taking water to Meg." She gripped Luke's sleeve. "Meg's alive!"

"It's possible," Luke said, standing up. "Come on. We'll search the house."

"We won't find Meg there," Kelly said, as she grasped the situation. "He must have her somewhere where there's no water supply."

"But he may have moved her here."

"Look," Kelly said, pointing at two faint circles next to the jugs. "Two jugs are missing." She sighed with relief. "Enough water for several days." She saw the worried look on Luke's face. "I know what you're thinking. We don't know when he brought that water to Meg. It could have been yesterday...or weeks ago...or not at all."

They went to the house. Luke kicked in the back door, and they entered the kitchen. He set down his gym bag, bulging with tools, a flashlight, and a camera. They quickly checked the entire house to see if Meg was there.

"Now we'll start a thorough search with the kitchen," Luke said. "Just remember, the span of our search warrant covers only items related to the missing women. So don't let your curiosity run wild."

"Who, me?" Kelly asked. She immediately explored the pantry. Luke opened the cabinet doors beneath the sink. Lying on the floor, he rapped his knuckles along the panels. "I found something," he said. Kelly knelt by his side. Luke prodded the panel with a screwdriver, and it slid sideways.

Kelly gasped. Belvista bus schedules. Latex gloves. Duct tape. Night-vision goggles. "Tools of his sick trade," she said.

"Come on," Luke said.

"Let's see what else we can find." They explored the cellar. Nothing.

The dining room and living room. Nothing.

The bathroom and smaller bedroom. Still nothing.

Kelly looked through Alex's bedroom closet. "Every square inch is paneled, just like his room," she said. "It's as if he's sealed himself inside a coffin."

"Kelly, come here!" Luke was running his hands along the baseboard near the bed. "It's a false wall." He tapped with a hammer and put an ear to the wall. "Hear the hollow sound? There's a large space behind the paneling. I think we've found his hiding place." He rose, scanning the wall, testing the panel's seams. "There's no entrance here."

Luke and Kelly hurried to the closet. Luke carefully parted Alex's dark suits, which hung from the clothes rod. On the wall behind the suits were three hooks. A pair of black jeans hung from one hook. A black T-shirt hung from the second, a black jacket and ski mask from the third.

"These must be the clothes he wore when he kidnapped the women," Kelly said.

"They never stood a chance. He crept out of the night like a shadow." Carefully, Luke lifted the black jeans from their hook. "There's a latch," he said. He slid the bolt and cracked open the door. Switching on her flashlight, Kelly prayed, *Meg, please be alive. Please.*

Luke took the flashlight and stepped into the room.

"Jeeze!" he exclaimed. "It looks like a shrine."

"Meg? Is Meg there?"

"No."

Kelly gripped Luke's arm and peered into the room. Women's clothing and shoes were lined up neatly.

"Stacy Deems," Kelly said, nodding toward the black pants, white shirt, and black shoes. "That's what she was wearing when she was kidnapped." She pointed toward the jeans,

T-shirt, blue plaid shirt, and sneakers. "Kim Eberly was last seen wearing those."

"Mary Waverly's red skirt and top," Luke surmised. "According to Sam, she was known to like bright colors."

Kelly's voice trembled. "There's the framed picture of Meg and me in the flower shop."

"Don't touch anything," Luke warned.

Kelly took several steps toward a long, narrow bench. A hand towel rested on the bench. "Luke, something's underneath that towel. See where it's bumped up?"

Luke pulled a pen from his pocket, stuck the tip under the corner of the towel, and slowly lifted the pen. "Shiny," he said. "Silver."

"My beaded bracelet!" Kelly gasped.

"From the Mariners' Museum back lot," Luke said. He slowly lowered the edge of the towel.

"That maroon shawl," Kelly said. "It matches the dress Julia Newcomb was wearing. He took it from the casket." A wave of nausea overcame her as she looked around. "My God! He took souvenirs from the women who died of natural causes too."

Luke walked past the necklaces and bracelets. He stopped at the rosary beads and prayer books. "What a heartless monster Alex Bradford is. I've seen enough. There's no doubt who the kidnapper is. I'll photograph everything. If Bradford sees we removed any of this, he'll bolt and—"

Kelly cut in. "He'll do away with Meg and any trace of her."

While Luke retrieved his camera, Kelly studied the clothing.

"Luke, everything looks clean and pressed," she said when he returned. "The women didn't wear these clothes for very long."

"Don't draw the wrong conclusion," Luke said as he snapped photos. "It doesn't mean he kills his victims immediately. He might make them wear other clothes. It could be part of his compulsive ritual."

Kelly caught sight of something in a corner. "Shine the flashlight over there," she said.

Three pet collars, three leashes, and three pet dishes sat in a row. Luke snapped several photos.

Kelly frowned. "I didn't see any signs of a cat or dog."

They returned to the kitchen, trying to leave everything as they'd found it, hoping Alex wouldn't realize they'd found his secret room. Luke set a true copy of the search warrant on the kitchen table.

"Do you have to leave that?" Kelly asked. "I wish Alex didn't have to know that we're on to him."

"Me too," Luke said, "but it's procedure."

They left by the back door.

"I didn't take anything, so I don't have to leave an inventory list," Luke said, taking Kelly's hand and walking with her toward the property line. "He won't know for sure what we saw."

Kelly took a deep breath and exhaled as she ducked beneath a branch. The air seemed heavy and hard to breathe. Her throat was tight with fear for Meg's safety. What a naive fool she had been. On Sunday morning, her second day in Belvista, she had found the button to Meg's blouse and some pink chalk and proudly thought she could find Meg all on her own. Now she knew better. She was up against an evil she had never even imagined. She needed Luke and all the help she could get if she ever hoped to see Meg again.

Luke's cell phone rang. "Abbott...yes." He quickly told what he and Kelly had discovered at Alex's house. "You finding anything at Duprey's studio?" His expression went from surprise to anger. "In Saunders' studio? Take his cameras and photos, and write up the inventory. We're on our way."

"What did he tell you?" Kelly asked as Luke rushed her toward his car.

"They found photos of Meg in Saunders' studio, dated the Saturday she disappeared. She's wearing her daisy pajamas."

He turned the key in the ignition and roared out of the library parking lot.

"Is Meg alive in the photos?"

"Yes."

"Alone?"

"Yes."

"Who took the photos?"

"We don't know yet. But when we do, all hell is going to break loose."

Kelly could hardly breathe. The world as she knew it was spinning out of control.

THIRTY-THREE

Greg Saunders' Studio

LUKE AND KELLY RUSHED into Greg Saunders' studio.

"It looks as if a paint bomb went off," Luke said. Massive canvases, consisting of colorful dots and swirls, covered every inch of wall space and were stacked against the furniture.

"Saunders calls it Abstract Expressionism," Officer Simpson said, holding up a brochure with photographs of Saunders' work.

Kelly liked the bold, daring look but wondered if rage motivated Greg Saunders to paint like that.

"Here's what you're looking for," Detective Abbott called out.

Kelly rushed to the dining area, where several photos lay on a table. "Meg. It is Meg!" she exclaimed.

Kelly's eyes darted across all twelve photos. Meg, barefoot and wearing her daisy-trimmed pajamas, looked so beautiful in the deserted cemetery. The soft light of early evening glistened on her face. Her tousled hair tumbled over her shoulders.

Luke came and stood beside Kelly. "Anything significant about this part of the cemetery?" he asked, running his fingers beneath three photos.

"Yes," Kelly said. "Those are the Bradford family tombstones. Michael told me Meg had been there. He said she thought it was a great setting for his paintings."

"And this," Luke said, pointing at another group of photos, "is the mausoleum area that Bill Kalinsky mentioned at his funeral home."

"Alex Bradford's pride and joy," Kelly said.

"It keeps coming back to Bradford," Luke said. "Hold on." Luke picked up a photo and held it up to the light coming in the window. "There's a car parked on the perimeter road. It sure looks like—"

"A black Lexus," Detective Abbott cut in. "We wanted you to have the fun of spotting it, too. From what we can make out, there's no driver or passenger."

"Why would Meg be wearing her pajamas in St. Anne's Cemetery?" Kelly asked, more concerned with Meg than the car. "And what is she doing there? It's such a creepy place." She looked at the photos again. "Beautiful to an artist or photographer, I suppose."

"Looks like she's posing for pictures," Officer Simpson said.

"Let's ask Saunders," Luke said. "Either he's the photographer, or he knows who is."

"I'm betting it's Duprey," Officer Simpson said. "He was the last to see her. These are his souvenirs. Sick creep."

Luke frowned. "Simpson, call Saunders and tell him to come to the police station asap. Don't take any excuses. We need to grill him and Duprey until they tell us what they know about Meg and the cemetery."

Luke paced back and forth in front of Saunders' paintings. "Here's a new wrinkle. What if Alex Bradford kidnapped the first three women, and Duprey or Saunders or both took Meg? Bradford didn't have Meg's pajamas at his house, but he had the other three women's clothing. Maybe he doesn't have Meg after all."

Luke headed for the door. "Let's take all this and the photos of Bradford's secret room back to the police station." His eyes narrowed. "We've got most of the pieces of the puzzle, but we don't have the full picture."

Kelly looked around the studio and felt unnerved by the explosions of color. "I hope Saunders, the mystery man of this case, has the missing pieces of the puzzle," she said.

THIRTY-FOUR

Ritter and Dunbar

"KELLY, YOU'RE HERE because of the special circumstances," Chief Clemmens said, greeting her cordially as she and Sam Chambers approached the interrogation room. "But let's get something straight, Chambers. You call yourself a specialist on criminal behavior, but in my opinion, you don't belong here. Luke requested it." The chief cracked his knuckles in Sam's face. "I think your psychobabble is a crock. Next thing you know, we'll be calling in fortunetellers."

"I'm all in favor of that," Sam said, "if they can help us find Meg. Olivia Moon would be my first choice."

Chief Clemmens clenched his fists. "Don't get me started on that tea-leaf nutcase."

Sam opened his briefcase. "You should be annoyed at yourself, not me or Olivia." He waved the article about poor young women who were called gold diggers. "You went along with the Business Club. To please them and save your job, you pushed the idea that Meg had run off with a wealthy man. If only—"

"Belvista is a small town. Everybody knows everybody. A serial killer is the last—"

"Chief Clemmens," Kelly interrupted. "Please cut Sam some slack. He's come here, against his doctor's advice, to help Luke interpret the information we're going to hear."

Chief Clemmens was still muttering when Kelly and Sam left him and walked past the interrogation room into an adjoining room marked private. Cramped and windowless, it was furnished with four dilapidated chairs. They faced a wall containing a small window.

Kelly leaned against the glass and peered into the interrogation room. She watched Luke busily reviewing a pile of folders. The top two buttons on his shirt were undone, and his jacket was slung over the back of a chair.

"Luke is clever," Sam said as he and Kelly sat down. "He doesn't really need me here."

"Then why did you come?"

"Luke doesn't want you to be alone, in case…you know… something upsetting is said."

"You're a good friend, Sam." The door to the interrogation room opened. "Mr. Ritter, have a seat," Luke said. "You're a watchman at the Mariners' Museum, am I right?"

James Ritter sat down and lowered his eyes. "I'm going to lose my job, ain't I?"

"Let's just cut to the bottom line," Luke said.

"It was an accident," Ritter blurted out.

"I need to hear some specifics."

"He told me to scare her, send her packing. So I loosened the boat rigging. I didn't mean for the boat to break loose and come crashing down. I just wanted to let her think it could. Anyway, the boat missed her. She tripped and hurt herself. It was her own clumsy fault." His watery, bloodshot eyes studied Luke. "I've seen her since. There ain't no scars. Women are born hardheaded. That's a fact."

"Did you write a message in the sand for her?"

"Big deal. Two words, *Leave Belvista.*"

"She was knocked out. Weren't you at all concerned about her?"

"Somebody was there, creeping around. Whoever it was sneaked away when I checked on her. I stayed until she began to moan and come to. I saw she was okay." He tapped his chest. "I've got a heart."

"Did you see who was creeping around?"

"No." He gave a wry smile. "Figured it was just some creep."

"So you left her there alone."

Kelly shifted on the uncomfortable chair in the observation room. "So my tripping actually saved my life. That boat could have killed me."

"Look on the bright side," Sam said. "Ritter scared away Alex Bradford. I'm convinced Alex followed you there. That was him you caught a glimpse of at the gate. If Ritter had arrived a few minutes later, you wouldn't be sitting here. You'd be Alex's prisoner, in some hellhole."

Luke continued to fire away with questions. "Tell me, Ritter, who asked you to scare away Kelly Madison?"

"Hal Dunbar, who else? He's the big cheese in this town. He looks after us little cheeses."

"Why would he want to send away a woman he hardly knew?"

"She was poking her nose where it didn't belong. She and that sister of hers are bad for business. They could've given people the idea that Belvista was a dangerous place. Hal Dunbar has big plans for the town." Ritter motioned Luke closer. "I'll let you in on something, if you'll forget about that boat accident."

Luke smiled. "Forgive and forget—that's my motto."

"Hal Dunbar's going ahead with his plans to build an auto-service complex behind the cattail marshes. He's going to make a fortune from the maxi-mall traffic. Pumps. Car wash. Auto repairs. Mechanics up the ying-yang. I'm going to be the head watchman during the construction." He hooked his thumbs into his belt loops and sat back.

Luke leaned into the hallway. "Chief Clemmens," he said, "send in Dunbar."

"I PASSED JAMES RITTER on his way out," Hal Dunbar said, brushing past Luke and settling himself in his chair in the interrogation room. "Ritter can't be trusted. Drink exaggerates his stories. Ha! The last fish that got away from him wouldn't fit in this room."

"Very funny, Mr. Dunbar, but this isn't about James Ritter."

"That's a relief!" Dunbar's breath whistled through his teeth. "I was afraid you thought Ritter and I were friends. He might have said some things that would make you think that. But it's not true."

Luke paced behind Dunbar's chair. "I asked you to come by so I could apologize for being brusque with you at times. But also because I need your help."

"Apologies accepted, and I'm glad to do my civic duty," Dunbar said.

"I'm still feeling my way around this job and this town. I'm trying to get a handle on the relationship between the town council and Belvista's business owners." He leaned close as if to confide a secret. "I want to protect the interests of men like yourself in case of fraud. But the malarkey of petitions has me confused. Everyone tells me you're the man to ask."

"Fire away! I attend every council meeting, and I do business with most of the people in Belvista."

"So I've noticed," Luke said, and he dropped several folders onto the table. "I've been reviewing the town council's minutes, and I see several petitions signed by you and Henry Erdlinger. Seems like an ideal partnership."

"Sure is. He's got the capital, and I've got the land."

"So, you intend to build an auto-service center on the property behind the cattail marshes."

"That's right."

"Let's go back fifteen months. You and Henry Erdlinger petitioned the council to drain the marshes so that a mall can be built."

"A maxi-mall. Right."

Luke opened a folder and ran a finger halfway down the page. "I see you petitioned the town council, asking them to relinquish the city's right-of-way between your property and the cattail marshes."

"A road there will make it easier for visitors to get to my auto-service center."

Luke thumbed through several more pages. "I'm a city man. I can't make head nor tail of this."

Dunbar scrutinized the page. "Grass, Detective Campbell. Here in Belvista, the sun shines, and the grass grows. Then it needs to be cut. I offered to maintain the strip of land between the cattail marshes and my property until the city's easement is terminated and the land is officially ceded to me."

"Why, Mr. Dunbar, I wasn't aware of your grass-roots commitment. Not many men of your standing in the community are willing to dirty their hands pushing a lawn mower."

"Not me, personally. Look right here." He tapped the page. "I agreed to hire someone to maintain the lawn."

"And who was that?"

"Alex Bradford."

In the observation room, Kelly leaned close to Sam and whispered, "I thought Luke would never get around to Alex."

"Luke couldn't ask Dunbar outright about Alex," Sam said. "Dunbar has a big mouth. If Alex found out these interrogations centered on him, he might skip town and—"

"And let Meg starve to death."

Luke stopped pacing the length of the interrogation room and crossed his arms. "I thought Alex Bradford worked at a funeral home."

"He does. But apparently he shares my civic concerns. He began attending council meetings after the mall concept was introduced. He spoke to me privately and volunteered to maintain the property."

"That explains everything." Luke turned a page and ran a finger horizontally across the print. "At the next meeting, a council member thanked you and Alex Bradford. I couldn't figure why you and Alex would be mentioned in the same breath. You're so important. Alex is—"

"We are worlds apart. That was the first time we ever spoke. Since then, he mows, clips, whatever, and I stay out of his way. He's an odd duck, but a civic-minded duck."

"Thank you, Mr. Dunbar," Luke said.

"Luke sure played that to the hilt," Kelly commented to Sam as she stood up, eager to leave the cramped room.

Sam nodded. "Luke knows you can catch more flies with honey than vinegar."

"If only Alex Bradford would fall for such tactics," Kelly said wistfully.

THIRTY-FIVE

Father Shaunassey

"LET'S TALK ABOUT the Bradford family drownings," Luke said.

"That happened seven years ago." Father Shaunassey tugged his clerical collar away from his neck.

"According to Mrs. O'Rourke, the housekeeper at the rectory, you returned to the rectory the night before the Bradford funerals looking as if you'd seen a ghost. She says you were up all night, sick to your stomach."

"The sight of eight relatives lying in caskets..." Father Shaunassey wiped the lenses of his glasses with his handkerchief. "I'd never experienced anything like that."

"I think you have," Luke said calmly. "Belvista has known other disasters that took the lives of several family members." Luke checked his notepad. "The school-bus accident four years before the Bradford tragedy. A fire that swept through the Winwood Apartments two years later. Shall I go on?"

Father Shaunassey shook his head. "You've made your point."

Luke poured a glass of water and slid it toward Father Shaunassey. "Now, why don't you tell me what frightened you?"

Father Shaunassey took several quick swallows. "I visited Preston's Funeral Home late in the evening for a private goodbye with the deceased. I'm a frequent visitor. I have my own key. The caskets weren't in the receiving room, so I went to the preparation room."

He glanced up. "I expected to be alone, but I surprised Alex.

He spun around, eyes blazing. He held an empty sack in his hands. He was wearing surgical gloves and a rubber apron. All eight caskets were open. Right away I saw the dead kitten in each casket, lying across the deceased's chest."

"Did Alex say anything?"

"He said to keep my mouth shut or he'd tell the Monsignor lies."

"What kind of lies?"

"That I had abused him when he was a youngster." Father Shaunassey crooked his neck as if his collar were strangling him. "Alex can be very convincing. I couldn't let him jeopardize my life's work."

"So you kept quiet."

Father Shaunassey nodded. "Ever since then, Alex has tried to unnerve me during my sermons—jingling coins, rattling papers, dozens of little tortures. He's made a mockery of everything I hold dear."

"That will be all, Father. For now."

In the adjoining room, Kelly turned to Sam. "Officer Simpson said Alex brought home eight kittens the day his family drowned."

"Alex killed the kittens and put them into the coffins," Sam said. "That's why no one ever saw them again."

"Now I get it," Kelly said. "The Bradford family's footstones have matching symbols. I thought they were arrowheads. I was wrong. They're cats' whiskers. Why would Alex bury kittens with his family?"

"I don't know for sure," Sam replied. "But based on what I know about other predators, Alex is punishing his family for something they did to him."

"Chief Clemmens!" Luke called into the hallway.

"What's up?" The chief lumbered into the room.

"Send some men to Alex's old neighborhood. I want to interview the neighbors right away."

"Looks as if Luke is one step ahead of us," Kelly said.

THIRTY-SIX

Mrs. Antoinette Agressi

IN THE PRIVATE ROOM, Kelly and Sam leaned forward, curious about Mrs. Antoinette Agressi. They had never heard her name mentioned until now.

The plump woman with gray curls bustled into the interrogation room. "My dear departed Angelo would have a fit if he knew I were called here like a common criminal."

Luke offered her a chair. "Mrs. Agressi, I don't consider you a criminal, common or otherwise. I'm hoping you're a keen observer of your neighbors."

"If you have something on your mind, just ask me. 'Clear the air'—that's what my Angelo always said."

"Consider the air cleared, Mrs. Agressi. I need your help with an old case I'm working on. Think back eighteen years. A young boy about ten. A mother cat and her litter of eight. Does that ring a bell?"

Mrs. Agressi folded her hands and plopped them onto the table. "You're speaking of the Bradford family. Little Alex loved those kittens."

"What happened to them?"

"I don't know."

"What do you think happened to them?"

"I can't say."

"Can't…or won't?"

"Mr. Bradford told me never to mention those kittens."

Luke shook his head. "Come on. Mr. Bradford didn't boss around a strong-willed woman like you."

"Life is never simple, Detective Campbell. My Angelo worked for Mr. Bradford at his furniture store. Their best salesman. Citations all over the walls. One afternoon Mr. Bradford came to my house. He said if I ever mentioned those kittens, he would fire Angelo. He was mean enough. I knew he would carry out his threat."

"Mean?" Luke repeated. "A woman's life may depend on what you can tell me. Any details would be helpful."

Mrs. Agressi closed her eyes for several seconds as if to gather her thoughts. "For years I heard screams coming from that house."

"Alex was screaming?" Luke asked.

Mrs. Agressi nodded. "His father beat him. He beat Alex's mother too. I thought about reporting him to the police, but my Angelo told me to mind my own business." She sniffled. "My Angelo couldn't afford a cut in pay." We convinced ourselves that the other neighbors could report the beatings, but nobody did. It's that kind of neighborhood."

"What kind is that?"

"Hear no evil, see no evil, speak no evil."

Luke's mouth turned into a grim line. "Coming back to the kittens. You never mentioned them again?"

"Not until today, to you."

"Tell me about the kittens."

"I think Mr. Bradford got rid of them."

"Why?"

"Alex sobbed something about the marshes. Then he said, 'Nobody helped the kittens. Nobody helped me. They'll all be sorry.'"

In the private room, Sam and Kelly locked eyes.

"Years of abuse," Kelly said, "and years of silence from his mother and neighbors. What a deadly combination that turned out to be."

THIRTY-SEVEN

Greg Saunders

"MR. SAUNDERS, thanks for coming in," Luke said, and he pointed to a chair.

In the adjoining room, Kelly and Sam studied the artsy Saunders, wearing black jeans and a black silk shirt. His gelled hair, slicked into a ponytail, hung halfway down his back. He moved gracefully, like a dancer.

"I hear Meg Madison might have been abducted," Saunders said as he sat down.

"Where did you hear that?"

"My fiancée, Rita Duprey, heard it from her brother."

"You know Meg?"

"Not very well." He toyed with his dangling silver earring. "I talked to her a few times."

Luke put his hands on the table and leaned close. "She was seeing your friend, Michael Duprey."

"The way Michael tells it, he's seeing every beautiful woman in Belvista."

Luke dropped the photos of Meg onto the table. "How do you explain these?"

Greg lined up the photos, changing the order, then sat back. "I photographed Meg in St. Anne's Cemetery. She asked me to. She wanted to surprise Michael with them."

"Seems a bit ghoulish, don't you think?"

Greg shook his head. "No. Meg thought the macabre setting would give Michael's work a sharper edge. All that pink powder-puff stuff he pumped out? It was boring to anyone with a contemporary eye, including Meg. I suppose she wanted him to be successful—you know, more into the current scene."

"Like you," Luke said.

Greg shrugged off his smile.

In the observation room, Kelly said to Sam, "Luke told me that Greg Saunders and Michael Duprey are jealous of each other."

"I heard that too from the artists I interviewed when Meg went missing," Sam said. "Greg's jealousy could slant everything he says. I don't trust him. I don't think Luke does, either."

"Okay, Saunders, whose idea was it for her to pose in pajamas?" Luke asked.

"Meg's. She was thinking nighttime. She wanted Michael to paint the scene dark and foreboding." He glanced up at Luke. "I know what you're thinking. It looks creepy, as if someone is about to rise up from a grave. Or murder is about to be committed. But it's posed to give that impression. Look at Meg's makeup." He slid a photo toward Luke. "Black eyeliner, pale face powder. It's very artistic in a clichéd way. Sort of *Night of the Living Dead* meets *The Others*."

In the observation room, Kelly felt uncomfortable with this talk of death and cemeteries. She'd been so startled by the photos that she hadn't even realized that Meg was wearing stagy makeup, but Saunders was right.

"Did you and Meg leave the cemetery together?" Luke asked as he picked up the photos.

"Yes. I drove her back to my place. She changed into jeans, and I dropped her at Pruitt's Inn."

"What happened to the pajamas she was wearing in the photos?"

"She took them with her in a bag."

"Was that the last time you saw her?"

"Yes."

Luke paced but never took his eyes off Saunders. "Did Meg mention her plans for the evening?"

Saunders nodded. "She was going somewhere with Michael. She didn't say where."

Luke stopped pacing and crossed his arms over his chest. "Did you ever see the pajamas again?"

"No." Saunders shot Luke a quizzical expression. "You think I have a pajama fetish? Puh-leeze."

"Whose idea was it for Meg to hold a handful of daisies?"

"Meg's. I suggested a single rose and a black negligee. But, no, she goes for schoolgirl pajamas with daisy trim, and she holds field daisies. Oooh-la-la! Really over-the-edge, daring stuff!" He massaged his temples dramatically as if to ease a migraine.

"What time was it when you took her to Pruitt's Inn?" Luke asked.

He pushed up the cuff of his shirt. "I don't wear a watch. I live by instinct."

Luke sneered. "Just tell me what time it was."

"Sometime between five and six-thirty."

Luke frowned. "Why didn't you give the photos to Duprey? That's what you say you promised Meg."

Greg steepled his fingers and seemed to be searching for words.

"What I'm thinking," Luke said, "is you didn't want Duprey to have them. You thought he could paint something great with them. It was all about jealousy, wasn't it?"

Greg opened his mouth to speak, but Luke beat him to it.

"You can go, Saunders, but I strongly suggest you don't leave town until you hear from me."

THIRTY-EIGHT

The Bus Station

L<small>UKE CAME INTO</small> the observation room. "Kelly, I'd like you to take a half-hour break."

"But I don't want to miss anything," Kelly said.

"This is awkward," Luke said. "My men want to discuss sensitive issues about the case, and—"

"Okay."

Luke gave Sam a knowing glance.

"I'll stay with Kelly in the courtyard," Sam said. "We could both use some fresh air."

"Don't wander off," Luke warned.

W<small>ALKING WITH</small> K<small>ELLY</small> toward a bench, Sam pulled out his cell phone. "Hazie Moon left a message. She says it's an emergency." His voice was agitated. "It must be about last night."

Kelly stopped short. "What happened?"

"Jeff Traskell, the guy whose email she found about the Cinderellas, attacked her."

"Oh, no. Was she hurt? Is she okay?"

Sam ignored her questions and punched in numbers. After a hasty "What's up?" he said, "She's right here," and he passed the phone to Kelly.

Hazie spoke rapidly. "I'm at the bus station with the Muffin Men. My bus leaves in ten minutes. Come right away. I found something of Meg's. I want you to have it."

"What did you find?" Kelly asked, startled by the unexpected news. "Is it—?"

"Hurry!" Hazie cut in. "And don't bring the police with you!" The phone went dead.

Kelly tugged at Sam's elbow. "Come on. We need a plain-clothes detective right away."

"Tell me what Hazie said."

"No time now." Kelly ran into the police station and nearly crashed into Detective Andy Quinn. "Detective! Come with Sam and me. Hurry!"

"What's the matter?"

"Hazie…at the bus station…she has something of Meg's. She said no police. Her bus is about to leave."

In a whirlwind, Detective Quinn rushed Kelly and Sam to his beat-up Chevy, pulled out his cell phone, and cleared everything with Luke. "Don't worry, Luke. She'll never be out of my sight. Sam either." Five minutes later they roared into the bus-station parking area. They hopped out and plowed through the crowds toward the buses.

Jittery, Kelly looked around, knowing this was where the kidnapper most likely found his victims. She didn't see Alex or any officers or anyone familiar who might be the undercover policewoman Luke had assigned to the area. She was glad to have Detective Quinn on one side of her and Sam on the other.

"I can't believe the crowds," Kelly said, struggling against an onslaught of rambunctious teenagers lugging suitcases and musical instruments.

"Midweek special for New Jersey marching bands competition," Sam said, steering clear of a tuba. "I read about it in the *Bugle*."

"There's Hazie." Kelly pointed to one of the buses in the departure area. "Detective Quinn, don't let on—"

"I know how to play this," the detective said. "Go, collect what she has of Meg's. Don't do anything crazy. You either, Sam."

Kelly and Sam willingly agreed.

Taking Sam's hand, Kelly skirted around the crowd and hurried toward Hazie. Detective Quinn stayed close. Bob and

Bill, the Muffin Men, stood guard on either side of Hazie. They gave friendly hellos, but their eyes darted in all directions, obviously on the lookout for trouble.

People were loading onto the bus.

"I had just about given up on you," Hazie greeted Kelly and Sam. She reached into her backpack and pulled out a camera.

Kelly stared in disbelief. Meg's digital camera!

"Where did you find it?" Kelly asked.

"At the café. On a shelf in Mom's consultation room. Mom remembered Meg having it. Meg must have set it on the shelf when she had her fortune told."

"All aboard!" the bus driver shouted.

From the corner of her eye, Kelly saw Detective Quinn. He was pretending to read a bus schedule.

Hazie plowed on. "The camera got shoved to the back, along with everything else. I went looking for my favorite book of poetry this morning. That's when I found the camera. I tried to call you and Sam."

"Our phones were turned off," Kelly said.

Hazie patted the camera. "I figure whatever or whoever Meg photographed might lead you to her."

"Thank you," Kelly said, fighting back tears of gratitude. She carefully put the camera into her purse.

When Hazie turned to check on the bus, Kelly saw several bruises on her neck. "Sam said Jeff Traskell attacked you. Are you okay? Those bruises look painful."

Bill punched a fist into his hand. "He's going to pay for hurting our Hazie."

"Hazie, please tell me what happened," Kelly said.

"That jerk Jeff sneaked up on me in the college parking lot," Hazie began. "He said 'I know you have my email. I want it.' I played dumb. Before I knew what happened, Jeff had his hands wrapped around my throat, squeezing hard, blabbing something about the Cinderellas. I gave him a karate chop to the rib cage and left him yelping in pain with my laughter ringing in his ears."

The bus driver honked the horn and pointed at Hazie.

"One minute!" Hazie called out.

"Did you report it to the campus police?" Kelly asked. She saw Detective Quinn fold up his bus schedule.

"No, I told Mom. She decided I should leave town until all this Cinderella stuff blows over. Mom's afraid I can't take care of myself." Hazie rolled her eyes. "What planet is she living on? I'm going to my Aunt Trudie's on Long Island. She's a poet. She's cool."

Bill flexed his muscles. "Bob and I are going to have a little chat with Jeffie boy."

Hazie stepped toward the bus. "Kelly, let me know what Meg photographed. After all, I'm not clairvoyant."

"Good luck," Kelly said, and she hugged Hazie good-bye.

Kelly and Sam headed toward the parking area. Detective Quinn was close on their heels. "Who knows what Meg's camera will reveal?" he said. "This makes my day."

"Mine too," Kelly said. She stepped off the pavement onto the grass to let dozens of teenage musicians pass by. A car horn beeped several times. Kelly looked toward where the sound was coming from. She froze. "Detective Quinn, there's a black Lexus with tinted windows parked across the street, wedged between two SUVs."

The Lexus was backing up, trying to pull out. Kelly gripped the detective's arm. "We can't miss this chance to find out who the driver is."

"Kelly, Sam, I can't leave you on your own. Stay close to me," Detective Quinn said sternly. "All I want is the license plate number. We'll be real casual, get the job done, and leave without calling attention to ourselves. Anything else and he might bolt. Need I remind you, Meg's life is at stake." He speed-dialed his cell phone. "Luke, a black Lexus with tinted windows is leaving the bus station, south side. I hope to get the license. Send a squad car. No sirens. Stop the Lexus for a broken taillight, whatever. With luck, we can find out who the driver is without tipping our hand."

Heart pounding, Kelly linked arms with Sam and strode across the street behind Detective Quinn. They were approaching the Lexus when a wave of teenagers rushed by. Detective Quinn, Kelly, and Sam stopped short. The Lexus' horn blared. The teenagers jumped away, whooping and shaking their fists at the driver. The car jolted to a stop. The window rolled down.

Her breath coming at a dizzying speed, Kelly steeled herself and didn't move.

"Miss, I could use some help" came a man's voice from the car.

"Okay, sir." Kelly crouched and found herself face-to-face with the driver. It wasn't Alex. It was the director of St. Anne's Cemetery.

"Miss, please tell those kids to get out of my way," the man said impatiently. He didn't give any hint that he recognized her.

"Sure thing," Kelly said, feeling Detective Quinn's breath on her neck. Willing herself to stay calm, she shooed the teenagers away.

Kelly wanted to scream, "Where's Meg?" but Detective Quinn shot her a warning glance. "Have a nice day," she said.

"You too." The man forced a smile. "Teenagers," he muttered as the window rolled up.

Kelly stood rooted to the spot, trembling from head to toe as the Lexus bolted ahead. Detective Quinn was scribbling the license plate number in his notepad. Kelly caught a glimpse of the car as it pulled away. It wasn't a New Jersey plate. It was from Maryland.

"That was too close for comfort," Sam said, and he exhaled loudly.

Detective Quinn quickly called Luke. "Cancel the squad car. Do *not* intercept the Lexus. I'll explain when I see you."

"That was nice work, Kelly," Detective Quinn said. "Both of you stayed cool under pressure. My blood pressure is probably off the charts."

"I don't know that man's name," Kelly said, "but I saw him in church talking to Alex and again at the cemetery. Alex said he was the director of St. Anne's cemetery. He gave a thumbs-up to Alex. I assumed that was for Alex's meticulous preparation of the grave. But maybe he was approving the next victim. Me!"

Detective Quinn steered Sam and Kelly toward his car. "I'm betting this is the Lexus in Greg Saunders' photos taken at St. Anne's Cemetery."

Kelly hurried to keep up. "Maybe this man and Alex Bradford are both involved in the kidnappings. Greg Saunders could be in on it too." The possibilities made her head spin.

Detective Quinn opened his car door, and Sam and Kelly hopped into the backseat. "Luke needs to hear about this," he said, and he plunked down in the front seat. "I'll call him." He speed-dialed again, ran lots of details past Luke, then passed his phone to Kelly. "Luke wants to speak to you," he said. "I'll drive while you talk."

"Alex isn't the only kidnapper," Kelly said. "Alex has an accomplice. He's the director of—"

"Detective Quinn told me everything," Luke said. "I just wanted to hear from you that you're okay."

"I'm okay."

"I'm not," Luke said.

"What's wrong?"

"I'm thinking about what could have happened. I'm a candidate for a heart attack."

"See you in five minutes."

"I'll be on a stretcher, getting CPR."

THIRTY-NINE

A New Direction

DETECTIVE QUINN PULLED INTO the police station parking lot. He took the camera from Kelly and rushed it into the station. As Kelly and Sam got out of the car, Luke strode toward them.

"I want to thank you both for bringing in Meg's camera," Luke said. "It's sure to help us find her. And thanks for following Detective Quinn's every word. That whole scene with the Lexus could have gotten messy." He shook Sam's hand. "From the day you arrived in Belvista, you tried to cut through the Cinderella crap and get this case re-opened. I appreciate that. I know you kept things from me and encouraged Kelly to keep secrets too, but I understand your reasons. You were protecting Hazie and her mother. None of you had confidence in the police department. I want to work on changing that, but it will take time. For now, I'd like you to stick around and continue to help with this case. Can I count on you?"

"You bet," Sam said.

"Good."

"I made mistakes," Kelly said, "and I'm sorry."

"This entire case has been riddled with mistakes by many people," Luke said. "I include myself. From now on, let's all agree to do what's best for Meg."

Luke took Kelly's hands in his.

She gazed into his eyes. "How's your heart?"

He smiled. "It skipped a few beats, but it's still ticking."

"Good."

"Jeannie Wilkins gave me mouth-to-mouth resuscitation.

That worked like a charm," Luke said, and Kelly swatted him with her purse.

Detective Quinn rushed into the parking lot. "The Lexus belongs to John Grant, the director of St. Anne's Cemetery. He manages a string of cemeteries in New Jersey, Delaware, and—"

"Maryland," Luke cut in. "That explains the Maryland license plate. Good work, Quinn."

"Thanks. I'm going to tail Grant and find out where he goes, what he does, who he knows."

"I'll free up two officers—your choice—to look into Grant's whereabouts when the other women went missing." He patted Quinn on the back. "We've got to move fast on this." He pointed toward the police station, and everyone headed that way. "The dead women's clothes are in Alex's house. Alex obviously put them there. Grant could be an accomplice or the mastermind. I want his phone records, computer, the works."

"I'd like to contact local authorities in the towns where Grant has cemeteries," Quinn said. "They can fax us info about graves dug during the months the women went missing. Grant could have transported the bodies there. It's a long shot. Lots of risks for Grant, but—"

"Get right on it," Luke said.

"May I offer an opinion?" Sam asked, walking by Luke's side.

"Go ahead," Luke said.

"Sexual predators work alone. I'm convinced we're looking for a sexual predator, since the victims are all pretty young women. In all my research, I never found a partnership. Serial killers can come in pairs—Bonnie and Clyde, Leopold and Loeb, and so on—but not sexual predators."

Kelly fought back her tears. *Sexual predator.* She hadn't allowed herself to think in those terms. My God. Meg at the hands of...

"We made duplicates of the disk from Meg's camera," Detective Jessup called from the steps. "We uploaded it onto your computer, Luke. We're ready to roll."

"Let's go see what Meg photographed," Luke said.

EVERYONE GATHERED AROUND the computer monitor in Luke's office. One by one, the people and places that Meg had captured on camera appeared.

"That's the Mariners' Museum," Jones called out.

"That's the library," Smith said.

The Belvista officers identified every setting, building, and landmark. Kelly recognized Pruitt's Inn and the cattail marshes. When a shot of Michael Duprey painting in the marshes appeared, several officers booed. Photo after photo rolled by, many of the beach and park. Several featured people they all recognized: Tim Ramsey, Benny and Justine Pruitt, and Michael Duprey outside his studio with other artists. Greg Saunders stood in the center of the group, smiling.

"There's the boardwalk," Luke said. "Finally, a crowd scene." He took off his glasses and wiped them on the front of his shirt. "Let's look at faces and cars." He put his glasses back on. "Come on, Meg," he encouraged, "give us something to work with."

Scenes of the boardwalk rolled by.

"Stop," Luke said, leaning forward. "Enlarge that one."

Kelly peered at a row of cafés, wondering what he had seen.

"There he is!" Luke exclaimed. "That's Alex Bradford, plain as day, lurking in that doorway."

"He was stalking Meg," Sam said.

More photos passed by. "Let's see that one again," Luke said. Kelly recognized Dunbar's Department Store on the boardwalk. "It's Greg Saunders," Luke said, peering closely. "That's Saunders' reflection in the window. Quite a coincidence." Luke nodded to one of the officers. "Smith, tail Saunders, and don't lose him!"

As the last photos came up, Officer Jones said, "I didn't see the cemetery guy, John Grant, or his car, in any of the shots."

"Let's make sure of that," Luke said. "Go through them again, Officer Simpson. Find something for us. Don't overlook the obvious. Could be Alex Bradford borrowed Grant's car."

Luke checked his watch. "Okay, everybody, until Detective Quinn comes in with the goods on Grant, it's time to go back to where we were, focused on Alex Bradford but open to any possibility. Let's hustle."

FORTY

Closing In

EVERYONE MOVED TO THE conference room, and Luke got right to business. "Before we review our plan to trap Bradford, I'd like to hear what you found out while I was conducting interviews."

Time flew as they gave their reports, ending with Detective Jessup. "I didn't find anything unusual in the cattail marshes," he said. "The clam boat was right where you said it was. There was no sign of digging. And no hiding place where Bradford could keep a prisoner."

"First thing tomorrow, we'll look at the area that abuts the cattail marshes on the north. That's the piece the city has a right-of-way on. Dunbar wants it ceded to him. I want to see what Bradford is landscaping there and why." Luke raked his fingers through his hair. "Good work, everyone. Nothing came up to change our minds, but we have lots of paperwork to please County Chief Prosecutor Attenborough. Bradford is the man we're after."

Luke glanced out the window at the darkening sky. "I'm wagering Bradford will get itchy to visit Meg. Isn't that the way it works, Sam?"

Sam nodded. "Sexual predators have compulsions and rituals." He looked from one detective to the next. "They repeat them with each new victim. They will do anything to keep the vicious cycle going. Naturally, they prefer moving about under the cover of darkness. He'll make his move soon."

The words sent a chill through Kelly. Sam wasn't holding

back anything. There wasn't time. A confrontation with Alex Bradford was close at hand.

"Let me review our plan to trap Bradford," Luke said. "He knows Kelly will be at St. Anne's Church hall tonight for the covered-dish supper. She told him so. Originally, she intended to question the guests about Meg. We can skip that now. I don't want Kelly wandering from my side. As many of us as possible will be there too. Once Bradford leaves his house, Detectives Waters and Jessup will follow. If he stops off at St. Anne's to check on Kelly's whereabouts, they'll keep their distance until he's on the move again. Then I'll send reinforcements. Bradford might double back, so some of us will stay at the hall." Luke looked at Kelly. "Bradford will be followed every step of the way. He'll lead us to Meg. We'll get him. Meg will be free very soon."

There were a few questions and suggestions. Then there was an uneasy silence.

"What if...?" Kelly's voice trembled.

Luke spoke for her. "What if Bradford decides to kidnap you and Jeannie before he visits Meg?"

Kelly fought the fear that gripped her. "Do you think he would come for us at St. Anne's?"

"His mind is so twisted, he might. It could be one more way of getting back at Father Shaunassey. But if he looks in and sees all of us at the potluck supper, enjoying casseroles, cake, and pie, as if nothing unusual is expected, he may go to Meg and come for you later. We'll be ready for anything."

Kelly's jaw dropped. "Cake and pie! In his note, the kidnapper said we'd come to him 'easy as pie'!"

"How did I miss that?" Sam clapped the heel of a hand against his forehead. "Bradford dropped that clue intentionally."

"Why would he do that?" Detective Ryan asked.

"He's challenging us," Sam explained. "He's convinced he can get away with anything, so he'll try anything. Do not—I repeat—do not underestimate this murderer."

"He's only one man," Luke said. "We're a team. And, believe me, he's met his match!"

"If he comes," Kelly pleaded, "let him kidnap me. He'll lead you straight to Meg."

"We've been over this a dozen times," Luke said. "It's too dangerous. If he lays a hand on you, we'll arrest him on the spot. Do I make myself clear?"

Kelly nodded her agreement, but her thoughts were racing. *Meg. Meg. Meg.* Her sister's name echoed through her mind.

FORTY-ONE

St. Anne's Hall

KELLY SAT AT A TABLE with Luke and three officers and their wives in St. Anne's Church hall. She'd been pretending to have a good time, but her nerves were frayed. Detective Andy Quinn and his team were still working the John Grant angle and were tailing him. Grant had been out of state at his other cemeteries when the first three women disappeared. Now the detectives were investigating where he was when Meg went missing. Detectives Waters and Jessup were watching Alex Bradford's house. So far, Alex was staying put. Officers were tracking Duprey and Saunders, but they hadn't reported anything suspicious.

Luke's cell phone rang. "Quinn, what have you got?" Luke listened intently. "Could be something. Thanks." He clicked his phone shut. "Quinn found out that Grant's been married three times. Divorces, no murders," he said as if reading everyone's mind. "But Quinn found out that Grant has a lady friend in town. With a black eye. Seems Grant plays rough. She told Quinn his first two wives had threatened to file assault charges but never did."

"So Grant could be involved in Meg's disappearance?" Kelly asked.

"Could be, but my men finished scrutinizing Meg's photos. Grant didn't show up."

Officer Browning piped up. "My guess? Grant lets Bradford catch the women, bring them to him, and keep the clothes as souvenirs. Then Grant takes over."

"That's enough, Browning," Luke said firmly.

Luke's phone rang again. "Quinn? You have something?" His brow furrowed with worry. "Stay on it."

"What did he tell you this time?" Kelly asked, preparing herself for the worst.

"Grant is at his Wednesday night poker game. Quinn's team is watching and waiting. Quinn searched Grant's car and found a notebook filled with poems. Grant wrote and dated them. One says something like 'when the daisies turn the hillsides white.' There are daisies in several poems."

Kelly gasped. "Grant is involved!"

"We don't know for sure," Luke said. He leaned across the table toward Browning, Delgato, and Rendell. "Go tell Quinn's news to the other officers. Let them know we're staying right here as planned until Bradford makes a move."

Kelly watched the officers go from table to table. She felt the tension in the room. Theories were flying around. There was the eerie feeling that something was about to happen... and it wouldn't be good.

Father Shaunassey came to the microphone. "The talent show will begin in ten minutes," he said nervously. The lights were turned up, causing him to squint. "Performers, please report to the reception table."

A flurry of activity followed his words. Girls in sparkly costumes carrying batons rushed from their tables. What a hoopla! Dozens of performers. Tap shoes. Harmonicas. Magicians. Jugglers.

"I'll be right back," Kelly said. "I need to use the restroom."

"Lock yourself in." Luke's hand lingered on hers. "And hurry back."

As Kelly walked toward the restroom, she looked over her shoulder. Luke was headed toward Jeannie and Detective Ryan. They had positioned themselves at the front door, where the reception-committee women were briskly selling tickets for a cake raffle.

The talent-contest winners were noisily crowding toward

the reception table. Parents hurried after their children, giving last-minute advice. Several men struggled to push the piano toward the makeshift stage.

As she passed the kitchen, Kelly nodded to Detective Abbott. He was chatting with the brigade of casserole women. He poised his fork midair, eager to dig into the macaroni dripping with cheese, and saluted her. Kelly was tempted to take a cup of coffee to Officers Simpson and Jones, who were stationed outside, but she had promised Luke to stay indoors, where she would be safe.

Father Shaunassey's voice blasted from the microphone. "Five minutes to show time!" He sounded awkward, unaccustomed to being the master of ceremonies.

Alone in the restroom, Kelly locked the door behind her. She stepped across the drainage grating, careful not to catch the heel of her boot. Above her right shoulder was the only window in the room. It contained a single panel of frosted glass. It was too small for anyone to climb through.

The unsettling feeling came over Kelly that Alex Bradford was hiding in one of the three stalls. She pulled her cell phone from her purse, just in case. She crept forward, bent down, and peered along the floor. She held her breath, expecting to see Alex's boots. But the stalls were empty.

To calm down, Kelly walked to the sink, set down her phone, and splashed cold water onto her face. A soft clicking noise sent chills up her spine. She jerked around and stared at the stalls. Could Alex be standing on a toilet seat? She pushed each door back slowly. Her breath quickened. Nothing. Only her imagination.

Another noise, muffled, dull. The utility closet. Alex could be hiding in there. She tiptoed toward the door. She tried to turn the knob, but it was locked.

She exhaled. Locked. Thank God.

Kelly paused in front of the mirror. She checked to see that her honey-colored top was neatly tucked into her matching tiered skirt. Then again, that same soft clicking sound. Directly behind her. In the mirror, she thought she saw the utility closet doorknob turn. She spun around. The door flew open.

"Good evening, Kelly," Alex said. "I've been waiting for you." He lunged toward her and clamped a hand over her mouth. Reaching for her phone, she felt the sting of a needle in her arm.

"Help!" she screamed, but the word was only in her head. She sank into blackness.

FORTY-TWO

Captured

THROUGH THE COBWEBS that floated in and out of her mind, Kelly tried to focus on her surroundings. Thick darkness whirled against the windows as she lay on the floor of a car, behind the driver's seat. Alex's voice pierced through the engine's hum.

"Terrible music," he muttered, and he changed the radio station. The car rattled as it raced along a bumpy road.

Kelly had no idea what time it was or where she was headed or how far she had traveled from St. Anne's Church. She had to stay calm. Figure things out. The car veered left and right, time and time again. The potholes were bad, like those on Hospital Road. She caught a glimpse of dim stars and a pale snippet of moon. There was no sound of traffic. They must be on a lonely country road.

Kelly tried to raise herself, but grogginess kept her rooted to the floor. Her head ached. Tape bound her wrists together. A handkerchief was pulled so tightly across her mouth, she couldn't wedge her fingers underneath to pry it loose. Kelly saw the outline of Alex's features as he glanced over his shoulder. She held her breath and kept still. There was no one in the passenger seat. Maybe John Grant was waiting for them wherever they were going.

Kelly looked to her right. Jeannie wasn't in the car. Alex had said in his poem that he would capture two women. Kelly prayed that Jeannie was safe at St. Anne's. But maybe Alex had kidnapped Jeannie too. He could have already hidden her somewhere.

Alex veered to the left. Picking up speed, the car veered right. Two more right turns, and the car slowed. The thin slice of moon dipped below feathery clouds. She heard dull thuds. Something brushed by, bouncing against the side of the car. Cattail stalks! Alex was driving on the road beside the cattail marshes. There were no streetlights. No cars. No one. She was all alone. Except for Alex. She had to think and act fast.

Kelly groped beneath the blanket that covered her. Her purse lay near her knees. As the car slowed to a snail's pace, Kelly knew that Alex was heading toward the picnic tables. The road ended there.

Kelly fumbled with the clasp of her purse and guided it open. She had to get her cell phone. She searched frantically. Gone. Alex must have taken it. *Don't panic.* She searched her purse again. Her fingers felt her sewing kit's cross-stitched daisies. Unfastening the snap, she withdrew both scissors. Her eyes glued to the back of Alex's head, she struggled up. She tried to tuck the scissors into the top of her left boot.

One pair of scissors slipped. Landed on the carpet. A muffled noise. Alex looked over his shoulder. She held her breath. He turned to the front again. Kelly groped for the scissors. Found them. Moved both pairs to the top of her boot. Her heart pounded. The tips of the first pair of scissors slid inside her boot and rested snugly against her anklebone.

"Not that song again," Alex muttered. As the car slowed, Kelly rammed the second pair of scissors into her boot.

Alex parked in the grove of maples behind the picnic tables. He climbed out and yanked open the back door. He pulled the blanket off Kelly, tossed her purse into his sack, and pulled her to her feet. She stumbled.

"Shall we visit Meg?" he asked, his voice smooth as satin.

Kelly breathed deeply, trying to clear her head. She wondered how long it had taken Luke to notice that she was gone. Had he seen Alex? Were he and the detectives following? She listened. No sounds of car engines.

"I asked you a question," Alex murmured.

Kelly nodded, staggering, still woozy from whatever drug he'd injected her with.

"Good," he said, and he pulled her toward the thick, tangled underbrush.

Think hard. A delay would improve Luke's chances of finding her. Kelly pulled away, clenching her hands into a single fist. She pummeled Alex's chest.

"It's no use," Alex said. "You're no match for me. None of you are." He grabbed Kelly around the waist. She tried to struggle free but was too weak.

Alex pushed Kelly forward. He ducked beneath a maple tree and rolled back a torn section of a chain-link fence. "Crawl!" Alex ordered. He pushed her to the ground.

Hands bound, Kelly crawled awkwardly through the opening.

"Stop right there!"

Kelly looked over her shoulder. Alex was pulling the torn section of fence back into position. It was close to the shortest maple tree. That must be how he'd located it so quickly in the dark.

Still on her hands and knees, Kelly moved her left ankle. The scissors were still there, but she was too weak to use them. And what if she were to kill Alex? She might never find out where Meg was imprisoned. *Be patient. Find Meg, then attack Alex.* She crawled forward, telling herself that soon she would be stronger. Strong enough to wound Alex and rescue Meg. But what if John Grant was with Meg? How could she overcome two men? Panic gripped her.

"On your feet!" Alex ordered.

Fear rose in Kelly's throat as Alex roughly helped her rise and prodded her along. Luke had had his suspicions about this section of property, but on such a dark night, he wouldn't see the torn fence. Alex had her purse. She had no compact to leave behind as a clue. No scarf or beret she could drop on the ground. Like the other missing women, she would disappear without a trace. No. Not true. She had an advantage. She knew a great deal about Alex that the other women didn't. But could it save her? Would it save Meg?

She must now be standing on Hal Dunbar's property. She peered into the darkness as Alex kept prodding her along. It seemed as if they walked for miles. Was she imagining things? There, a short distance away, the turrets and pitched roof of a house materialized. Wooden planks crisscrossed the windows. The spooky house must be abandoned. It sent shivers of fear through her.

"Home, sweet home," Alex said as he took a key ring from his pocket. He unlocked the back door and pushed Kelly inside. He took a flashlight from a hook by the door and switched it on. A beam of light shot out. Eerie shadows raced through the empty rooms, chasing a pair of squeaking mice into a hole in the baseboard. "Home at last," Alex said, and he untied her gag.

Kelly spun toward him. "Where is my sister?"

Alex grasped Kelly under the chin, pressing against her windpipe. "I'll tell you when you may speak. Do you understand?"

Kelly's knees buckled. "Yes," she rasped.

"Good. Now you may visit Meg." He inserted the largest of the three keys into a lock, and the cellar door creaked open. Rickety wooden stairs descended into a black cavity. Kelly heard the door slam shut behind her.

She turned quickly, intending to claw Alex's eyes. He grabbed her arm. "Don't you dare touch me," he said. His eyes flashed mere inches from hers.

Kelly descended the stairs, gripping the railing, stumbling and tripping over the hem of her skirt. The stone foundation and stone floor loomed ominously. The acrid, musty air stung her nostrils. She fought back tears as her courage slipped away.

At the bottom step, Alex yanked Kelly to his side and led her toward the far wall. The arc of light traveled across the room, illuminating what appeared to be a dull gray-brown wall. Then Kelly realized she was looking at tattered blankets, covered with spider webs and dust, hanging side by side from lengths of clothesline stretched across the width of the cellar.

Alex ducked beneath one of the blankets, dragging Kelly with him. Another blanket. Another. Four, five, six blankets flapped in Kelly's face. When she could finally stand, she faced a long brick-and-mortar wall. Directly ahead lay a double-wide wooden door barricaded with a plank that slipped through a handle.

Alex lifted the plank, and the door swung toward them. Kelly covered her mouth to stifle her scream. There was Meg! My God, what had Alex done to her?

FORTY-THREE

Meg

MEG WAS CROUCHED in a damp, windowless room the size of a garage. A single lightbulb dangled on a cord attached to a crossbeam. She was ghostly pale, disheveled, glassy-eyed. Her pajamas were streaked with dirt.

"Meg!" Kelly cried, but Meg didn't respond.

Meg shielded her eyes from the flashlight beam. Her handcuffs glistened. A chain ran from her handcuffs to a pole sunk into a slab of concrete in the middle of the room.

"Meg!" Kelly cried again. She shuddered at the gruesome sight behind Meg. Light flickered off pet dishes, duct tape, and handcuffs that lined the shelves of a utility cabinet missing its doors. Cameras and boxes of film sat on a table near the cabinet. A hospital gurney was shoved into a corner. Beyond the lightbulb's eerie glow lay shadowy darkness.

"Hello, Meg," Alex said softly.

"Hello," Meg murmured. "May I have some water, please?"

Tears welled in Kelly's eyes.

Alex pulled a water jug from somewhere in the darkened corner. Kelly recognized the jug. Alex had dozens just like it in his garage.

In the split second that passed while Alex glanced away, Kelly saw Meg's dead eyes come to life. Was she imagining a hint of the defiant Meg she knew? Alex looked up, and the dullness quickly returned to Meg's eyes.

"Ready," Meg said, and she held out her hands, cupping them. Alex poured water into her hands, and Meg drank greedily.

"Thank you," she said sweetly. "Kelly," she murmured. Droplets of water glistened on her cracked lips. "We must obey him."

"Help!" Kelly screamed. "Help!"

"Scream all you want." Alex smiled. "No one will hear you. These walls silence everything." He patted a wall, then slapped dirt off his hands.

Kelly realized that the walls, ceiling, and floor were composed of dirt.

"No one knows about this old root cellar except me," Alex said proudly.

Kelly gathered her courage. "Not even Mr. Grant, your partner in crime?"

"Partner?" Alex's eyes filled with fury. "This is my plan! If you mention the word *partner* again, I'll—" He grabbed Kelly around the throat. "Do you understand?"

"Yes," Kelly said, wincing with pain. Now she knew for certain, Alex was doing this all by himself. She might be able to wound one man. Two, impossible.

Alex turned toward Meg. "Tell Kelly our plan."

Meg slunk to the floor and rested her back against the wall. Her pajama top hung loosely from her shoulders. Kelly could see that in three weeks of captivity Meg had lost ten to fifteen pounds.

"My sweet Kelly," Meg said. "Now that he has brought you home, I'm going away, and you'll take my place."

Alex withdrew his key ring and dangled it in front of Kelly. "We must prepare."

Kelly lunged for the key ring, straining at the tape that cut into her wrists.

Alex shoved her to the floor. "Wait in the corner." He set a camera on the gurney.

Time was running out. Kelly knew she must seize the opportunity and act. Quickly.

Kelly tensed every muscle in her body. *Ready*.

Alex unlocked Meg's handcuffs.

Kelly took a deep breath. *Soon. Very soon.*
Alex knelt next to the pole and unhooked her chain.
Now! Kelly screamed to herself.

FORTY-FOUR

Escape

KELLY REACHED into her boot. Scissors in each hand, she dove for Alex's face. Blood spurted from his cheeks. "Run, Meg!"

Meg cringed, her eyes wide with terror.

Wildly, Kelly stabbed Alex again and again. She got him. Chin, neck, shoulder, chest. "Run!"

Alex howled and fell to the floor. Writhing in pain, screaming, he pulled out the scissors. Staggering to his feet, arms flailing, he tripped over the table and fell into the cabinet. Handcuffs, duct tape, everything flew from the shelves and hit the earthen floor.

Kelly grabbed Meg's hand and shoved her toward the door. "Hurry, Meg." Tripping and stumbling, trying to avoid the jumble of things on the floor, Kelly saw her scissors near the cabinet. Staying clear of Alex, terrified he might spring up at her, she scooped them up and went back to Meg. "Cut me free," she ordered.

Meg, dazed and disoriented, took the scissors. With trembling hands, she worked the blade back and forth across the tape that bound Kelly's hands. "Try harder," Kelly pleaded, arching her fingers away from the blade.

The tape ripped, and Kelly's hands broke free. She grabbed the flashlight and key ring. In what seemed like one seamless motion, she struggled to the door, opened it, pulled Meg through, slammed the door shut, and shoved the plank into the holder. She flicked on the flashlight.

Meg collapsed against Kelly, covering her face with kisses. Kelly hugged her and burst into tears. "Thank God you're alive."

Meg sobbed. "He said he was going to kidnap you. I couldn't stop him."

"You're safe now. That's all that matters." Kelly longed to console Meg, but she saw the toll the imprisonment had taken. She grabbed a blanket from the line, shook it, and wrapped it around Meg's fragile body. "We need to get you to a doctor."

Swinging the flashlight beam back and forth, she guided Meg toward the stairs. "Lean on me, and keep moving," she said.

"I can't climb them." Meg wiped away her tears. "Get help, and come back for me."

"I'm not leaving you here."

"I'll try," Meg said.

With Kelly's help, Meg limped up the stairs, pausing after every two or three steps. "That night, I went for a cigarette in Justine's yard. Alex grabbed me, drugged me, brought me here, and—"

"Shhh. Save your strength," Kelly said, but Meg couldn't stop talking about Alex's rituals. She conquered several more steps. "How long have I been here? I couldn't even tell night from day."

The flashlight beam flickered.

"Put all that out of your mind," Kelly pleaded, hoping to keep Meg quiet. Meg was on the verge of hysterics. If she collapsed, Kelly didn't know if she could get her to safety.

The flashlight died. Kelly rapped it with her knuckles. The beam came on, weaker now.

Kelly slipped the key into the lock and opened the basement door. "Come on, Meg. The fresh air will make you feel better." Like in a nightmare, where everything happens in torturous slow motion, Kelly led Meg through the kitchen and out of the house. Meg breathed the cool air in deep gulps as if she were trying to inhale the night.

"I thought I'd never see stars and sky and grass ever again."

Her tears, glistening in the moonlight, streaked her dirt-encrusted cheeks.

Kelly guided Meg toward the fence. "We have to get out of these marshes and get you to the hospital." She tucked the blanket around Meg's shoulders.

"Kelly, I'm afraid to tell you something."

"What is it?" A chill traveled up Kelly's spine.

"I just remembered. There's a hidden exit from the cellar."

Kelly's knees nearly buckled. "Don't worry," she said, hardly recognizing her own calm voice. "Alex isn't in any shape to haul himself out of the cellar."

Kelly tried to hurry Meg along as they continued toward the fence, but it was difficult to see. The flashlight beam was faint. The fog had risen from the marshes and crept across the grass, obscuring rocks and hollows. They stumbled time and again. Finally Kelly spotted the short maple tree marking their escape route. The fence materialized an arm's length away in the woolly-thick fog. Kelly pulled back the torn section and pushed Meg through.

"You'll make better time without me." Meg's words were etched in weariness. "I'll wait here."

"Just a little farther," Kelly encouraged, and they continued walking.

There. In the faint flashlight beam. Alex's car. Maybe her phone was in his car. "Come on, Meg." Kelly helped Meg to Alex's car. She looked in the window. No cell phone. No keys.

Noises close by, like branches cracking underfoot.

Alex! Was he here, somewhere in the dark? Meg was too weak to walk farther. Where was Luke? Where were his detectives?

From somewhere behind them came a chilling shrieking. "You won't get away!"

Kelly turned off the flashlight. She knew the beam had pinpointed their position. She put an arm around Meg's waist and walked her toward the edge of the marsh. "I know where we can hide," she whispered.

Peering into the swirling fog, Kelly barely made out the roofline of the picnic shelters. She located the middle one and stood in front of it. Then she walked toward the cattails, pulling Meg along. After a short sweep left and then right, Kelly found Alex's clam boat. It was still camouflaged with the reed blanket, just as it was when she and Luke discovered it.

"Stand back," Kelly whispered to Meg. Struggling, she flipped the boat over and picked up the oars. She steadied the boat while Meg crawled in and slumped near the stern. Kelly stepped into the rocking boat and with her right foot shoved away from the edge.

"Stay low," Kelly whispered. Crouching, facing Meg and the stern of the boat, she rowed through the tangle of cattails. She swerved into one of the crisscrossing channels that cut through the marshes, hoping to get as far from the upland as possible. They would hide near the center of the marshes, where the water was deep, until help came. Alex couldn't reach them there.

But with the fog, Kelly couldn't see far. She kept steering the dory into clumps of cattails, where it lodged. Meg helped as best she could, but she was too weak. Kelly did most of the work, pushing and guiding the boat free each time it got stuck.

Kelly felt the boat rock under them. It nearly capsized. She pulled in the oars, afraid they would be pulled from her hands. She stared in horror. This couldn't be happening! Alex rose from the pitch-black water behind Meg.

He hurled himself at Meg.

Meg lurched forward and slid to the bottom of the boat.

"Stay down," Kelly said. Pumping the oars, she rowed away from Alex.

Alex thrashed in the water, then flung himself toward the boat. Kelly tried furiously to row toward shore. Alex grabbed the boat's bowline. The boat jerked and rocked from side to side at the abrupt halt. Kelly yanked the left oar into the boat. Gripping the right oar, she crawled over Meg and struggled to her feet. Alex lunged at her.

"Stay away from us!" Kelly cried, and she swung the oar. He ducked, grasped the side of the boat, and tried to haul himself over the edge. Kelly grabbed the oar again and jabbed him on the side of the head. He slid back into the black water, sucked into the slimy muck below the reeds.

As Kelly rowed, Meg swathed her hands in the blanket and batted a path through the cattails. They got themselves as far from Alex as possible.

"Kelly! Kelly Madison!" came a shout from a bullhorn.

"Over here!" Kelly shouted. "It's Luke Campbell, a detective," she told Meg. "Thank God, he's found us."

"Help us," Meg cried weakly.

The dory slammed into dry land. Kelly stumbled out, pulling Meg along with her.

"Help!" Kelly called over and over. She and Meg clung together, shivering from the cold and the sheer terror of their harrowing ordeal.

"Keep calling!" Luke shouted.

Finally, headlights broke through the fog. More lights. They twisted and turned, heading their way toward the cattails.

"Luke!" Kelly cried. "This way!"

Luke and the detectives came along the bumpy road fronting the marshes. Beacons of searchlights shone from their car windows. Encouraging words were shouted from the bullhorns.

Kelly kept shouting, "Help! Over here!"

Brakes squealed. Doors slammed. Luke and the detectives jumped from their cars. They battled their way through the tall cattails, following her cries.

"Kelly, thank God you're safe." Luke cradled her in his arms.

"I hit him with the oar." Kelly sobbed. "I think he drowned. He's out there somewhere."

Luke hugged her with all his might. She reached out to Meg. She felt herself falling as if she'd never stop. Falling like a leaf toward a soft, grassy bed.

FORTY-FIVE

Belvista Hospital

KELLY'S EYELIDS FLUTTERED as she awakened from a dreamless sleep. She stretched lazily in the warm afternoon sun that streamed into her room at Belvista Hospital and opened her eyes. Luke dozed in a chair by her bedside. A peaceful expression graced his haggard face. She remembered Luke racing through the cattails. Suddenly the memory of Alex and last night's terror flooded over her. Shoving the covers aside, Kelly struggled to sit up.

Luke awoke and sprang from his chair. "Kelly, you're safe. You're in the hospital." He kissed her cheek. "Lie back and rest."

"Where's Meg?" Kelly asked, her eyes wide with fear.

"She's in the next room. She's sedated, but she's fine."

Tears pooled in Kelly's eyes. "Did Alex…assault her?"

"No."

Kelly wiped away her tears.

"Jeannie has been watching Meg around the clock."

"And Jeannie?" Kelly's voice trembled. "Please tell me Alex didn't hurt her."

"She's fine. She'll come by to see you soon." Luke lifted her fingertips to his lips. "You gave us quite a scare. All things considered, you're in good shape. But Alex is a sorry-looking mess." He chuckled. "You could train Belvista's finest in scissors-stabbing and oar-bashing."

Kelly laughed in spite of herself. "Where is Alex?" she asked anxiously.

"Don't worry. He's locked up. He'll end up in a maximum-security facility. He won't get near you or Meg ever again."

"How did he slip past the detectives who were watching him?"

"Bradford's car never left the garage. So Detectives Waters and Jessup assumed he was staying put. But he sneaked out and drove a car he'd borrowed and hidden a few blocks away. He was familiar with the layout of St. Anne's and had a set of keys he'd stolen from the rectory." Luke shook his head. "I underestimated his ingenuity. He entered the hall through the basement. He pulled down a ladder that went to the kitchen utility closet and the adjoining restroom utility closet. He climbed the ladder, hid in the restroom side, and waited, knowing he could escape through the restroom, kitchen, or basement, if anyone came looking."

Kelly blinked away her tears. "I was so scared. I didn't think you'd find us…in time."

"When you didn't return from the restroom, we broke down the door. Seeing you weren't there, we rushed to Bradford's house. Obviously, he wasn't there. We raced from St. Anne's Cemetery to both funeral homes. Finally we tried the cattail marshes, all the places we'd connected to Bradford. Not knowing where you were or what was happening to you… The thought of losing you…" His voice faltered. "Sam Chambers is on his way here to see you. Chief Clemmens gave him an exclusive interview with Bradford. Sam spoke briefly with Meg, too. He's pieced together what happened."

"Meg spoke to Sam? What about me? I want to talk to her."

"You've been sleeping. You'll see her very soon."

"How did she sound? Was she hysterical? Is that why she's sedated?"

"Try to relax," Luke said tenderly. "Meg is going to be okay."

"John Grant wasn't involved after all," Kelly said.

"No. Detective Quinn discovered that Bradford often drove Grant to the airport in Grant's black Lexus and then drove around in it until Grant returned. Grant knew from the mileage that Alex was driving it, but he overlooked the little joy-rides. He considered Bradford his best worker and didn't want to lose him."

"Michael Duprey and Greg Saunders weren't involved either, were they?"

"No," Luke said.

Minutes later, the door creaked open. Sam came in, holding out a bouquet of mixed flowers. "No chrysanthemums," he said. "I figured you'd rather not see any more of them for a while." His face was drawn. The interview with Alex had obviously taken its toll.

"I'm really glad to see you, Kelly." Sam set the flowers on the nightstand. "I still can't believe the strength you found to rescue Meg and yourself. You're very brave." His voice faltered as he kissed Kelly on the cheek. "Now I know where Meg got her courage to survive."

"I'm worried sick about her," Kelly said. "Will she ever recover from this nightmare?"

"Her doctor thinks so. The bad memories won't disappear, but they'll eventually fade. And she'll cope with them over time."

"I can rest easier knowing that. Now, please, Sam, what did you find out about Alex?"

Sam pulled up a chair. "One day, Alex's father came home and saw that the new litter of kittens had made a mess on the rug. In a rage, he made Alex, just a young boy, put the kittens into a sack, take them to the cattail marshes, and drown them. Alex never forgave his father. He began to fantasize about how it would feel to drown. That's what he wanted his father to experience. That's what he believed his father deserved. Then he expanded his fantasy to include his entire family."

"Why?"

"They didn't stand up for Alex and try to reason with his father. Alex said they would be sorry."

"Alex drowned his family, didn't he?" Kelly said quietly.

Sam nodded.

"And the missing women?"

Luke smoothed Kelly's hair away from her forehead and kissed her tenderly. "The officers started dragging the marsh at dawn. We recovered the remains of the missing women early this morning. They were wrapped in burlap sacks and weighted down with stones."

Kelly cringed. "Meg was next. Then me."

And then Jeannie," Sam said. "We found a poem in Alex's car, which revealed his plan."

"What did it say?" Kelly asked.

Sam pulled his notepad from his pocket and read aloud:

I've got the woman in white.
Stole her in the dark of night.
Put her with the one in blue
And the dear daisy girl too.
With all these picks
I'll have my six.

"Six," Kelly said. "It's all a blur. Help me sort it out."

Sam moved his chair closer to Kelly. "Six women died in the hospital. Alex had kidnapped four women, including Meg, by the time you arrived in Belvista. You were his fifth victim. Jeannie would make six."

"So your theory was right," Kelly said. "For every woman who died, one disappeared."

"His murderous impulses resurfaced with Hal Dunbar's proposal to drain the cattail marshes. It terrified Alex and brought out his territorial instincts. The cattail marshes were his because his kittens were buried there. Shortly after the town council considered Dunbar's proposal, Rose D'Amici died in the hospital. Preston's Funeral Home, where Alex worked, handled the arrangements. For the first time ever, Mr. Preston asked Alex to transport the body to the funeral home. To

Alex, that was a mark of honor. Of power. During that ride, his compulsions grabbed hold.

"Let me backtrack. As a boy, Alex was racked with guilt about drowning his kittens. As he grew older, his hatred for his father festered. By age twenty-one, he had drowned his father and every person in his family without any feelings of remorse. At that point, he identified with his father's power and justified his own actions. When that first pretty young woman died in the hospital of natural causes—helpless as his kittens, helpless as he had been—Alex broke from reality. He reasoned that if chance or accident or illness could take a young woman's life, he could too. He convinced himself that he needed to arrange the deaths of pretty young women, as his father had arranged the deaths of pretty young kittens. It was his privilege, his right of passage from powerful, to more powerful than his father, to all-powerful. A son competing with his father. Very Freudian."

Sam rubbed his temples and continued. "His compulsions came with rigid rules that regulated his behavior. He couldn't kidnap until a pretty young woman died in the hospital and he was involved in the funeral preparations. After the funeral of Rose D'Amici, Alex went to the bus depot and studied the women that stepped off the bus. He wanted to kidnap a loner who wouldn't be missed and drown her in the cattail marshes. But it was February, a snowy day according to his poem, and the ground was frozen solid. As the weather turned warmer, Alex began to prowl the bus station, looking for the perfect catch, fantasizing about what he would do. He even practiced."

Kelly shuddered. "Practiced?"

"He put on dark clothes, parked his Toyota Corolla at a strategic spot, and followed young women, deciding in minute detail how to execute his plan. When the next woman, Lisa McFarland, died—it was April, and the ground had thawed—Alex sprang into action. He chose pretty Stacy Deems, a young woman who was traveling alone. His murderous rampage had begun. In the back of his mind was always the need to match a kidnapping with that first death, Rose D'Amici."

Kelly clenched her jaw. "When Luke introduced newer methods of solving crimes, Alex wanted to prove he was unstoppable."

Detective Ryan rapped on the door and motioned Luke outside. Kelly strained to hear the whispered conversation.

"We've finished exhuming the Bradford family," Detective Ryan said. "The medical examiner says Alex made it look like accidental drownings, but the broken bones tell another story. County Chief Prosecutor Attenborough has an airtight case."

Kelly turned back to Sam. "I feel better knowing what happened and why. I'll always be grateful to you, Sam."

Jeannie bustled into the room. Kelly was so happy to see her. She hugged her and thanked her for taking care of Meg.

"Meg's asking for you, Kelly. She's tired but hungry as a bear. She's going to be fine."

"How can you be so sure?" Kelly asked.

Jeannie laughed. "Meg was looking out the window—she can't get enough of the beautiful scenery—when who should pull up in a fancy car but Michael Duprey, who painted all those pictures of her. Well, he wasn't alone. There was this older woman, all coy smiles and loving glances. She kissed Duprey, and I could tell she wasn't an aunt or cousin. A few minutes later, there's a knock on the door. 'May I see Meg?' Michael Duprey asked, cool as a November morning. He told Meg how much he loved her, how he missed her, right there in front of me. He said he hated to ask, but would Meg appear at an exhibition of his paintings? He thought her mingling with potential buyers could help him sell the paintings of her." Jeannie laughed heartily. "Meg threw a tray at him. She missed, but he got the message."

"Sounds like the Meg I know and love," Kelly said, relieved that Meg was already becoming her old self.

"Well, guys, if you'll excuse me," Jeannie said as she ushered them away, "I need to get Kelly out of bed." Jeannie fluffed Kelly's hair. "It's time to go visiting." She bent close to Kelly. "I'll go to the cafeteria while you and Meg talk. I know Luke and Sam will stand by in the corridor in case you need them. Luke's a lovesick puppy. And Sam is devoted to Meg. He's fascinated by her place in his Cinderella cover-up theory. He's quite proud of himself and deservedly so."

"He'll always have a special place in my heart," Kelly admitted. "He was the first person to take Meg's disappearance seriously."

Luke came back to Kelly's room and sat on the edge of her bed. "There's some things I wanted to say."

"Me, too," Kelly said.

He stroked her arm. "All the words I just rehearsed seem to have flown away."

"Why, Luke Campbell," Kelly said teasingly, "I've never known you to be at a loss for words."

He cupped her chin with his hand and lifted her face toward his. He kissed her tenderly. She lingered in his embrace, content to be in his arms, to feel his strength. She gazed over his shoulder into the amber light of autumn. So much had happened since she had first come to Pruitt's Inn. She smiled as Luke kissed her gently on the cheek and fussed with her pillow.

Kelly knew the horror was over. She tried to concentrate on the pleasant memories, the new friends made, Meg whole and happy, and Luke. Wonderful Luke.

Kelly gazed into Luke's eyes. "Meg and I are going to stay on for a few days with Jeannie until Meg is stronger. I'll be coming back to Belvista as soon as I submit my design plans to my New York client."

"Something special drawing you back?" Luke asked. He gave her an encouraging glance.

"I'd like to open a design shop," Kelly said. "I've seen the ideal place on Front Street."

"I hope you won't be too busy to see me."

"Not a chance. New York, Atlantic City, Belvista, wherever. I'll find you."

"Promise?" he asked.

"Promise."

* * * * *